ROSEMARY AND THE BOOK OF THE DEAD

SAMANTHA GILES

AGORA BOOKS

ABOUT THE AUTHOR

Samantha Giles is known and loved by millions of viewers for her popular portrayal of *Emmerdale*'s Bernice Blackstock. She has also been a regular character in three series of *Where the Heart Is* and *Hollyoaks*, as well as lead guest roles in many other well-known TV programmes.

She started writing about four years ago, inspired by a dream she had about the four witch characters that feature in her debut, *Rosemary and the Witches of Pendle Hill*. Other than acting and writing, she also has her own website where you can find out more about Samantha and her books as well as purchase her spell kits:

www.thesamanthagiles.co.uk

Samantha is a big country music fan and is also a patron for Animal Aid charity in Liverpool, and PaganAid charity.

ALSO BY SAMANTHA GILES

Rosemary and the Witches of Pendle Hill

ROSEMARY
—AND THE—
BOOK OF THE DEAD

SAMANTHA
GILES

This is a work of fiction. All characters and events in this work, other than those clearly in the public domain, are entirely fictitious. Any resemblance to any persons, living or dead, is entirely coincidental.

Printed and bound in Great Britain by Clays Ltd, Elcograf S.p.A.

Cover Design By: Allison Li

First published in Great Britain in 2021 by Agora Books

Agora Books is a division of Peters Fraser + Dunlop Ltd

55 New Oxford Street, London WC1A 1BS

For Mum and Dad

1

POSITION VACANT

"Ready, everyone?" Dad grinned, not waiting for an answer as he cleared his throat like he was a newscaster about to give us the most important piece of information ever. I pulled a slight cringy face while he continued to read:

> *"Position Vacant.*
>
> *"Wanted: a fun-loving childminder with rules. Must have own transport. Must like children. And cats. Flexibility required and some late nights. Please reply to PO Box 22, Bootle."*

Lois glanced at me and even she looked slightly puzzled. There was silence.

Dad continued to grin expectantly.

Mum bit her lip.

Lois farted.

I sniggered.

"Lois!" Dad berated. "Well, come on, troops, don't you think that's a winner?"

"Mmm," Mum said doubtfully. "Surely you don't need to say 'must like children', do you, darling? I mean, why be a childminder if you don't like children?"

"Haven't you ever seen *Mrs Doubtfire*, Rae? I mean, it's on all the bloody time!" Dad continued. "There's a whole host of unsuitable people who apply to look after the children."

Lois nodded her head wisely. "And look at Nanny McPhee."

"No, Lois," I corrected her. "Nanny McPhee isn't evil. She's kind and nice."

"Yeah, but she looks scary."

I sighed. "I don't think it matters what the childminder looks like, does it, Dad?"

"No, of course not," Dad replied firmly.

"Well, we don't want some scary-looking individual looking after our children, do we, John?" my mother added cautiously.

I tuned out as I heard them arguing over what did or didn't constitute "scary-looking", with Lois, I think, having the deciding vote that anyone with copious amounts of hair on their chin or more than one wart might not make the grade.

If the Aunts and Uncle Vic and Mr Foggerty were still living with us, we wouldn't be in this mess.

It was now June, and we hadn't seen any of the four witches and wizards who used to live with us since November last year.

I thought back fondly to how Lois, Adi, and I had found Phyllis (one of the Aunts who had gone missing), and how together we had defeated the evil

Mal Vine, who had turned out to be Phyllis' brother and had been seeking revenge for something that had happened hundreds of years ago. Thankfully, once we had found her and my parents sorted out their differences, Mal was stopped from causing any more destruction, and his group had been disbanded.

I knew it wasn't necessarily forever, though. I remembered Phyllis' words to me when I had asked her how we would stop Mal from reforming the "No-Laws" and potentially continuing his reign of hate.

"It is down to each and every one of us to continue this fight in our own little lives. We do this by living each day with love and kindness and compassion . . . Where there is light, we can always defeat the darkness."

I hoped with all my heart I would never have to see Mal Vine's cold flinty eyes again, or his two-fingered salute that made my skin prickle with fear.

I glanced once more at my family. Mum was attempting to re-write Dad's advert, Dad was patiently waiting for her to finish so he could ignore all her suggestions and just press "send" to the childcare website, and Lois was scratching her bottom with Bea's nose. (Bea being her cuddly grey rabbit that she never goes ANYWHERE without.)

How I longed to see the Aunts, Uncle Vic, and Mr Foggerty.

All I had to remind myself that they had ever existed at all was just one measly postcard that Frances had sent from Egypt where they had been holidaying.

I missed them so much.

"I must admit, I'm worried about leaving this to you, John," Mum frowned anxiously as Dad's finger hovered over the 'send' button.

"Rae, I'm more than capable. Remember, I'm used to interviewing people."

Mum raised her eyebrows at me and Lois, who had drawn a round smiling face on a piece of paper — presumably her contribution to the nanny debate.

"Just be nice to them, John," Mum added, knowing as we did that social skills were not one of Dad's strengths.

"Don't worry," he grinned, pressing "send" with a flourish. "I'll find us the perfect person."

2
MUM'S BIG JOB

So, the reason my parents were looking for a childminder for us was mainly because of MUM'S BIG JOB.

Mum and Dad had sat us down one evening — Mum bursting with excitement, despite trying to look like a serious grown-up in control — and Dad had uttered the words, "We want to tell you some exciting news about a rather big job that Mum might be doing."

We had fallen about in fits of laughter as, in our house, if anyone talks about a BIG JOB it's usually a poo.

After Lois' hiccups had subsided (a direct consequence of too much laughter), we finally found out what the news really meant.

"I've been offered three months' work on a soap opera, girls!" Mum had squealed. It was so high-pitched that even Bob and Maggie, our cats, who were sleeping side by side on the couch, had folded their ears back and flicked their tails in protest.

They had probably thought one of those dog whistles had gone off.

"Mum, that's amazing!" I'd shrieked.

"What's a soap opera?" Lois had asked simultaneously, with a quizzical look on her face.

Mum had flicked a glance at Dad, who was looking proud.

"Well," Mum had continued, "it's a programme that's on pretty much every day, all year round. People get hooked on it, as they like to follow the characters' lives, and they are usually set in fictional towns or villages and feature lots of regular characters who live in that place."

"Does this mean we'll have to move to this programme's village then?" Lois had frowned, her eyebrows creasing in confusion.

"No, darling!" Mum had laughed. "It's all pretend, silly. It's a made-up village, and I'm going to be playing one of the regular character's sisters who is just visiting for a few months. So, I'll still live here, but it means I've got to travel quite a long way to get into work and might sometimes have to stay overnight."

"Oh!" Lois' face had dropped at the mention of overnight stays.

"Listen, darling, I haven't even got any kind of filming schedule yet, so let's not worry about something that hasn't even happened. I might only be in for one day a week, and so you'll hardly notice I've gone."

"So how long is this job for then?" I'd asked carefully, feeling slightly uneasy about the idea of Mum working 'quite a long way' from home.

"Only three months, so it will fly by. But listen, the good thing is television work pays much better than theatre, so we might be able to afford a little holiday at Christmas or something!"

"Oooh, we could go to India!" I'd blurted out, thinking of how my best friend Adi had plans to go with his family later this year for Diwali festival.

"India?" My dad had looked puzzled. "I don't think Miss Fussy Pants would be able to get her baked beans and digestive biscuits there, do you?"

"Baked beans are in the university," Lois had added smoothly.

"I think you mean they are universal," I'd corrected her, shaking my head.

"You can get them everywhere, too," she'd continued innocently.

Dad had rolled his eyes. "Yes, sadly I think you might be right. Anyway, enough about holidays. You never know, Mum might end up staying there a while, and I could jack my job in!"

"Why would you want to leave your job, Dad?" I'd asked, frowning, noticing my mum's surprised expression.

"I could be a man of leisure. Play golf, practise my guitar, do up the house."

"I don't think that's going to happen, John. And anyway, why would you not want to work? You'd be bored at home."

Dad had shaken his head. "Wouldn't have time to be bored."

"Mmm, well, this is the first I've heard of this 'jacking in the job' nonsense." Mum had raised an eyebrow. "Plus, I don't think with all the time in the

11

world you'd get round to repainting the bedroom or fixing a lock on the bathroom door."

"We don't need a lock on the bathroom door. It's dangerous."

"Dangerous?" we had all chimed.

"Yes. What if you got locked in there and couldn't get out?" Dad had looked very pleased with himself at this suggestion.

"Dad, we're nearly ten and six, not two and three."

"Anyway," Dad had added, looking down for a moment, "maybe it's time for a career change. You know, to find a job I really like ..."

Mum looked like she had swallowed a snail, and I swear when Dad had started talking about his job that the greeny-blue colour around him had dulled. (Did I mention I could see colours around people that show how they are feeling or give clues about their personality?)

And so, only a few days after this discussion, Mum had toddled off down the M6 for costume fittings and make-up tests and medicals for her new job on the popular soap *Brightside*.

She'd had to leave at 6.30 a.m. in order to get there on time but assured us she would be back to pick us up from school. As we only had one car, Dad had walked us to school and then had to cycle to the station so he could get his train to Manchester, a journey that I know he HATED.

"Those bloody trains are a joke. Never on time, always overcrowded. Some snotty-nosed individual with a cough spluttering into your face or tickling your cheek with the edge of their newspaper," Dad had moaned as we reached the school gates.

As we had said our goodbyes, I flicked my eyes up to the space above his head. No, it was okay. His cloud most definitely hadn't returned.

Phew. That was a relief.

When Dad was feeling low, a raincloud would appear, hovering above his head. Sometimes it was white, sometimes it looked grey and threatening, and other times it was full-on pouring with rain.

No one else could ever seem to see the colours I saw around people. I didn't dare tell anyone — except, my mum knew. Apparently, she had the same thing when she was my age. She said it disappeared when she became a teenager, so I never want to turn thirteen. I don't want to lose my gift. It makes me feel special, and even though it makes me odd and an outsider in some ways, I'd rather be different.

My best friend Adi understands me quite well, considering he's a boy. I guess we did go through a lot together last year when we went on our quest to find Phyllis after she had mysteriously disappeared.

We used to have a "portal" via a mirror in our house, which is a kind of gateway to another dimension where our witch and wizard houseguests would go. Adi cleverly found a way for us to access it, and that's how we got ourselves the job of finding Phyllis.

The sad thing is, since the witches stopped living with us, the portal is no longer there, so that's another thing that's changed, along with our house-guests disappearing, and Mum getting this new job.

Sometimes I wish things could have stayed the same.

So, at break time, I had been sitting in the "apple", which is the contemplative space in our playground, telling Adi about Mum's trip to Birmingham. Adi had listened to me droning on intently, every now and then pushing his oversized glasses further up onto his nose. He'd recently developed a new habit of wrinkling up his nose, as if that would hold his glasses up. I was fascinated by the wrinkling and wanted to tell him to stop, because I could see right up his nose, but didn't want to hurt his feelings.

"So why aren't you pleased about your mum doing this job then, Rosemary?" Adi was the only one of my friends who called me by my full name.

"Isn't it obvious?" I'd answered him. "Mum will be away from home. For ages, I expect. First, we lose our houseguests, and now we're losing Mum all over again."

"You haven't heard any more from any of them then, since the postcard?"

I'd shaken my head sadly. "Frances promised us she would see us again. Why is it that grown-ups are always breaking promises?"

I had been exaggerating slightly there for effect, as my parents usually were pretty good at keeping promises. Although I had been very suspicious when Mum had said that we would hardly notice that she'd gone.

Adi looked thoughtful. "Well, if Frances said

she would definitely see you again, then you have to trust her and wait for the right time. 'We can't change the direction of the wind, but we can adjust the sails.'"

It was another of his Indian sayings. I had looked at him for clarification.

"It means you may not be able to change the way things are, but you can change your mindset."

I'd pulled a face.

"If Frances said she would see you again, she will. So, start believing that, Rosemary. Come on!" Adi had said, dragging me up by my arm. "Bell's gone."

I'd followed him back into class thinking about how right he was. Frances had made a promise that she'd see us again.

I had to stop worrying and have faith she would return to us when the time was right.

3

BRIGHTSIDE (BUNGALOWS)

A few days later, having spent two days after school with Mrs Sykes in the office while waiting a WHOLE HOUR on the first day and TWENTY MINUTES on the second for Mum to collect us, we had all realised the current arrangement wasn't going to work.

Mum was continually getting stuck in traffic on the M6 rushing to get home, or her scenes "over ran", or Donna Watlington was late going on set. The excuses were endless, and while I felt for my mum, as she was clearly distressed at having been late several times, I also felt annoyed and embarrassed that Lois and I had to sit on the floor in the office, doing boring old word searches while Mrs Sykes kept eyeing us impatiently over her glasses.

"Darlings, I'm so sorry about this week," Mum had cried as she negotiated the Fiveways roundabout and nearly crashed into a white van. "Whoops!"

"Why is that man waving at us, Mummy? Do

you know him?" Lois had asked curiously, winding her window down so she could shout "hello".

"Wind the window back up, Lois. He's not waving; he's, erm, he's doing a rude sign at us!" Mum had shouted, getting her gears in a muddle, so the car made a crunching sound. "Lois, no! Stop it, please!"

But it was too late, Lois was already blowing raspberries and making faces at him.

I had looked the other way, just desperate to get home so we could try to fix this nightmare of no one picking us up from school in time.

When we'd finally got through the front door, things weren't really any better. There was a rather large pool of sticky wee in the kitchen by the rocking chair. Bob had clearly had one of his fits while we were all out, and guess who trod straight in it? Yes, Lois.

"Eurghhhh, Mum!" she had shouted, tears already forming. "I've stepped in Bob's fit. It's all over my socks!"

I could hear Mum was on her mobile sounding stressed. "Yes, er, okay, well, that's going to cause me a few childcare problems as it's their inset day, so my girls aren't at school."

"Lois, shut up!" I'd shushed her. "Mum's on the phone. Don't mess up this job for her."

Lois' face had crumpled, and that was it. She always was soooo good at turning on the water-works. I had to cuddle her for a whole minute until she calmed down, by which time Mum had finished her call and was looking worried.

"Rosie said I'm messing up your job," Lois

cried, throwing herself at Mum. "She's being mean to me, I've stepped in Bob's fit, and my socks are stinky."

"For goodness' sake, Lois, don't be so silly. You haven't messed up anything, except possibly the carpet by traipsing round with wee-soaked socks. Take them off immediately, please."

Lois bent down to remove the offending items, which had been white at the start of the day and were now black, grey, and yellow, tinged with cat urine.

"But listen, girls, I'm in a bit of a pickle. I've now got to work on Monday as Donna's got a hospital appointment on Tuesday, so they've had to move the scenes around. I'm going to have to see if Dad can stay at home that day or something."

"Don't worry, Mum." I squeezed her arm. "I'm sure we'll work it out."

"I'm afraid Donna seems to get the schedule moved around rather a lot for different things," Mum added grimly.

Suddenly, I remembered. Donna had been in the play with Mum last year, I was sure of it.

"Isn't she the same Donna who was in *Who's Afraid of Virginia Woolf* with you last year, Mum?" I'd asked.

Mum had nodded her head. "She got very lucky straight after that and got a regular role in *Brightside*, so she's suddenly become one of their leading ladies."

"Well, it's nice for you to have a friend there at your new work, Mummy," Lois had added sweetly, as if the entire crying over treading in Bob's wee had never happened.

"Mmm, isn't it?" Mum had replied, but I'd noticed she didn't look pleased at all, in fact, quite the opposite.

I had started to realise that weekend how Mum being in a soap opera wasn't as exciting as we had all first thought.

She was absolutely exhausted all the time with the constant travelling, a bit snappy, and she suddenly seemed to be worried about whether the house had been hoovered or washing done, when ordinarily she never seemed to bother too much about this kind of stuff.

I'd wondered to myself whether it was really worth earning "good money", as Dad had put it, when she was too tired to spend it. However, Monday morning soon arrived, and Lois and I had waved her goodbye at 7 a.m., wondering how strange our inset day was going to be at home with Dad, who had a host of "Zoom" meetings booked in.

A few hours later, after we'd had crisps, biscuits, and watched too much YouTube, we decided to FaceTime Mum.

The two of us were really excited about seeing her at work but hadn't bargained for the sight of a heavily made-up older lady peering at us from beneath her downward dog yoga position, just to Mum's right.

"Oh hi, girls!" Mum had giggled nervously and

seemed to be sucking in her cheekbones and barely opening her mouth as she spoke. "Sorry, Harriet, my two are on an inset day," she'd added apologetically to the bottom housed in tan tights, which was almost on a parallel with Mum's face.

She hadn't sounded like our mum at all. Her usual purple colour kept crackling with flashes of white and yellow and looked like it might burst into flames.

Harriet had remained in her yoga pose, her face bright red with exertion, sweat trickling down from the small of her back. "Oh, darlings, don't mind me, just doing my daily stretch before we start another day at the sausage factory."

Lois and I had exchanged a look of confusion.

"So, everything all right at home, girls?" Mum had finally asked, glancing at Harriet, who was hoicking herself up from her downward dog.

"Do you know this programme used to be called *Brightside Bungalows*?" Harriet interrupted as she started to peel her tights off.

We'd shaken our heads, wide-eyed with surprise as she'd started to disrobe in front of us.

"All set in a street of bungalows, isn't it? Well, do you know why they had to drop the *Bungalow* bit from the title?"

Lois and I had shaken our heads again in unison.

I'd noticed Mum was silent, probably wondering if Harriet was also going to remove her knickers and bra (thankfully she didn't).

"I'll tell you why, shall I?"

I think we had realised that Harriet was going to tell us whether we liked it or not.

"Because bungalows don't have anything going on upstairs, do they?"

"They don't have an upstairs at all," Lois had added proudly.

"Exactly," continued Harriet, pulling a robe around her. "And nor do most of this bloody cast either. Nothing going on upstairs, thick as pigs' muck. So, they had to drop the *Bungalows* from the title and just leave the *Brightside* bit."

There had been silence as we'd collectively watched Harriet's skinny frame disappear from the screen and heard the door of the dressing room slam.

Finally, Lois spoke. "I don't think that lady likes this job very much."

"Well, she's been here twenty-five years," Mum had murmured.

"Why would she still be doing it if she hates it as much as she seems to?" I'd asked, confused.

Mum had shrugged and looked as baffled as we were. "The money?" she'd said tentatively, as if thinking that could be the only thing that would keep her there.

"She must get paid a whole bunch of money then!" Lois whistled under her breath. "At least a hundred pounds." She'd paused, then changed the subject. "Who else do you share your dressing room with, Mummy?"

Just at that moment, we'd heard the briefest knock, and in had walked Donna.

Mum looked like she'd been stung by a wasp.

She'd stuttered and fawned about Donna, and I noticed little yellow sparks were spiking out of her body, as if she were jumping with nerves.

Donna, on the other hand, had looked like the cat who'd got the cream. I didn't like the fiery red glow that surrounded her body.

"Rae," she'd drooled, tossing her luscious dark hair off her shoulder and glancing at us disapprovingly through the screen. "Your children, I presume?" (Imagine instead of "children" she had been saying the word "rats".)

"Yes, let me introduce you." Mum's voice had been all breathless and soft, as if she was afraid to speak at normal volume. "This is my eldest, Rosemary, and this is Lois."

I had given a small smile, and Lois had just stared and wiped her nose with Bea, something she liked to do if she was assessing someone.

Luckily Mum hadn't noticed. "This, girls, is Donna."

"Donna Marie," Donna had corrected.

"Oh, yes, sorry. Forgive me." Mum had touched her forehead with her hand, embarrassed.

"How quaint," Donna had continued.

I had no idea what she'd meant by that.

"Got to get changed now, ladies. I think you need to go to make-up, Rae. There's only so much they can do in an hour ..."

Mum had looked so wounded, and I'd felt furious with Donna, suggesting that our mum needed more time in make-up.

"I'll call you in a bit, girls," Mum had whispered. And then she was gone.

I'd had an uncomfortable feeling in my stomach. Mum hadn't seemed herself at work. She'd been surrounded by two women who were clearly unhappy, and their dissatisfaction seemed to be dulling Mum's usual excitement for the job she longed to be doing.

An hour or so later, after Dad had hurriedly made us sandwiches and then hot-footed it back to his tiny office, Lois had decided she wanted to try making oaty biscuits.

We'd scrambled around in Mum's recipe books for the scrap of paper that Lois had been convinced the instructions was written on.

Dad was no help whatsoever. Every time we'd lingered in his office doorway to ask him a question, he'd raised his palm up as if to say, "not right now".

So obviously, we did what any self-sufficient kids would do: we'd taken matters into our own hands.

Finding the ingredients and making the mixture was easy — though melting the butter in the saucepan had nearly caused chaos as we'd left a tea towel next to the hob that almost caught fire. We'd even very carefully patted the oat mounds into circles and put them in the oven AND tidied up the kitchen.

I'd felt certain that Mum and Dad would have no fears about leaving us home alone, should the necessity ever arise — in an emergency situation, of course.

I guess it had all started to go wrong when we'd got so engrossed in a Mario Kart game that we'd forgotten about the biscuits.

"Can you smell something funny?" I'd asked Lois as she prepared herself for game three.

"Nope," she'd replied.

The smell had got stronger until something prompted me to go and ask Dad what it was. As soon as we'd left the lounge, we'd seen smoke coming from the kitchen.

"Oh my god! Lois!" I'd shouted.

"Dad!!" we'd both screamed at the top of our voices, while trying to waft a tea towel to dispel the smoke in the kitchen.

Dad, it turned out, had been upstairs in the loft, of all places, trying to find an old file, and on hearing our shouts had dashed down the stairs, missed the last two and landed on his bum with a thump.

To say he was not best pleased had been an understatement.

"For crying out loud, you two, why didn't you tell me you were making biscuits!" he'd shouted, pulling out a tray of blackened rocks from the oven.

Lois had disintegrated into tears. "I was really looking forward to eating those."

At that moment, Mum had chosen to FaceTime us again, and Dad's computer was buzzing with yet another Zoom meeting about to start.

Mum's face had dropped when she'd seen the smoke in the kitchen and Lois' tear-stained face.

"Don't worry, Mum," I'd said as soothingly as I could muster. "It will all be fine by the time you get home."

"One day I ask Dad to look after you, and it's a

disaster. The kitchen could have burnt down! We cannot go on like this," Mum had replied.

It had been distressing hearing Mum so upset. It was only some burnt oaty biscuits, but I guess sometimes grown-ups overreact to things. I'd been about to offer her more words of reassurance when we heard a knock at her door and a voice asking her to go on set.

She'd sighed heavily and raised her hand to her forehead. "I've got to go, girls. Please, no more disasters."

And it was then that I noticed a yellow mist had wrapped itself around her arm.

I had to look twice, for as she'd lowered her hand the mist faded, and I swear to you there was a hole the size of a ten-pence piece about midway up her forearm.

A hole that I could see right through.

4

PALOMA AND THE POP SOCK

T he events of that day, with Mum's stress levels going through the roof and Dad's embarrass-ment at the jungle backdrops behind him that he couldn't remove during his Zoom meetings, were what prompted my parents to advertise for a childminder.

So, you can imagine that it was with a heavy heart I made my way up to bed that night, knowing whatever Lois and I wanted was never going to happen.

We were going to be stuck with some bossy childminder who my parents would choose. Our post-school hours would be full of dread, rather than fun walks home with our mum, pointing out herbs and their uses, and making up silly songs.

Before I slid into bed, I crept into Lois' room and gazed at her sleeping form.

Suddenly, she opened one eye, which startled me. "What are you staring at?"

At least I think that's what she said. She was talking through her doe (dummy), which, yes, I'm afraid she STILL insists on at bedtime, even though she's six.

"I said, what are you staring at, Rosie?" Lois repeated.

"Nothing. I'm just thinking about this child-minder Mum and Dad have advertised for. I don't want a stranger picking us up from school."

"Don't worry, Rosie," Lois replied sleepily, snuggling into Bea. "Paloma said it would be someone nice."

"Paloma?" I questioned, shocked. Paloma was the pesky raven who seemed to have formed an un-likely mutual appreciation society with my little sister. "I suppose you'll be telling me next that Paloma talks to you all the time!"

"Well, yes, she does." Lois grinned knowingly at me.

"What?" I asked. "How does Paloma know we need a childminder?" I didn't wait for her to reply. "We could end up with some right nightmare person stopping us from having any freedom whatsoever."

Lois rolled over, leaving me with a view of her back. "Paloma knows everything, and she said it will be fine, chill pill." And with that, she snuggled down into the duvet.

I guess that was her way of signalling that the conversation was over.

How on earth could Paloma be back? We hadn't had sight or sound of her since we were in the wormhole looking for Phyllis. Why had she turned up now?

I felt a frisson of excitement, as well as anxiety.

Paloma had been Aradia's bird, the woman who was the gatekeeper to the portal, which sadly no longer existed in our house. Aradia had been sacked, because she had been found to be helping the enemy, Mal Vine.

Was Paloma still with Aradia? Could she be spying on us and then relaying information back to Aradia, who would then tell Mal Vine?

My mind was full of questions as I settled down to sleep and finally, when I succumbed to the darkness, my dreams were unsettled.

I dreamt that Phyllis and Frances were arguing about a broomstick. Phyllis wanted to paint it yellow in honour of the Beatles song "Yellow Submarine", and Frances kept saying in her soft Scottish burr, "No, no, hen, we'll be spotted if it's yellow. You don't want Mal to find us again, do you?"

Then both witches were silenced as a booming voice echoed around. Its chilling words were etched in my mind.

"I will unleash the forces of the book. I will seek vengeance for all you took. This is my time. Witches of the night, prepare to fight." This was followed by laughter.

Without even seeing his face, I KNEW it was the voice of Mal Vine.

I woke, sweat dripping down my forehead, totally unsettled by my nightmare that had felt so real, in spite of me telling myself it was just a dream.

I glanced at the clock: 3.33 a.m. It was going to be impossible to go back to sleep now.

What did it mean? What book was he referring to? I had been thinking about our absent house guests and Mal Vine before I went to bed, prompted by Lois talking about Paloma. Surely it was just an anxiety dream?

I got out of bed and went to my window and looked out on our garden. I could see Maggie, one of our cats, sitting on top of the fence, gazing into the night, as cats do.

Suddenly, she was swept up from her position by something that literally flashed across the garden. The energy that it created left behind some white smoke and bright yellow sparks.

I scanned the sky for a sign. There was nothing. Nothing at all.

I stood by the window for what felt like an age, hoping I'd see something, another flash of whatever it had been. But the night was still. Apart from a gentle breeze that caused the wind chimes to make the odd sound, there was no sign of life. Not even a glimpse of our Maggie.

I crept downstairs and let myself into the kitchen, where we kept the cats at night, in case Bob had one of his epileptic fits.

It was quiet. I could just make out the sleeping Bob on the rocking chair, but no sign of Maggie.

Suddenly I jumped, as the cat flap flipped open, and Maggie eased her enormous furry body through it. She walked nonchalantly past me toward her food bowl, then started coughing and spluttering.

Typical! She was obviously about to bring up a fur ball.

I readied myself with a dishcloth to clear it up and followed her around the kitchen until she had finished bringing up a rather squelchy combination of fur, grass, and semi-digested biscuits. I grimaced and gathered the offending mess, ready to throw it into the bin, when I suddenly gasped. For there, in my hand, covered in goo, was the unmistakable nylon mass of a flesh-coloured pop sock.

My tummy flipped over. Who wore pop socks?

Frances, of course.

I skidded over to the back door and unlocked it, quickly surveying the skyline. It was chilly for June, a clear night. The moon looked full and seemed to be glinting at me cheekily. I blinked and shook my head in an attempt to dispel those daft thoughts. The moon didn't glint — that wasn't real. But the pop sock that I retrieved from the bin most certainly was.

I carefully locked the back door and headed out through the kitchen, back upstairs to bed.

How on earth would I sleep now?

But strangely enough, as soon as my head hit the pillow, I felt myself drift off into nothingness once more.

I woke up the next day with that feeling you get when something exciting is going to happen but you're not sure what.

It was Friday, and we had no plans for the weekend, apart from a family dinner, as Mum, who had already gone to work, would be home around 6 p.m., and it seemed like a nice way to start the weekend.

The sun was shining weakly, and it looked as if it was going to be a warm June day.

I washed and pulled on my checked blue summer school dress and went downstairs. Nobody else seemed to share this fizzy feeling that I could feel in my tummy.

Lois was hogging the rocking chair, eating panny cakes (her new addiction), which she had toasted, plain, and cut into four.

Dad was always quiet in the mornings, and today was no exception. He was hugging his coffee and studying his tablet.

"Oh!" he cried out in surprise.

Lois and I looked up.

"Looks like we've got a reply already to my advert!"

I threw Lois a troubled look, which she returned with a grin and her impersonation of an angry baby rhinoceros. (You have to put your face down towards your chest and pull your eyebrows into a frown and then do an overbite with your bottom teeth.) I know it was supposed to make me laugh, but all I could manage was a weak smile.

"Great!" Dad continued, starting to type. "I'm going to reply and tell her to come for an interview tonight at 5 p.m., as I'm working from home today."

"If we don't like her, we don't have to have her, do we, Dad?" I asked quietly, knowing it was a long shot.

"Look, Rosie," Dad smiled at me, "if you two don't like her, then I don't suppose I will either. And there will be loads of replies, don't worry.

We'll probably be seeing quite a number of potential childminders."

Dad frowned.

"What is it?" I asked nervously.

"Nothing really, probably just a typo. I asked for a confirmation of their DBS certificate from any applicants, and she said she has a CFW certificate." Dad shook his head, confused. "Probably a new thing I haven't heard of ... Crime Fighting W..." He trailed off.

"Clever Friendly Woman?" Lois offered up, munching on her panny cake.

I raised my eyebrows. "More likely Clueless Forgetful Whinger ..."

"Look, girls, whatever it stands for, it will be something sensible, no doubt, and nothing like anything you two can guess."

Nevertheless, the interview with the potential new nanny occupied my thoughts all day.

At afternoon break time, Adi and I sat in the contemplation "apple" space.

"What's wrong, Rosemary? You've barely been listening to what I've been saying," he complained.

"Sorry, Ads. I've been thinking about the new childminder, and I'm dreading who will turn up tonight at 5."

"Don't call me Ads."

"Soz."

Adi looked up into the sky. I wasn't sure why; perhaps he was looking for some inspiration.

"Did you listen to anything that I said before?" he asked me seriously.

I paused. He didn't look annoyed that I hadn't

been listening, so I guess it was safe to tell the truth. "Sorry, no."

He tutted and shook his head. "I just might have the answer to your childminder problem."

"What?" I must admit I was a little suspicious.

"Why don't you look in your mum's spell book and do a spell to summon back all your old house-guests or something?"

I found myself grinning, a smile that started slowly as I realised what he was saying, and which now was beginning to reach my boots. "Amazing idea, Adi! You're a genius."

Adi blushed. "Yeah, I'll take that."

5

THE NEW NANNY

As soon as Lois and I got home after school, I made the most of Dad being upstairs while he helped Lois take her uniform off. I dashed into his small office, where I knew Mum kept her *Book of Shadows*, which is basically a book containing spells.

I ran my finger down the index quickly.

Spell to Find Love. No.

Spell for Protection. No.

Spell to Get Rid of Warts. Eugh. No.

Spell to Give you Confidence. No.

This was hopeless. Then I remembered *Francesca's Finds*, which must have been Frances' book. That was where we had got the spell we used last year to try to get rid of slimy Marcus, who had tried to worm his way into our family.

I found it wedged in the bookshelf in between a book of *Ear Worms You'll Never Erase* by Curly Slitherer and Dr Ranj Singh's *What's That Rash?*

This is why I most definitely believe in fate. Because I opened the book up and there, right in front of me, were the words I had been searching for: Summoning Spell.

I flicked my eyes over the ingredients.

Lemonade and liquorice root.

Was that it?
I read on quickly.

This is a simple ritual that can be used as a summoning spell, and one which you can use to gain control over others — so use it wisely.

On a waxing moon, drink a glass of lemonade rapidly and then burn a piece of liquorice root. Once you feel the burps about to start, make sure you loudly say the name of the entity you wish to summon while burping. These vocal eruptions give the spell its power.

When all your burps have been expelled and the root is burned, bury the ash facing west and lie down for ten minutes to allow the gases to settle.

I was about to check the cupboards to see if we had any lemonade when Dad reappeared.

"Sorry, Rosie, no computer time for you. I've only got forty minutes before this lady arrives for her interview, so I need to get on."

I sloped out of the office, feeling utterly defeated. I didn't even know if it was a waxing moon, which if I remember rightly was after a new moon and leading up to a full moon. As for liquorice root,

I hadn't had a chance to rifle through Mum's dried herb collection.

I took myself up to my bedroom to get changed, noticing on the way that we did have a big bottle of lemonade on the side. Well, that was something. At least we could practise the 'speaking while burping' part of the spell.

At 5 p.m. exactly there was a sharp rap on the front door, and my stomach flipped. I didn't know whether to rush downstairs and see what this prospective nanny was like, or whether to remain hidden in my bedroom.

"Come on, Rosie, let's go down and see who it is," whispered Lois loudly, as she stuck her head around my bedroom door. She was clutching Bea (as usual) and had her T-shirt on inside out.

"Lois, your T-shirt's on the wrong way," I said frowning, trying to make out what it said.

Lois shrugged casually. "Well, I'm going down." She turned swiftly, and I heard the pitter-patter of her feet going down the stairs.

I crept out of my room and leaned over the bannister, cautiously sneaking a look as Dad opened the door.

"Hello, come in. Ah, let me help you with that."

I watched through narrowed eyes as Dad turned back into the hall carrying an enormous tartan hat box, which completely obscured his face. And following him, looking as if she was bursting to tell a big secret, trying not to grin from ear to ear, was Frances!

I stared open-mouthed. I really was in total

shock. I had to check myself to make sure we hadn't actually done the summoning spell.

No, we really hadn't, and yet Frances was following my father into the lounge, her familiar Scottish burr reverberating around the house like a warm glow.

"Thank you so much, Mr Pellow. I'm not very good at travelling light, I'm afraid, and I've given up on the traditional handbag." She chuckled as if she'd just told a great joke. "I can never find anything in mine anyway!"

"Do sit down, Miss Fothermiddle," I heard my Dad say.

"Muddle," Frances corrected him.

"Yes, I am in one, rather. That's working from home and trying to look after the kids, eh?" Dad laughed.

"No, no, dear, it's muddle. My name is Fother*muddle*, not middle. Although I do have plenty of middle, too. Must be my age!"

I could imagine Frances patting her rotund tummy as she said this.

Then the door closed, and I skidded down the stairs, nearly knocking Lois over, who had been crouched on the bottom step, hiding behind the menagerie of coats that were hanging over the bottom of the bannister post. We shared a look of mutual delight and excitement.

"Did you know about this?" I whispered curiously.

With her eyes wide, she shook her head.

I pulled her up, and we crept over to the door to try to listen in.

"And you have your own transport, you say?" we heard Dad ask, trying to do an authoritative voice.

"Oh yes, there's nae problem there," Frances chuckled. I cringed, just knowing she was referring to her broomstick. "And I have my CFW certificate here."

We could hear she was rummaging around in her hat box.

"Here we are."

There was silence.

"Child Friendly Witch?" Dad said very slowly.

Lois and I looked at each other, horrified.

"Er, no, no, misprint. It's meant to say, 'Child Friendly Which Is All You Need!' It's the, er, new thingy out to replace the old checks ..." Frances trailed off with a nervous giggle.

"Right," we heard Dad reply.

"I am very flexible, as well," Frances continued, clearly ticking off each of Dad's requirements from the advert.

"Quick, let's get in the room before she starts doing a back bend or something," I said, grabbing Lois and pushing her through the door.

"Er," Dad looked towards us, "these are my girls. This is Miss Fothergiggle," he said, nodding towards Frances.

I don't know about Fothergiggle, but I could barely hold *my* giggle in.

Frances looked horrified. "Just call me Frances, Mr Pellow. Easiest all round, methinks!"

"Well, yes, where was I? I'm sure I needed to check on a few more things." Dad looked vacantly at me and Lois and then back to Frances. He paused, looking as though he was unable to take his gaze away from her.

Frances, meanwhile, sat comfortably on our sofa. Maggie had already jumped up and was treading her lap. Frances had clearly tried to dress more 'conservatively', as she had on a dark blue skirt and a cream shirt with a blue blazer, so she looked rather like some eccentric Girl Guide mistress. Yet the familiar pop socks were half-mast, and she wore her big black boots.

She smiled benignly at Dad, winked at Lois, and glanced at me conspiratorially.

Finally, after what seemed like an age, Dad spoke. "Well, when can you start, Frances?"

"How about now?" she replied sweetly.

6

THE BOOK OF THE DEAD

Dad went back to his office somewhat confused looking, as if he wasn't quite sure whether he had imagined the entire encounter. I could see that, to a non-believer like Dad, meeting someone like Frances would feel a bit like an out-of-body experience.

Usually non-believers (in magic) couldn't see witches or wizards like Frances and our other ex-houseguests, unless of course they chose to show themselves to them.

"Come here, my wee girls!" Frances whispered, holding her arms out to us as Dad left the room.

"Oh, Frances," I gulped through my tears, "I thought we were never going to see you again! I've missed you so much."

"Me too," Lois added, snuggling into Frances' cuddly frame. "Although Paloma told us someone we knew would come and be our childminder."

"Did she now?" Frances said thoughtfully.

"Where are Phyllis and Mr Foggerty and Uncle Vic?" I added, hoping that the arrival of Frances would mean the others wouldn't be far behind. "And how have you managed to get all your clothes and everything in that hat box?"

Though large, it was certainly not big enough to contain Frances' vast array of clothes, shoes, and toiletries.

"One thing at a time, my love," laughed Frances, securing her hat box with a click. "Uncle Vic is at our new headquarters, and Phyllis and Mr Foggerty are down in London."

I pulled a face. "That's miles away," I said, completely dejected.

"Not as far as you think, young lady ..." Frances tapped her nose. "And our new headquarters are in Liverpool city centre, so not far at all. But this means, my loves, I won't be staying here like before. So, I haven't got any of my clothes with me this time. They are all back at headquarters." Frances stroked my hair, noticing how disappointed I looked. "Hey! You know we had to close the portal down in your house, don't you, hen?"

I nodded.

"It wasn't safe, not with ..." She hesitated, as if worried saying his name might conjure him up, "... Mal Vine having found Phyllis. He knew there was a way through to your home, and so we had to close down and re-open elsewhere."

"Frances, do you have any Scottish batteries?" Lois said, completely changing the subject. "Only, our fridge magnet has stopped working, and I thought as you come from Scotland you might be able to fix it?"

"Oh dear," Frances replied, looking a little bemused. "Remind me to take a look at it sometime. By the way, where is your mum, girls? Will she be back soon?"

"Mum's got this three-month job on a soap opera, so she's a bit busy right now," I said glumly.

"Oh yes, that's right! I expect she'll be home soon, and I don't want to get in the way of your family meal tonight. Let's go into the kitchen and see if we can do anything to help before she gets back."

We followed Frances into the kitchen and sat at the table while she peeled potatoes. (She said she was sure Mum was intending on us all having sausage, homemade chips, and beans for tea.) I didn't like to remind Frances that beans were often a no-go area in our house, due to Lois' copious amounts of wind.

We chatted companionably for a while, though I could tell Frances was avoiding telling me much about what they had been doing.

"So why were you in Egypt?" I asked, glancing towards the postcard that was still attached to our fridge by the Scottish fridge magnet. It was true that it had mysteriously run out of battery since the portal had closed down. Previously, whenever anyone pressed it, Scottish music played, and everyone had to stop what they were doing and join in with Scottish dancing for the duration of the tune.

Lois and I had tried on many occasions to press it, usually to avoid some sort of 'chore' we had to do, or if we thought Mum and Dad were about to have an argument. Yet it remained oddly silent.

Frances barely glanced up but continued peeling potatoes furiously. "We were on our holibobs, pet, that's all."

"So why aren't you all together now you're back? Why are Phyllis and Mr Foggerty in London?"

Frances shrugged casually. "They just are for now ... Like I said, since the portal had to close, we've all had to disband a little and spread ourselves around a wee bit."

"Are you saying we won't see them again?" I probed, looking serious.

"No, no, no, dear, just they have a very important job to do right now, that's all."

"Is that horrible man back? Phyllis' brother who was trying to hurt us all?" Lois piped up.

I opened my eyes in surprise. I had thought she was drawing a picture of Bea. She had obviously been earwigging. Sneaky moo.

Frances looked cornered. "Oh no, don't be a daftie. He's long gone. We'll no' be hearing from him for a wee while!"

I studied her pallor, which had gone grey. I knew she could feel my eyes boring into the back of her head, and she shifted uncomfortably.

The silence was broken by my dad appearing, hovering nervously in the doorway of his office.

"Everyone okay?" He looked from me to Lois to Frances and grinned. "Getting to know one another all right?"

Frances met my eye and looked slightly uncomfortable. "Oh yes, Mr Pellow, we're already great friends, aren't we, girls?"

"Please, call me John," Dad said, looking at Frances as if he were trying to work out why she seemed familiar in some way.

"Yes, Daddy, we are great friends. It's almost as if we've known Frances ALL OUR LIVES," Lois said with a butter-wouldn't-melt expression on her face.

"Great." Dad smiled, nodding his head at nothing in particular. "Well, ladies, Mum should be home soon, and then by all means feel free to go, Miss Fumblemaker."

"*Frances*, please..." Frances trilled, sounding cross, which almost made me giggle.

Dad, still looking a bit dazed, shuffled back into his office.

"Frances, what's wrong?" I queried with a whisper. "You don't quite seem your usual self today. Is something bothering you?"

The mask that she had clearly been putting on was starting to slip. I watched fondly as she bent over to pull up her flesh-coloured pop socks, which were currently flapping about in a wrinkled mess down by her ankles.

"Sorry, Rosie, you're right. I am a bit ..." She fumbled around for the word. "Jumpy. Yes, that's it. I'm jumpy. I don't know why. My mother always used to say to me when I was like this, '*What is wrong with you, child? You're like a piggie who's been grabbed by the tail.*'"

"A piggie?" Lois exclaimed.

"Aye. Well, I was a little chubby as a girl."

I gave Frances a questioning look.

44

"I cannae explain it, girls. I just feel a wee bit out of sorts, that's all. I cannae put my finger on it."

"I can!" Lois guffawed, putting her index finger on the end of her nose and then crossing her eyes as she attempted to fix her gaze on it.

Thankfully, we were interrupted by the sound of a key in the door and a heavy *thwump* as my mum surrendered up her numerous bags.

Lois and I grinned at each other, wondering if Mum had also known that Frances was coming. However, the look on her face as she entered the kitchen told us everything we needed to know.

"Oh!" she gasped, looking at Frances as if she had seen a ghost.

I just heard Mum snarl under her breath, "What the heck are you doing here?" when Dad popped his head round the door again.

"Hi, love. Meet our new childminder, Frances Feathersnatcher."

"Just Frances, dear," replied Frances through gritted teeth, as she held out her hand to Mum, fixing her with a beady stare.

Mum recovered herself quickly. I don't think Lois noticed, as she had her tongue firmly out of her mouth while concentrating on colouring in Bea's nose with a pink felt-tip pen.

"Pleased to meet you, Frances. I hope the girls have been behaving for you?" Mum said. "So, thank you for coming, and I'm sure we'll see you again soon."

Frances looked a little confused and started blinking furiously.

Dad had by this point returned to his office. Lois was still colouring in, and I was aghast at the strange way Mum was speaking to Frances.

"Mum? What are you talking about? It's Frances!" I said in a loud, embarrassed whisper. "Our Frances. Our Aunty. This is great, isn't it?"

Mum sort of pursed her lips together and attempted a smile. "Of course it is, darling. Frances, could I have a very quick word before you head off?"

I felt so sorry for Frances. She had by now taken her jacket off, which really was not "her" at all. I could see the beginnings of sweat patches forming under her armpits, and her poor, forlorn pop socks had no chance of staying up whatsoever. She grabbed her jacket, looking totally lost, and dropped a kiss on top of my and then Lois' head with a whisper.

"See you girlies soon. Ta-ta."

I could have sworn I saw tears in her eyes. Even Lois looked up from her picture and said, "Oh, bye, Frances. See you soon. I've missed you." But then she went back to her drawing, so she might have just as well said, "Bring me a biscuit, will you?"

I watched Mum take Frances' arm, rather too firmly for my liking, and usher her out into the hall.

So, what did I do? I crept to the kitchen door that she'd closed on her way out and listened with my ears pricked up like a meerkat. It was quite tricky to make out everything that they were saying, so I peeked through the keyhole in the door, which somehow helped.

Mum was standing with her hands on her hips scolding Frances.

"I've moved on, Frances. This witchcraft nonsense could ruin my career now. I want no part of it, please."

"But Rae, how can you deny what your calling is? All the good you do with your spells, how beautifully you took on the role of Guardian of the Portal — what a role model you are to young Rosie and Lois."

"Frances, you're not listening!" Mum hissed. "The portal is no longer. I have a proper job, okay, for three months only, but who knows if it might get extended? We need this. *I* need this. I need to turn my back on Wicca now and get with the real world."

"But, my dear, Rae, Wicca is the real world. It's the world we live in, and we must cherish it and protect it and harness its powers to help us defeat the darkness."

"You're sounding like a lunatic, Frances. The world I'm now in — of TV and show business — thinks it's all mumbo jumbo. If I'm to be taken seriously, I need to be more like the others. I need to fit in." Mum sounded desperate now.

Suddenly, I saw Frances glance at Mum's wrist, where I'd noticed the "hole", and I knew she'd seen it, too.

As Mum was talking, a greenish mist emanated from the hole, and I'm pretty certain, as it started to fade, that the hole was bigger.

"Don't lose yourself, Rae," Frances whispered,

touching Mum's arm, which she pulled back, re-
coiling as if she had been burnt.

"And I don't want my girls' heads filled with
nonsense of moons and stars and witchcraft. You're
here to childmind, just keep it at that, please." And
with that, Mum ushered Frances out the door.

I couldn't believe what I was hearing. Mum
LOVED Frances, Phyllis, Mr Foggerty and Uncle
Vic, didn't she? They were our family, weren't
they?

I couldn't understand why Mum was being
like this. She had always embraced her "witchi-
ness", as she called it. She loved helping people
with her spell kits and her herbal remedies. She
always told us the importance of spreading light
out into the world with kindness and using the
power of nature to bring goodness to any
situation.

I felt confused about what it all meant. Mum
knew I could see colours around people, so did this
mean she'd be angry towards me, too? This "ability"
wasn't something I had chosen — it was just part of
me. But maybe I needed to try to keep it hidden
right now, until I felt Mum had returned to her
normal self.

I watched her for a moment longer. She stood
in the hall looking at herself in the mirror, the
mirror that had been the starting point for the portal. I couldn't see what expression was in her eyes,
but I felt that she was behaving in a way that really
wasn't her.

Suddenly there was a pop, and the TV
switched on.

Lois and I both jumped as it was showing the main news channel, which we never have on.

The headline caught my eye.

The *Book of the Dead* stolen from Ancient Egyptian collection.

Egyptian. *What a coincidence*, I thought. Egypt was where Frances and the others had been.

I felt a cold shiver go down my neck and listened to the newscaster.

"The highly collectible and prized Book of the Dead has mysteriously been stolen from the British Museum. The Book of the Dead is said to be a detailed guide from Ancient Egypt that enabled the deceased spirit to find their way through the underworld and into the afterlife. The book has been sought after by collectors all over the world, and the police are treating this very seriously. Museum staff believe this may have been an inside job and are questioning employees, as no alarms were set off and the infra-red cameras showed no sign of any deliberate break in."

The local reporter then started showing various Egyptian artefacts that the museum housed, which concluded with the empty lectern that presumably had contained the *Book of the Dead*. The surrounding glass was untouched — no force had been used — so the untidy-looking museum curator agreed that its disappearance was indeed a mystery.

I did a double take.

The untidy museum curator was wearing a badge with the initials B. Foggerty on it, and standing just behind him was a tall, slim, older lady with a grey perm and blue-rimmed spectacles: Phyllis.

What on earth were Phyllis and Mr Foggerty doing in the British Museum?

7

ADI'S BOMBSHELL

I didn't dare mention anything to Mum about having seen Phyllis and Mr Foggerty on the TV in the British Museum. I thought that Mum would probably say my eyes were deceiving me or something.

She certainly wasn't herself all weekend. She had been tired and stressed out with all the lines she had to learn, and Dad had raised his eyebrows secretly at me more than once as he tried to reassure her that all would be well.

"You don't understand, John. This is such an important job. I have to fit in. I have to know what I'm doing. I have to make a good impression," Mum had said.

"Love, you wouldn't have got the job in the first place if you hadn't made a good impression. Just relax and do what you do," Dad had suggested, squeezing her arm.

I'd kept my gaze very firmly planted on her arm with the hole. I was sure it had got bigger. I was going to keep a watchful eye on that.

I knew this week was a full-on week for Mum — she was working every day *and* having to stay over Tuesday and Thursday night.

Lois and I were not happy. The only positive I could see was that Frances would be with us every day, thank goodness, and perhaps she would be able to shed some light on why Phyllis and Mr Foggerty were working at the British Museum.

Monday morning, Mum didn't have to leave until after we'd gone to school, and she was very teary saying goodbye to us at the school gate.

"Don't be sad, Mummy," Lois whispered, hugging her. "I'm going to be busy today playing with Daisy, and I'll see you tonight. You can take Bea with you to work, if you want to, as long as you bring her home for me later."

"Thank you, darling, that's very sweet, but I think Bea would prefer to stay cosy in your bed today. I'll see you soon, girls."

Mum hugged us both and smiled a watery smile. "Sorry if I was grumpy this weekend. I'll get used to the hours, I expect. Be good for Frances."

All the way through maths, I kept trying to catch Adi's eye, but of course we were doing fractions, which he loved, so I didn't have a chance.

Finally, at lunchtime, he sauntered out into the playground, completely oblivious to the stares I'd been giving him.

"What?" he asked me, screwing his face up so his glasses stayed up on the bridge of his nose. I tried hard not to be distracted by a flapping booger up his left nostril.

"Adi, I've been trying to catch your eye all morning. We need to talk."

He looked totally blank and shook his head at me as if to say, "no idea what you're on about."

"The aunts ... Mr Foggerty ... Phyllis ... They're BACK!" I whispered pointedly.

"Back?" Adi replied open-mouthed.

Now I'd got his attention.

"Yes!" I hissed, dragging him over to the "apple" contemplative space.

"When?" he replied. "Why didn't you message me?"

"Too complicated," I sighed, plonking myself on the bench.

He was all ears while I explained to him that Frances had replied to Dad's advert for a childminder, and thankfully Dad had given her the job before he'd realised that he hadn't actually interviewed anyone else for it (nor had we received any other replies, strangely enough).

"That's brilliant, isn't it?" Adi asked.

He soon lost his smile once I'd shaken my head.

"Well, it should be brilliant, but Mum was acting so weird around Frances, and she basically told her that she was turning her back on everything witchy, because she was worried people at her work would think she was odd," I explained.

The irony of this wasn't lost on me for one second, as the images of Harriet doing yoga in her underwear flashed into my head. Maybe Mum needed to not worry so much about appearing "weird".

"Plus, the TV then switched on by itself and showed this newsflash of some famous Egyptian book that's been stolen from the British Museum, and Phyllis and Mr Foggerty were there being interviewed as they were working there!" I continued.

"What's the name of the book?" Adi asked, his face taking on a serious expression.

"Did you hear what I said, Ads? The TV switched itself on." Okay, so he was used to the strange goings on in our house by now. I tried another tack. "Phyllis and Mr Foggerty were there. I mean, what's that—"

"Rosemary, tell me the name of the book!" Adi interrupted me, and I was startled by the look in his eyes.

"Some Egyptian book about dead people, I think," I replied casually.

Adi looked like he was going to be sick. I giggled nervously.

"It wasn't," he paused and swallowed dramatically, "the *Book of the Dead*, was it?"

I don't know why, but my mouth went dry, and all I could do was move my head up and down like one of those nodding dog figurines.

Adi took his glasses off and proceeded to try to clean them slowly with part of his shirt. His brown eyes looked troubled, and I noticed as he replaced his specs that they looked dirtier than when he'd taken them off.

"This is serious then," he finally concluded.

I was beginning to feel like I might get the giggles at any moment now. The urgency of the situation had totally escaped me. A book had been stolen from some museum. I mean, really, how serious was this likely to be?

"Why?" I asked him, quashing my laughter as I tried to think of sad things like dead puppies and kittens.

"If that book gets into the wrong hands, we are all in very grave danger. The *Book of the Dead* contains some of the most feared creatures of the underworld, and if they are released into the world, heaven help us all."

My stomach flipped over. "You need to tell me EVERYTHING about this book now!"

"I don't know everything about it, Rosemary. I think we are going to have to ask Frances about it. The fact that you saw Mr Foggerty and Phyllis working at the British Museum suggests they must have known the book was in danger of being stolen. And didn't you say the postcard you got from them all was from Egypt?"

I nodded.

"Doesn't that seem a bit of a coincidence to you?" Adi continued. "They were all in Egypt, and now suddenly this book from Ancient Egyptian times goes missing?"

It did seem more than a coincidence. "What is the book about though, Adi?"

He glanced at his watch. "We haven't much time before the bell goes. But listen, it's basically a book that explains how a dead person's soul, which is the essence of the person—"

"Yes, it's the person you are inside, the person you are without the shell of your body, I suppose," I interrupted.

Adi hurriedly continued, "So the book gives instructions as to how a person's soul, you know, once they are dead, can make the journey from this world to the afterlife. But on the way, they have to pass through something called "the underworld", which is full of scary things. If they pass these tests and get through it, they make it into heaven or the afterlife. It's what the Egyptians believed in, so when they mummified people — which is a process of preserving their bodies, because they felt after death that the souls would still need them — the *Book of the Dead* gave them instructions on how to get to the next stage of their journey."

I was puzzled. "But surely someone would only need this book if they were dead and their soul needed to find the way to the afterlife? No one alive would need it, unless they were collectors who wanted to maybe try to sell it or something ..."

"What about someone who might want it to unleash the creatures of the underworld so that they could destroy us all?"

For a few moments I pretended Adi was having me on. "Oh, Adi, don't be daft! We're not in *Star Wars*. Who on earth would want to unleash evil monsters on the world?"

"Someone who wants to destroy things," he said.

"Well, I don't think Jabba is quite up to that yet ..." I joked about Adi's little brother who was both a pain in the bum and liked to break everything in sight.

"I'm not talking about Jabba, Rosemary. I'm

talking about someone else, someone who we knew might reappear at some point."

I looked at Adi, knowing exactly who he was referring to, a feeling of dread in my tummy.

"Okay," I said, knowing I was delaying facing up to the inevitable. "Who would want to destroy the world by unleashing the creatures from the book?"

"Mal Vine," Adi replied, and my blood ran cold.

8

THE RETURN OF MAL VINE

All afternoon my mind wandered, to the point where Mr Bobbin, our music and RE teacher, started to go sweaty and red in the face as he told me off for the third time.

"Rosemary Pellow, this is most unlike you! Will you concentrate, please? You've only got to bash the triangle. Poor Treena's got to blow the penny whistle just before Justin's bongo solo, and you keep messing up!"

"Sorry, Mr Bobbin," I mumbled.

When the end of the school day finally came, I whispered to Adi in the cloakroom, "I'm going to speak to Frances when we get home. We have to find out what's going on here. I need to know if Mal Vine is back."

I shuddered inside as I remembered his brown flinty eyes that would bore straight through me as he tried to threaten my family. I couldn't understand how he could be back so soon after we had defeated him.

"I'll come to yours, Rosemary, if that's okay?"

Adi questioned eagerly. "I have to know how serious this is."

I nodded, grabbed my bag, and walked briskly out into the playground. I saw Frances straight away — thank goodness she was back in her own eccentric attire. Today she was wearing a bright yellow velvet dress, which thankfully came down to her mid-calves, so we were spared the top end of her pop socks. However, I did wonder how long they would stay up for on the walk home.

She was smiling slightly anxiously, and I could see she was trying to avoid all contact with other parents.

I briefly wondered whether it was tiring for her, making herself visible for all the grown-ups and non-believers, just so we could be allowed to be released from school.

I watched Lois rush up to her and hug her, and Frances planted a kiss on top of Lois' head, which she rubbed off, screwing her face up, and then proceeded to pull open the plastic bag Frances was holding, presumably looking for crisps or biscuits.

"Hi Frances!" I said quietly, as my mind was still focused on our fears about Mal Vine returning. "Is it okay if Adi comes round for a short time?"

"Of course, Rosie," she replied, scanning the playground for him. "Is he coming now?"

"No, he's just gonna go home and get changed and then meet us there."

"Right so, let's go, girleens, then," she continued, rummaging in her bag for crisps for me. Lois was already tucking into an oaty biscuit and had crumbs all stuck to the edges of her lips.

I walked home slightly behind my sister and Frances, who were singing the Beatles' song "Yellow Submarine", except Lois had managed to get Frances to sing "sumbarine" instead, which the pair of them thought was hilarious.

At last we got home, and don't ask me how he did it, but Adi was sitting on our doorstep in his jeans and a T-shirt reading a comic. He grinned at us and flared his nostrils, pushing his glasses back up on his nose.

"Slow coaches, aren't you?" he joked, standing back to let Frances open the front door.

Once Frances had helped Lois out of her uniform and said she could play on the computer, Adi and I loitered round the kitchen, waiting for her to come and sit down.

She eyed us suspiciously. "And what's going on with you two, mmm? You're like a pair of fidget spinners, and if I didn't know better, you're after something." She squashed her spongy bottom into Bob's rocking chair. (He wasn't on it, thankfully.) "Come on, spill the coffee."

Adi and I looked at each other and burst out laughing. "Do you mean spill the *tea*, Frances?" Adi hooted.

"Aye, whatever, just tell me what's going on," Frances replied rather crossly.

I sat down at the table in the kitchen and motioned to Adi to do the same. I took a deep breath and wondered whether she would tell me the truth. I knew I'd be able to tell, for if someone was telling a fib, brown smoke came out of their mouths.

"Adi thinks that Mal Vine might have stolen the

Book of the Dead from the British Museum, and we are worried that means he's back again and eager to hurt us in some way."

There was silence. Frances looked down towards her belly and raised her hand to her face and started wiping imaginary food from her mouth. (Well, that's what it looked like to me.) Afterwards, Adi would tell me it was a nervous reaction that proved she was unsure how to answer us.

"Is it true, Frances?" I whispered.

We both seemed to hold our breath until she slowly nodded her head.

"Aye, bairns, it's true. We are pretty sure he has stolen it. I don't know how he managed to get out of LIMBO, but he did and, well, Mr Foggerty and Phyllis, who are posted at the British Museum, are certain it's him."

"What's LIMBO?" I asked nervously, my mind conjuring up images of Mal Vine floating in the sky in between Earth and some other planet.

"Leeds Institute for Men Behaving Oddly," Frances reeled off. "It's a place where they put men who have done bad things — a sort of halfway house, instead of having to resort to the Tunnel of Eternal Darkness, which is the prison he was released from a while ago. I wouldn't be surprised if he'd conned his way out of there. These places are so short-staffed right now; there always seems to be some disaster going on somewhere else in the world, and Hecate orders folk to leave their posts and flock to sort out another catastrophe, not realising, of course, that we are left here picking up the pieces." She turned to look at us and gave us a wan smile. "I'm sorry, I'm going on and on, but what I will say—"

At that moment, we were both distracted by the front door being opened.

Mum was home earlier than we had anticipated!

"Hellooooo, girls, are you there? Good news, I was cut from my other scene, so I've got away early, which will make up for the fact I'm having to stay over tomorrow night." Mum appeared at the kitchen doorway smiling and holding her arms out to me.

We hugged, and then Lois joined us rather reluctantly as she was playing games on CBeebies.

By the way Frances jumped up, gathered her enormous hat box, and slipped her shoes back on, I guessed Mum had given her some kind of evil look.

How could Mum be cross with Frances when she was so kind to us? She was our family.

"Mrs Pellow," I heard Frances say by manner of greeting.

I couldn't believe what I was hearing!

At least Mum had the grace to reply, though rather stiffly, "Call me Rae, please."

I didn't really understand what was going on. After all, Dad was at work, and Adi had met Frances before.

"Mum?" I queried in a light-hearted voice. "We all know Frances. Dad's not here. We don't need to pretend."

Mum ignored me and brushed past us to turn the kettle on. "See Frances out, will you, darling, while I make some tea? Is Adi staying for food?"

"No thanks, Mrs Pellow. I'll get off now." And Adi took this as his cue to follow Frances and I out to the front door.

I felt quite choked up at the way Mum was behaving towards Frances — it was just so weird. I know I'd overheard her telling Frances that she didn't want to be involved with any more magic or Wicca, but how could she deny it all?

It was part of who we were.

Frances touched my head lightly as she stepped out of the house. "Tomorrow, I'll take you to see Phyllis and Mr Foggerty," she whispered. "We'll have an adventure."

"Really? That would be fantastic!" I said, feeling tears prick my eyes. "Can Adi come, too?"

"Of course! Adi must come. Remember, Rosie, the power of three ..."

I watched as Frances walked one way and Adi the other. I watched her until my eyes started to sting, and as I blinked away the soreness and looked for her yellow figure in the distance, I realised she had gone, and then it struck me.

Phyllis and Mr Foggerty were in London.

How were we going to get there and back in a couple of hours after school?

9
HOLY MOLY!

Mal Vine's rasping voice, the voice I'd heard in my dream, was still ringing in my ears as I sat at the kitchen table, sending shivers down my spine.

'*I will unleash the forces of the book. I will seek vengeance for all you took. This is my time. Witches of the night, prepare to fight.*'

Adi must be right; Mal Vine had stolen the *Book of the Dead*. It made sense that he would want to release the demons inside the book to the outside world. Yet wouldn't that also mean the end of the world not only for us, but for him, too? He was clearly still seeking revenge for Phyllis having left him as a child.

I ate my tea slowly and thoughtfully, glancing every now and again at Mum, who was sitting in the rocking chair with her script.

Funny, I could see right through her middle to the cushion propped behind her. It had an ugly blackberry-jam-looking stain on it, and I thought how it must have been Lois' work, as she was the only person I knew who managed to get food in the craziest places.

Hang on! I stopped my daydreams and focused once again on the cushion on the rocking chair. The cushion I *shouldn't* be able to see, because it was right behind Mum's back. OMG! There was another hole in her.

I flicked my gaze towards her wrists. Yes, the original hole was still very much present, and if I squinted, I could make out the greenish mist swirling very close to it. As I looked back to her stomach, I could see the hole was the size of the bottom of a mug. I felt as if I could have put my hand through it.

I thought back to last year when Dad was really depressed, and how I'd seen the dark shadow envelop him. It wasn't the same thing as this. I mean, my mum wasn't depressed, so what did these holes mean? Was Mum slowly disappearing? And if so, where was she going and how could I stop it?

I was pretty sure Frances had also seen them, thinking back to her reaction in the hallway when Mum had spoken to her. This both comforted me that I wasn't just "seeing things", but also alarmed me — if Frances could see them, too, then there was no denying that something was eating away at my mum. Could it be something to do with her sudden change of heart towards all things magical? I pondered whether I should tell Frances, but somehow it felt like that would be disloyal to my mum.

"Darling, are you all right?" Mum's voice broke into my thoughts. "You've been staring at my tummy for ages." Mum stretched her torso up and pulled her tummy in. "Have I spilt tea down myself or something?"

Could I tell her? No. Not yet. She was very touchy right now about EVERYTHING, and I didn't want to alarm her until I had figured out what was going on. Nor did I want to run the risk of her not believing me.

"No, of course not, Mum." I paused, wondering how to word this. "You haven't got tummy ache or anything, have you?"

"No! Why do you ask that?"

Luckily, I was good at thinking on my feet. "No reason, I just ... thought I heard it rumbling."

"Well, I'm starving so that's probably why. But I must wait for dinner and not be tempted to reach for the biscuit tin."

"Did someone say biscuits?" came a voice from the deep.

"She's had crisps, Mum, and a biscuit."

"Wait till dinner time, Lois, then you can have a biscuit for pudding as long as you eat all your mains."

"Well," I continued, trying to find a way of discovering whether these holes were linked to her sudden denial of magic. "Have you got any spells to do for anyone yet? I could help you like I usually do?"

I loved helping my mum put all her colourful bags of herbs and crystals together. It made me feel like we had a special connection.

Mum looked at me like she'd been slapped. "No," she replied in her "that's the end of the discussion" tone. "I've turned my back on all that now, Rosie."

I watched her fingers move up toward the chain she always wore around her neck — her five-pointed star, the symbol of Wicca — in a gesture she would often do if she felt anxious. I frowned slightly as I saw her replace her fingers in her lap.

The necklace was missing.

She had only ever taken it off once, that I could remember, when slimy Marcus from the play had given her a necklace with her initial on last year. Fortunately, once she'd realised how fake he was, she had put the necklace away and gone back to wearing her pentacle.

"Where's your necklace, Mum?" I asked, wondering if she had left it in her dressing room by accident.

"I, er, I've taken it off for now, Rosie." She looked down and thankfully had the grace to look a little ashamed.

"Why would you take it off? You said that Frances and Phyllis had bought you that when you first became Guardian of the Portal here and that you would treasure it!"

"Yes, darling, I know that, but life moves on. The portal is no longer here, so my services aren't needed anymore. I've spent my life believing in magic and following the practices of Wicca, and it's never done anything much for me, sweetheart." Mum moved towards me and cupped my face in her hands. "And now I've got a really great TV job, and I don't want people to think I'm odd or un-hinged. I have to try to find a way to fit in."

Her fingers felt sharp on my face, and I saw tears welling up in her eyes. This wasn't the mum I knew; that mum got sad about not getting the work she wanted, but was grateful when small miracles did happen, like getting an audition, or a reply to her letter, or even unrelated work things like the first rose blooming in the garden or the beloved pear tree in blossom. This mum, however, looked pinched and tired and had holes in her.

"But Mum," I continued quietly, "I don't understand. You've always said how important it is to be true to ourselves, to go with our feelings right deep down in our tummies, no matter what anyone says or thinks."

Mum looked into my eyes for what felt like an age. She didn't say anything at all. I could see little bubbles forming around her head in dark green that would collide into one another, and then the smaller bubble would be squashed. It was almost as if these bubbles were fighting with each other.

Finally, Mum spoke. "She told me the studio would think I was a liability."

"Who?"

"Donna."

She leaned back in the rocking chair and sighed, running her fingers through her auburn hair.

"Donna asked me what the symbol on my necklace meant, and I told her it was a pagan symbol to represent Wicca, and she freaked out."

"What did she say?" I was completely shocked that Donna could react like this to a way of life that Mum had always taught us to embrace.

The wheel of nature mirrors the wheel of life. I always remembered Mum teaching us that.

"She said I ought to remove it as the studio might get the wrong idea and think I was putting curses on people, etcetera," Mum said.

"But did you explain about how you only ever do white magic, as anything bad comes back on you threefold?" I asked.

"Oh, darling, if only it were that simple. Donna is one of the important people in the cast. She's just giving me the heads up so I can keep my job. I'm grateful to her, really, I am."

I wasn't so sure that Donna deserved Mum's gratitude. I remembered the way she'd looked at us when we had FaceTimed Mum. I didn't like the way whatever Donna said, Mum seemed to take notice of.

"Oh, Rosie," she added, turning away from me. "I wish I knew what the future held for me. And Dad, too. All this nonsense about wanting to change jobs. It's the first I've heard of it."

I wondered too about the future, and for some reason it didn't feel good right now. Even though Mum was saying she was renouncing her love of magic because she didn't want to lose her job, it just didn't ring true. A studio couldn't sack someone for their beliefs, could they? What about if you were wearing a cross or the Star of David or a crescent moon?

Surely we should be embracing our differences, not wanting everyone to be the same.

No, something was very wrong, and I needed to go about uncovering the truth.

10

THE TUNNELS

At 3.30 p.m. the bell went and Adi and I leapt out of our seats and headed towards the play-ground. I saw Frances immediately — she was wearing the bright yellow frock again, with her big Doc Martens, in spite of the fact it was June. Lois was already munching on a packet of crisps, and Frances rather thoughtfully had brought Adi some crisps, too, so he wasn't left out.

"Come along then, bairns. We haven't much time to lose. Let's be getting on so we can get to London and back before your Dad gets home later."

I really couldn't quite see how this was going to be possible. "Frances, Dad will be home about 7.30 p.m. How are we going to get to London and back before then? It takes over two hours on the train, so by the time we get there we'd have to have already left to get back home before Dad. It doesn't make sense."

"Aha!" Frances grinned, tapping her nose. "We'll see, won't we? Come along. Bus into town first."

We trailed after her, an excited Lois clinging on to her sleeves.

"Frances, are we going on your broomstick?" she said in a very loud whisper, just as we passed Mr Bobbin.

I giggled to myself as I saw him visibly recoil and touch the cross he wore around his neck while trying not to stare too obviously at Frances in her eccentric outfit.

Lois insisted on us all sitting on the top deck of the bus, and I felt a teeny bit sorry for Frances who puffed her way up the stairs giving everyone a view of her pop socks, as her dress had ridden up a bit. I did wonder whether I should give it a little tug down, but I could see Adi was already trying to avert his eyes, and so I decided it was best not to draw any more attention to it.

"I wonder how she's intending on getting us to London?" Adi mused, almost to himself, as we watched the local landmarks pass us by: the Picton Clock, Wavertree Town Hall, Hope Street …

"Maybe there's a new superfast train or something, Adi," I suggested.

He raised his eyebrows at me as if to say, "yeah right!" and simultaneously did the flared nostril thing as his glasses slid down his nose. I passed him a tissue that I had in my rucksack.

"Have you considered that Frances might use some magic to get us to London?" Adi whispered while snuffling around in his nose.

I turned away, watching as the bus flew past Lime Street Station. We weren't going by train then.

"Mum's told her she's not allowed to do anything magical with us," I retorted, then looked up to see Frances looking straight at me.

"Don't you be worrying, Rosie. Water seeks its own level." She winked and hoicked herself up from her seat, grabbing Lois' hand. "Come on, folks, this is our stop."

Water seeks its own level. What did that mean? I had a funny feeling it might mean she was going to be doing magic regardless. I looked at Adi, who shrugged, and we all hopped off the bus.

We were right near the huge John Lewis down by the docks, and we followed Frances at a trot as she strode out to cross the busy road. I wondered if we were heading for Albert Dock but no, she carried on along Dock Road until we reached a building that I had never seen before.

"Right, folks," Frances beamed, a little breathless, "here we are. This is George's Dock Building, where we go in. Now listen to me, under no circumstances must you draw any attention to yourselves, okay? Just follow me quickly and quietly and do as I say, do you understand?"

We all nodded obediently, though I was more interested in looking at the Egyptian-style carvings that had been drawn on the outside walls. As we entered the building, there was a very long queue for "Tunnel Tours", which, to my surprise, we joined.

The atmosphere was not unlike a library: quiet and serious. Frances fixed a smile on her face and turned to us with her finger on her lips, making the "shush" symbol.

At that moment, in the silent, stuffy foyer, there was a loud noise, as if a duck had been stamped on. People in the queue turned round with grim faces to look at us, and I knew exactly why they had such cross, disgusted expressions on their faces: Lois had farted.

Loudly.

"Lois!" I whispered. "Frances said specifically to be quiet."

"I didn't feel it come out, Rosie," she whined in retort and stuck out her bottom lip.

Adi looked like he was going to faint, even though it didn't smell, thankfully, and Frances looked worried.

"Never mind, pet, keep your bottom squeezed tightly shut just for now until we're past the queue."

For some reason (I cannot think why), the queue suddenly sped up, and before we knew it we were at the ticket desk being confronted by a burly looking man with a big moustache.

"Tickets. please," he stated gruffly.

Just as Frances started to rummage through her oversized bag, we heard a familiar voice. "It's all right, Reg, you can take your break now. I'll deal with this young lady ..."

Frances blushed and looked most relieved as Reg grumpily shifted his bulky frame out of the ticket-collector box and off through a door marked "Staff Only".

Standing in front of us, leaning up against the booth, smiling, in a brown checked suit that strained over his enormous belly, was our very own Uncle Vic.

"Uncle Vic!" Lois whooped excitedly, throwing herself at his stomach.

Uncle Vic looked pleased to be greeted so enthusiastically but was simultaneously looking around the foyer nervously. To be fair, it wasn't always easy to see where he was looking due to his crossed eyes.

"Hello, hello all. It's lovely to see you, but we must try to be a little quieter," he whispered, peeling Lois from his frame.

"But I really didn't feel it come out my bottom, Uncle Vic," Lois sulked.

"He's not talking about your noisy butt, silly. He's saying let's all shut up and do as he says," I explained patiently to my sister.

She was about to let rip at having been told off, when, thankfully, Adi pulled some food out of his pocket and handed it to her.

"I didn't realise it was going to be so busy today, Vic," murmured Frances anxiously, fanning herself.

"There's a big new attraction in the tunnel tours, that's why. But no matter, Frances, we shall go on our very own tour, shan't we, my friends?" Uncle Vic winked and turned the sign over in the ticket booth so that it read *"Tour full. Come back in one hour"*. There was no time on the notice, so how people would know when one hour was up was anybody's guess.

Uncle Vic watched while the last few people ahead of us were ushered into a room and handed fluorescent orange jackets.

"Why are we going on a tunnel tour, Adi?" I whispered, wondering how that was going to get us to London, as Frances had promised.

"I've been on one of these tunnel tours before with Jabba and my dad," Adi mused excitedly. "It was a few years back, but it was brilliant. You go right down to where the cars go through the Queensway Tunnel, which goes under the River Mersey and comes out on the other side, the Wirral."

I started to switch off as Adi was going on about the machines that extracted the noxious gases from the tunnels and replaced it with clean air. I was more interested in watching Uncle Vic, who was whispering away to Frances and gesticulating.

Finally, we started to move again, and Uncle Vic took us along a corridor and then down some steps that seemed to go on and on.

"Can I put one of those orange jackets on, Frances, please?" pleaded my little sister.

"No, no, no, young lady!" exclaimed Uncle Vic. "We don't want to draw attention to ourselves, do we now?"

Uncle Vic had stopped suddenly, and we all bunched up behind him.

"Oww, Rosie!" moaned Lois as I banged into her, almost knocking her flying.

"Sorry," I replied crossly. "I didn't know we were stopping so suddenly."

To our left was a red door with the word *Extractors* emblazoned on it. Uncle Vic pushed it open, and we descended more steps until we were in a huge underground room that was incredibly noisy, mainly due to the enormous fan in front of us.

"Right, lad and lasses," Uncle Vic shouted above the racket. "I'm going to very briefly stop this fan. See those numbers there?" He pointed to a number gauge to the right of the fan that was reading at 7563. "When that number hits 137, we are going to — one by one — jump through the gaps in the fan."

"Are you sure that's safe, Uncle Vic?" I looked at the speed the fan was going and couldn't imagine (a) it getting to a point where it was slow enough for us to time jumping through a gap, and (b) where on earth *were* the gaps?

"I do not think this is going to work, Rosemary!" Adi shouted in my ear, nearly deafening me.

"Can I go first, please, can I go first!" Lois shouted, jumping up and down like an excitable kangaroo.

"'Course you can, my darlin'!" whooped a delighted Frances.

This was bizarre. I was leaning towards Adi's opinion that there was no way this would work.

Frances and Lois strode closer to the fan, presumably waiting for Uncle Vic to turn the thing off.

I glanced nervously at Adi, who, for the second time, looked as if he were going to faint.

"I'm sure it will be okay, Adi," I added in my best reassuring voice.

At that moment, Uncle Vic pressed a button near the number gauge, and the deafening noise subsided as the fan started to slow down. We watched the numbers decrease rapidly. 7000, 6357, 5400, 4789...

"Uncle Vic!" I shouted, the butterflies in my tummy reaching fever pitch. "Where will this take us? Surely there's another way. This sounds so dangerous!"

3567, 2422, 1997 ...

"Don't worry, Rosemary! I'm a qualified first aider!" he chuckled, winking at me.

I was not reassured by this.

1002, 551, 137 ...

"Go, go, go!" screamed Uncle Vic to Lois and Frances.

The speed of the fan had decreased massively so that it was now going about as fast as the second hand on a clock. There were great blades in between each gap, and though the gaps were large enough to easily fit the cylindrical shape of a well-built adult, I still wasn't keen on taking my chances.

I half-closed my eyes in dread as Lois gave a huge whoop and threw herself through one of the gaps, followed by, to my amazement, Frances. The last I saw of her was a glimpse of her blue and white Scottish-flag underpants, as her dress completely flew up over her head when she dived through the fan.

"Come on, you two, go, go, go!" Uncle Vic motioned to Adi, then ushered me up. "We haven't much time. I prefer to switch this back on before I follow you through, in case I forget once I'm on the other side."

I think it was the fear of him switching it back on that made me push past Adi and just launch myself through. I was surprised to find that there was more room than I had anticipated. Adi followed me so closely I could feel him clinging desperately onto the back of my cardigan. We landed softly on a pile of cushions, with poor Adi's glasses completely skew-whiff, which made me want to giggle.

I looked up and saw Frances and Lois were already high-fiving each other triumphantly. Just as poor Adi was rearranging his glasses on his nose and about to speak, he was flattened once again by the flying arrival of Uncle Vic, whose face was now red and sweaty.

"Oowwwwww," grunted Adi, fumbling about on the cushions for his glasses.

"Sorry, young man!" puffed Uncle Vic, rolling his generous frame away from Adi and passing him his glasses that now had a broken arm.

"Oh man!" sighed Adi. "My mum's gonna kill me. This is the second pair of glasses I've broken."

"Don't worry, pet, give them here a wee second," Frances said, reaching for his glasses.

She made a very strange noise at the back of her throat, then conjured up an almighty amount of spittle, which she rubbed into the join where the lenses met the arm, and then handed them back to Adi.

"Er, thanks, Frances," Adi said cautiously, "but the arm's the wrong way round."

"Oh dear! How did that happen?" She tore the glasses from Adi's face and with further spit reglued them.

I noticed Uncle Vic had a look of utter despair on his face, whereas Adi looked like Frances had just offered to wipe his face with a flannel full of dog poo.

Glasses mended, I took the chance to look around.

We were in a small room with the fan, which, having been turned back on by Uncle Vic, was now whirling away full speed behind us — though we couldn't hear it, which was strange. In front of us was a glass partition, through which we could see a busy office.

Do you remember me telling you I could see colours around people? Well, the strange thing was, all of these people busy working on the other side of the glass were completely colourless, which was exactly how I saw Frances, Phyllis, Uncle Vic and Mr Foggerty. This made me think they also had to be witches and wizards, so I came to the conclusion we must now be in their new headquarters.

The people through the glass were mostly studying computers at desks, and ahead of them, dominating the room, was a huge screen with a world map on it. I could see the British Isles, which were lit up with a bright white flashing light, and then there were various lights in different colours all over the map.

I was dying to go into the room and find out what was happening, but Uncle Vic and Frances were striding ahead, already opening a door to the left of us.

"Come along, folks, this way. We are nearly there!" Uncle Vic ushered us all through the door, and we walked along a corridor, past the room with computers and maps.

I stared through the glass windows at the busy scene, searching anxiously for a familiar face, but no one appeared to take any notice of us all striding by.

"Frances, where are we now?" I asked her, curious to know what was going on.

"We're in our new headquarters, hen. It's got more office space and less recreational space, shall we say. No more beautiful gardens to party in, sadly." She looked off into the distance as if reminiscing about the old headquarters.

"And no Aradia either!" I added, remembering how the postcard we had received from our four friends had told us that Aradia, who was the gatekeeper of the portal, had been sacked for spying for the enemy. The enemy being, of course, Mal Vine.

"No Aradia," Frances echoed.

"But Paloma is still around," Lois added smugly.

I didn't have a chance to ask her further about this, as we came to the end of the corridor, which had widened out without me really noticing. There, ahead of us, were seven tunnels all going off in slightly different directions.

Uncle Vic took one of the tunnels to the right — was it the fifth or sixth tunnel?

As I looked behind, the corridor we had come from now looked just like all the other tunnels, which was a bit spooky.

We strode along for a few minutes, our feet barely touching the ground even though we were moving quickly, as if we were on one of those airport moving walkways. Then, suddenly, whatever had been propelling us stopped, and we were faced with a single iron ladder that sloped dangerously upwards.

Uncle Vic led the way, with me right behind him, followed by Adi, Lois, and Frances taking up the rear.

When I felt I literally had no breath left in my lungs, I could see we had reached a black ceiling. Uncle Vic pushed upwards on a small circular door, and I could see blessed daylight.

One by one we hauled ourselves out of the hole and onto a dimly lit walkway just under a bridge.

Uncle Vic stood proudly, dusting himself down, while Adi and I exchanged frowns, clearly wondering where we were.

I could hear lots of noise above us, the sound of hordes of people walking and cars and the odd beep of horns. The air felt thick and dirty, and there was a nasty smell from the river we were stood by.

As Frances dusted herself down, too, she glanced at Uncle Vic with a glint in her eye.

"Welcome to London," she said with a flourish.

11

THE BRITISH MUSEUM

"London?" Adi questioned, looking totally bewildered. "How did that happen?"

"Well, dear, it happened because Uncle Vic chose the correct tunnel to go under, otherwise we might have ended up on the other side of the Ganges, had it been down to me!"

"Hang on!" I added. "The tunnels go under the Mersey, though, so why haven't we come out on the Wirral? How can we be in London?"

"All a matter of carefully choosing the right tunnel, young lady. And lucky for all of us, I chose the tunnel that goes directly under the Thames, so here we are. And it's just a short walk to the British Museum now." Uncle Vic undid his suit button and patted his stomach as he started to head off once again.

We had no choice except to follow, with Frances and Lois bringing up the rear. Of course, it made no sense whatsoever that one minute we could be in the Mersey Tunnel and then, by choosing a particular path, end up bobbing up the other side of the Thames, but I guess I had kind of got used to the fact that when I was with the witches, anything was possible.

We must have looked a strange bunch following the rotund figure of Uncle Vic, who was clearly in a hurry to get to the British Museum. The rest of us were practically having to run to keep up with him.

I wondered if perhaps Frances and Uncle Vic were invisible here, as no one seemed to bat an eyelid at the five of us, but then again, we were in London, where apparently no one talks to you anyway.

At last we reached the magnificent British Museum, and Adi, Lois, and I gazed in wonder at the huge columns outside the front entrance. It looked very grand, and I felt a little fizz of excitement in my tummy as we had never been here before.

"Can we see the dinosaur skeleton first?" Lois asked eagerly, completely forgetting that only a few moments ago she was moaning that her legs ached.

"Wrong museum," stated Adi. "You're thinking of the Natural History Museum. Plus, the dinosaur has gone. It's a blue whale now."

Frances looked from Adi to Lois, clearly unsure what to say to defuse the situation as my sister looked furious that Adi was correcting her and upset that she wouldn't get to see her dinosaur.

"Never mind, pet," cajoled Frances. "We can see a mummy instead …"

"My mummy's here?" Lois asked, forgetting for a moment she was supposed to be turning on the waterworks.

"The Egyptian mummies. The ones wrapped

up in white bandages, remember?" I shook my head in disbelief.

Lois pulled a face. "Uurghhh, I don't want to see those, thanks. I want a piece of Madeira cake and glass of milk."

Uh-oh, here we go. I smiled to myself. Food again. Madeira cake was one of her new favourites.

Uncle Vic had already had enough of us all admiring the front entrance and was halfway up the steps leading to the door.

"Come along, everyone. I'm sure they'll have a café here, and if not, who knows, Phyllis and Mr Foggerty might have something to take your mind off the long journey."

"Phyllis and Mr Foggerty are here?" Suddenly Lois sounded brighter. "Oh goody, I haven't seen them for AGES!"

We trotted into the museum and soon found ourselves in the Ancient Egyptian area, where Phyllis and Mr Foggerty were "working". I was beginning to wonder if they had been posted here by Hecate to keep guard of the *Book of the Dead*. Perhaps she knew it was going to be in danger?

What didn't make sense to me was why Hecate hadn't been able to prevent it being stolen, if she had her suspicions it was going to happen.

I spotted our old houseguests immediately. Phyllis was addressing a group of tourists explaining the process of "mummification" in her high-pitched, warbly voice, and Mr Foggerty was standing awkwardly next to the empty display case. The case which had once contained the *Book of the Dead*.

It was too late to stop Lois. She flung herself at Mr Foggerty — who, I had decided, wasn't really a fan of children — and he reluctantly patted her on the back and even crouched down, probably in a desperate attempt to stop her from getting too excitable. Uncle Vic and Frances joined him and the three of them had a little group chat, which we were clearly not party to. Lois had wandered off to look at the jewellery, leaving Adi and I to discuss what was going on.

"Why has she brought us here, Rosemary?" Adi whispered. "Surely it's not just a trip out to see Phyllis and Mr Foggerty, is it? There has to be another reason." He looked around the high-ceilinged room, as if searching for inspiration.

Suddenly, Frances beckoned Adi and I over to them. I hugged Mr Foggerty somewhat awkwardly, and he shook Adi's hand, which made me want to giggle with the formality of it. At last Phyllis joined us, and after we'd hugged her and she'd remarked how much we'd both grown, Mr Foggerty spoke in a grim but clear voice.

"It's very good to see you all," he said. "I expect you're wondering why Frances has brought you here, aren't you?"

Adi and I nodded rapidly. "We know the *Book of the Dead* has been stolen because Rosemary saw it on the news last night," Adi said.

Mr Foggerty and Phyllis exchanged a look. He continued, "We don't know how it was stolen right under our noses, so to speak, as if it literally vanished into thin air. Of course, you can guess who we believe the culprit to be."

Phyllis gave a weak smile. "My brother, Mal Vine."

"We thought it might be him," I added softly, pausing for a moment. "Are you in danger again, Phyllis? Is Mal still seeking his revenge on you?"

Phyllis looked to Mr Foggerty and then to Frances, who squeezed her arm supportively.

"This is what we don't know, I'm afraid, Rosemary," she replied. "I'm sure he's got other things to think about rather than our history."

I paused, wondering whether to mention my dream or not.

I had to. I couldn't bear the thought of poor Phyllis being in danger again.

"I had another one of those dreams with Mal Vine appearing in it," I said urgently.

"What?" Mr Foggerty demanded.

Phyllis had gone white.

"It was his voice more than anything," I continued. "He said something about unleashing the demons in the book to get his revenge on the witches, and that you all had to prepare to fight."

"And fight him we will," Mr Foggerty insisted. "You know my thoughts, my dear," he said to Phyllis. "I am all for you going to the Tunnel of Eternal Darkness. It's the very last place he would think to look for you."

"That really is a last resort, Wolfie. I'm not sure I could take it."

Frances interrupted them, thankfully, as I could see Phyllis was getting more and more upset. "Listen, hen, you need to do what's safe. You know that.

And Jonathan's there now. He'll keep your spirits up, you can be sure of that."

"Jonathan, as in our Jonathan?" I exclaimed excitedly, remembering how fond we had been of the giant owl and his novelty pinnies.

Uncle Vic nodded. "Yes, we've all had a shuffle up, so to speak, and he's chief prison warden right now. And I'm sorry, Phyllis, but I happen to agree with Foggy, I'm afraid."

Adi pushed his glasses back onto his nose and cleared his throat. "Can I just ask what would be the point of Mal Vine releasing all the demons in the book? Surely if he was after world domination it would backfire, as the demons would destroy him, too."

Frances glanced at her watch. "We must be quick. We need to get back."

Phyllis nodded. "Yes, my thoughts exactly, my darling boy."

I could see Adi visibly blush at being called "darling boy".

"It's a little more complicated than that, though," Mr Foggerty continued. "You see, the *Book of the Dead* is the journey, the instructions for the deceased souls to make their transition into heaven, if you like, and it contains challenges to overcome — demons to fight, spells to help prevent you from losing parts of yourself to decay. Obviously, the Egyptians wanted their bodies to remain preserved, so that once they had succeeded in making their turbulent journey through the underworld, their bodies would be intact to take with them into heaven."

My mind switched off once I had heard the words "spells to help prevent you from losing parts of yourself".

Mum was losing herself.

If we three could find this book, maybe we could stop Mum from having any more holes appear in her body.

"Where would Mal have taken the book to?" I asked quickly, my mind racing.

"That we don't know," replied Mr Foggerty, sighing. "The trouble is, yes, we do believe he wants to unleash the demons to gain world domination, but he has to take control of them to do that, which isn't easy. And the biggest conundrum is how, against all adversity, he could have moved the book?"

"What do you mean?" I asked, screwing up my face in concentration.

Phyllis interrupted Mr Foggerty with a sharp cough. "What he means is that no one can take the book unless you have met with the Egyptian god Osiris, who resides within the *Book of the Dead*."

"It's impossible, Phyl," answered Mr Foggerty. "That means he would have successfully passed the serpent in the river and solved the labyrinth in order to meet Osiris. How can that be? We are missing something."

"The only thing we are missing, so far as I can see, is the bloody book!" joked Frances, diffusing the tension immediately. "We need to go now. Keep us posted. We will help in any way we can. Where's that girleen Lois?"

I turned around at the sound of giggles and

shook my head in disbelief, as Lois was posing in a series of Egyptian-style postures, pouting and smiling for the group of tourists who were snapping her every move with their cameras.

As we began to disband and follow Frances and Uncle Vic out, I grabbed Phyllis' hand in mine.

"What can we do to help, Phyllis?" I asked.

She looked thoughtful for a moment. "I'm not sure, my darling girl. I'm not sure. But one thing we are all certain of is that the three of you will have a very important job to do. What it is remains a mystery right now."

She bent down and kissed me gently on the top of my head, and as I turned to follow the others home, I felt a quiver of excitement.

If we could find the book and access the spells, we might be able to put our mum back together again.

12

THE AKASHIC LIBRARY

U ncle Vic had decided to remain in London for a while longer, so it was just the three of us plus Frances who carefully took ourselves down the single-rung ladder and back into the tunnel. When we reached the end where we were presented with a choice of tunnels, I noticed there were now eight to choose from, whereas I'm sure earlier there had only been seven.

Frances had somehow managed to find a piece of Madeira cake in her bag, which Lois was munching on, getting crumbs everywhere, when we paused.

"What's wrong, Frances?" I asked nervously. "You do know which tunnel leads back, don't you?"

"It's this one," Adi said confidently, pointing towards the tunnel that was second on the left.

Frances shook her head emphatically, muttering something about it being after 6 pm. "It's got to be the second on the right, Adi," she stated, smiling a little unsurely at us.

"What do you think, Lois?" I'm not quite sure

why I asked my little sister, as she was only interested in eating her cake.

Lois pointed casually to the third tunnel on the left. "It's that one," she said through her mouthful.

At least, I think that's what she said — it sounded more like "fit fat bum". I can't imagine she would have said this, but you never know.

"No, no, no, bairns," Frances insisted. "I've been here many times lately, and it's definitely this one." And with that, she started striding off to the tunnel she had originally pointed towards.

As we started walking, the conveyer-belt feeling beneath our feet started up again, so before we knew it, we were at the end of the tunnel.

But hang on... We should have passed the glass-fronted office and corridor. Instead, we were at a dead end with yet another single-rung ladder leading up to a porthole opening.

"Oh no!" moaned Frances, stamping her foot. "It's the wrong tunnel. I don't know why they don't just leave us a wee map."

"Is there not a simple key to the tunnels? Surely it's just a question of labelling the entrances so everyone knows which leads where," Adi stated, screwing up his face with confusion.

"It's not as straightforward as that, young man. You see, they don't like to signpost the tunnels in case we ever get invaded. We don't want to make it too easy for any enemies, do we?" Frances retorted, looking pleased with her answer.

"Doesn't it have *any* logic as to which tunnel leads where?" Adi asked with a painful expression on his face. He was, after all, a maths genius and the king of logic.

"I think it does, and then every now and then it changes, and I cannae keep up with it all. So, let's pop our head up through the porthole and see where we are. That will help us sort this mess out," Frances said cheerfully.

We all followed Frances' large frame up the ladder and collectively heard her say "Oooooooo" as she disappeared through the porthole.

When I emerged, followed by Adi, we exchanged a look of surprise ourselves, for we were right in the middle of the desert. A large river, covered with tall reeds on either side, flowed behind us.

"I'm soooooo hot!" moaned Lois, pushing out her lower lip and blowing to cool her face down. "Have you got a drink, Frances?"

Frances rummaged in her bag and brought out a bottle of water, which we all fell upon.

"Where on earth are we, Frances?" I panted. I had never felt heat like this before.

"Well," she replied, grinning sheepishly, "I do believe we are in the Sahara Desert, and this," she continued, pointing to the water, "is the Nile River in Egypt."

"Egypt?" Adi blurted out, clearly shocked.

For some reason, I really wasn't that surprised we were here. After all, the postcard Frances had sent us late last year had been from Egypt, so I knew something was going on here, even though she had said they were on holiday.

"What's special about Egypt then, Frances?" I asked slowly.

"We have a tunnel leading here, dear, because this is a very spiritual place where one can find the Akashic Library."

"Bless you!" giggled Lois.

Adi and I looked at her, bemused. "What?" I said, screwing up my face in confusion.

"Sounds like a sneeze, so I said 'bless you'," my sister replied, incredibly pleased with her logic.

Adi and I burst out laughing.

"I like that, Lois, very good!" I added, patting her on the head.

She struck a pose, put her head on one side, and moved her hair from her eyes in a flamboyant gesture. "Mmm, yes, flips hair," she added smugly.

I shook my head at her daftness.

"What's the Akashic Library, Frances?" Adi was back in discovery mode.

"Bless you!" Lois and I said in unison and then collapsed into laughter.

"The Akashic Library is, well, how do I explain it? Mmm. It's a huge library in another dimension, which contains records of every deed, every word, thought, feeling, or intent that has ever occurred or is going to occur at any time in the history of the world."

"Whoa!" Adi replied, sitting himself down on the hot sand. "That is awesome."

"Yes, it is rather, isn't it?" Frances smiled.

"So, are you telling us we could go and look up what anybody is thinking?" I asked, trying to clarify the enormity of this.

"Anyone can access their own personal records in the library. So, say you wanted to find out where you were going to live when you were thirty. You could go and have a wee look. It contains every soul's journey of what has happened, what is happening, and what will happen. So, it's a pretty big deal."

"Wow! Can we go and look up to see if I'm going to get a Nintendo Switch for Christmas, Frances, pleeease?" pleaded Lois, who suddenly looked as if she had revived herself at the thought of knowing what she was going to get for Christmas.

Frances laughed. "Oh, lovey love, it doesn't work like that, you know! The records aren't set in stone. They can change depending on what other things influence you. So today it might read that Mummy and Daddy are getting Lois a Nintendo Switch, then by next week, there might be a great offer on something else that they know you'd like, so they might get that instead …"

Lois pulled a face. "These records sound stupid then."

"Lois!" I berated. "But I know what she means," I added. "What's the point of them if they can change?"

"Good question, Rosie. The point of them is that you can see what's in store for now and then, I guess, go about changing it, if you want to."

"What about the past?" Adi queried. "I mean, you can't change the past, can you?"

"Oooh, now, young man, that's going beyond my capabilities to understand. I believe Uncle Vic would say that the past could be changed. Time doesn't go in a straight line where the Akashic Records are held. It's another dimension in another part of time — a place where events of today, for example, can be sitting right next to events from 1066." She held up her hands in surrender. "It's a tricky thing to get your head round. Now come on, I've a hungry lady here who'll be wanting her tea soon. Isn't that right, Lois?"

"Frances," Lois said, taking her hand, "you know me so well."

"Whereabouts is the library then, Frances?" I asked as we lifted the porthole, which had quickly become covered in sand again, to start our descent. "It sounds amazing!"

"It's a good half an hour walk west of here, underneath the hidden chambers of the Great Sphinx of Giza."

"The Great Sphinx ..." Adi mused. "I've read about that. It's supposed to have a secret door just underneath its ear that leads right inside it."

"Adi, you are such a brainbox. I'll not be needing to tell you anything." Frances chuckled.

As we walked back up the dark tunnel, away from Egypt and all its mysteries, I couldn't stop thinking about the Akashic Library. Somehow it felt significant, but I couldn't yet think why or how it would be important to us.

Once we'd arrived back at the opening where all the other tunnels met, Lois was so adamant that we took the tunnel she had chosen that we decided to give in.

"Let's just go with Lois, shall we? After all," I

whispered to Adi, "we'll never hear the end of it if she's right and we've ignored her."

"I just don't get her logic," Adi whispered back, not quietly enough as it happens.

"I know I'm right because Paloma told me I was," Lois said confidently.

"And when did you see Paloma, pet?" Frances asked her coaxingly.

"I didn't see her, she just told me which tunnel it was when we were coming back from London." Lois paused, preening herself, almost as if she were copying Paloma. "She also said that Aradia saw us leave that museum place."

There was a collective silence, broken only by a soft raspberry sound, which could only have come from Lois' bottom.

"Did you just fart?" I mouthed to her silently.

She ignored me.

"Aradia?" Frances said sharply. "Are you sure Paloma told you this, hen?"

"Of course I'm sure," Lois answered crossly. "She said she was just giving us some warning, as she's my friend."

"Who? Paloma or Aradia?" Adi asked seriously.

Lois rolled her eyes. "Paloma, of course. She's not friends with Aradia anymore, even though she still has to work out her conspac or something."

"Contract," I corrected. "How can we be sure that Paloma is telling the truth? What if she is spying on us for Aradia? Have you thought of that, Lois?"

"Rosemary's got a point, you know. How can

we trust Paloma? After all, she was never that nice to us, was she?" Adi motioned to me.

I nodded, remembering with distaste the nasty, runny poo she'd left on my shoulder.

"Look, Paloma is my friend. We talk. A lot. She wouldn't tell me fibs," Lois said.

And with that she marched ahead, leaving us with the stench of her windy bottom.

We followed, eager to escape the smell, and I was relieved, as well as surprised, to see that, after a while, it became a corridor once again.

It was so good to get home and have something to eat. It felt like we'd been away on a journey for days, not just three hours. Dad arrived back around 7.30 p.m., just as we were about to wash, ready for bed. I knew he was missing Mum, as she was staying in Birmingham tonight, even though he pretended to be cheerful for Frances.

"Right, thanks very much, Miss Fiddlefuddle. I can take it from here."

I saw Frances' eye start to twitch at Dad's inability to get her name right. I think by now she had given up telling him to call her Frances. Instead, she pursed her lips and gathered her hat box, planting a kiss on my and Lois' heads.

"Goodnight, Mr Pellow," she said through gritted teeth.

I was still mulling over all the information about the Akashic Library and the missing *Book of the Dead* when I went upstairs to read before bed.

How could we find out where Mal Vine had taken the book?

Suddenly, I had a lightbulb moment.

Of course! Why hadn't I thought of this before? The perfect way to find out where Mal had taken the book, was to look it up in the records at the Akashic Library!

If it was true that it contained the records of every deed, every intention, every thought that had happened and was yet to happen, then we would most definitely know where the book was.

I settled down to sleep, full of excitement and nervous energy. I couldn't wait to tell Adi, and moreover, I couldn't wait to go back to Egypt and find the Great Sphinx.

I could almost hear the desert whispering its secrets to me as I fell into a slumber.

13

THE VISITOR

Mum rang us early the next morning, just as we were about to leave for school. "Is everything all right, girls? I'll be home tonight, thank goodness."

She sounded really tired and weird.

"Are *you* all right, Mum?" I asked tentatively.

Her laugh had a hollow ring to it. "Oh yes, love, I'm fine. I'll be glad to get home," she whispered. "Donna and Harriet have had a spat, and it's not nice being in between them, I can tell you."

I thought how awkward it was for me whenever my friends Mae and Gloria had an argument. I was always caught in the middle. Adi didn't really have any friends other than me, so we never had to worry about him falling out with other people.

I managed to corner Adi just before registration to tell him my great idea.

His eyes lit up with excitement. "Yes, brilliant, Rosemary. We will have to go tomorrow though, as isn't your mum home tonight?"

"She is," I whispered back. "Mind you, I don't

think Frances will approve, do you? The only way we can do it is if we pretend we are doing some after school club so she has to look after Lois. We couldn't take her."

"But what about all that power of three stuff? Wouldn't we need Lois to get in?"

"Don't see why," I replied. "After all, it's not something we've been asked to do, is it? It's something we are doing for ourselves, and all we want is to get into the library and look up where the *Book of the Dead* has been taken. How difficult can that be?"

"Quiet, please!" boomed the voice of Mr Bobbin, who was covering for our usual form teacher, Miss Hick. He began to call out names alphabetically.

"Tomorrow, straight after school, we'll go," I continued. "I'll tell Frances tonight that we've got a club tomorrow."

"Rosemary Pellow!" Mr Bobbin interrupted.

"Packed lunch, sir," I answered automatically.

"I'm not asking whether you are having hot dinners or packed lunch, I'm asking you to BE QUIET! Move away from Mr Adani, please, and go and sit next to Dan."

Oh god. I sighed inwardly. If I was sitting next to daredevil Dan all day, I'd have to keep my wits about me.

When the final bell went to mark the end of the school day, I had been subjected to: bits of rubber being flicked at me, him constantly goading me to start humming like a fly, and him threatening to flush my plaits down the toilet. I was exhausted, and I wished Uncle Vic was meeting us so he might be reminded of what happened to him and his side-kick last year when they overstepped the mark.

As it was, Frances met us, looking rather subdued.

"What's wrong?" I asked, concerned.

"I'm not sleeping well, Rosie." She stretched out her spine and shook herself. "I'm a very light sleeper, anyway. Never mind. Perhaps I can have a wee nap on your sofa at home."

I squeezed her plump arm and trailed behind her and Lois, who was bending Frances' ear about some incident in school that involved glue and glitter and Miss Ulwin, the headmistress, not being able to speak for a day.

Once we had arrived home and Lois had been fed milk and cake, I casually mentioned the "Phantom Club" that Adi and I were attending after school tomorrow.

"Okay, hen, that's fine. Do you not need me to come back to school and collect you then when it's done?" She yawned, settling herself down on the couch, with Maggie purring on her lap.

"Oh no, that's okay, Frances. Adi said he'll bring me home. You can get on with sorting out our tea and all that. I'll be home by 6 p.m." I crossed my fingers, hoping this would give us enough time to get to the Akashic Library, find the information, and then get home.

Satisfied I had sorted out the plan for tomorrow, I switched the TV on in the kitchen and helped myself to a chocolate chip cookie from the tin.

As I turned my back on the TV to replace the

biscuit tin in the cupboard, I felt a shudder of energy behind me. I can only describe it as a fizzing sensation, the feeling that someone or something was standing behind me.

I spun round quickly. My breathing was shallow, and my heart was beating fast. There was no one there. Then, I just so happened to glance up at the TV and staring at me in glorious technicolour was none other than Mal Vine.

"Where is it?" he snarled, his brown eyes screwing up, the lines on his weathered face deepening.

I stared, frozen with fear.

"I said, where is it? Answer me, girl!" he spat, and I felt droplets of his spittle hit my cheeks.

"I don't know what you mean. Where is what?" I stuttered.

"The book!" he screamed.

"You know where it is. You have it. Why are you asking me?" I answered shakily, assuming he meant the *Book of the Dead*. My biscuit, already starting to melt, had made my fingers sticky, and I no longer had an appetite.

Mal stared at me for what seemed like an age, and then he started to laugh. At first it was a chuckle, then it grew and grew until he was guffawing and laughing so hard I thought he might burst.

I grabbed the remote control. I don't know how I managed to think to do this, given how terrified I was, and I switched the TV off.

There was silence.

I stood there, melted chocolate all over my

hands, wondering whether to switch the TV back on or not.

Of course, I had to check he had gone.

My breathing calmed. I aimed the control at the TV, my eyes half-closed in fear. Thank god, there was some programme on about science with those doctors who are twins. My relief was undeniable.

I sat down in the rocking chair and allowed my shaky body to calm down, before I washed my sticky hands and dissected the meaning behind Mal's appearance.

I was wondering whether to tell Frances when she suddenly popped her head round the doorway into the kitchen with a concerned look upon her face. "What's happened, Rosie? You're as white as a sheet."

"I've just seen him," I whispered, barely able to get the words out.

"*Mal?*" she mouthed.

I nodded.

"*What did he say?*" She continued to mouth the words silently at me, which reminded me of my Gran who would constantly mouth uncomfortable sentences, like "*what's that smell?*" and part of me wanted to laugh.

"You can speak normally, Frances," I managed to say.

"Come here, hen." She clucked around me, crouching down on her haunches so she could be closer to me. "Tell me what happened."

So I did. "Frances, it was so scary. And what did he mean asking me where the book was when he's the one who's taken it?"

"It's a double bluff, sweetheart," Frances stated, attempting to haul herself up from her crouching position. "He thinks if he appears to you asking where the book is, it looks as though he hasn't taken it. But we know he has, so take no notice of him."

"Yes," I agreed, "it's the kind of thing Mal would say to put us off his scent."

However much I believed this as I said it, there was still a tiny grain of doubt that set root in my mind. Why would he bother to scare me like this if he really did have the book?

The sooner Adi and I got to the Akashic Library and found out where the book really was, the better.

I heard a key in the lock and the sound of Mum calling out, "Hello, anyone home?" Only her voice sounded brittle and fake, and she had a dark-green energy that shuddered around her as she came through into the kitchen.

Then I realised why.

She was followed by Donna. Or should I say Donna Marie, who in her tight white jeans and pink T-shirt looked completely out of place in our kitchen.

I didn't like the way the colours around her were browns and ochres, and every now and again there would be a flash of lightning that made me feel constantly on edge.

"Hi Mum. Hi Donna," I said tightly, glancing at Frances to see if Donna had spotted her.

"Donna Marie," Mum added quickly.

Donna glanced around the kitchen. "Home

alone, are we?" She smirked, throwing a look of disapproval at Mum.

She obviously couldn't see Frances, and I thought how revealing it was that Frances hadn't made any effort to allow herself to be seen by her either.

I opened my mouth, unsure what to say, when I saw Frances sidle out with her finger to her lips, and Mum followed her exit with a quick glance. I noted, with interest, that despite Mum's protestations about turning her back on magic, she clearly *did* still believe, otherwise she wouldn't have been able to see Frances.

"The childminder has literally just gone. She texted me to say she had to dash a few minutes ago ... Family emergency," Mum added quickly. I could feel her eyes boring into me for support.

"Yeah, you've only just missed her," I added, which wasn't a lie. I could see Mum looked grateful.

"Donna Marie's just come back with me for the night to, er, have a break." Mum smiled, looking towards Donna for confirmation of this.

I wondered silently how Mum had ended up offering her to come here for the night. It would mean we wouldn't get any time with our mum on our own, as Donna-flipping-Marie would be hogging her.

"Lois!" I whispered, standing by Dad's tiny office as Mum started fussing round Donna. "Get off the computer. Mum's got Donna with her."

Lois finally looked up. "Donna from her work? The lady with the big lips?"

"Shhh!" I whispered, motioning to my noisy little sister that they were only in the kitchen. Lois pulled a face of dismay, which I mirrored.

Mum and Donna were already at the kitchen table nursing cups of tea, deep in conversation. Lois and I hid from sight in Dad's office and earwigged, occasionally raising eyebrows at each other.

"The thing is it's either my or Harriet's team you're on, Rae. People think she's the innocent one, but she's not. I'm afraid you have to choose." Donna sniffed dramatically and reached for a tissue.

"*Harriet*," I mouthed silently at Lois, who widened her eyes and pulled a silly face.

"Harriet who drowns dogs in her underwear?" she whispered back, loudly.

I shushed her and wondered how she could have translated the downward dog yoga position into "drowns dogs".

"Harriet's always seemed harmless," Mum said carefully. "I'd feel very uncomfortable choosing sides ..."

"Oh, you have no idea, Rae. She wheedles her way into your life, gets your trust, and then gets you sacked. We've got to get her off the show. I hope I can count on your support. It's been so awful for me ..." Donna continued, dabbing her eyes.

"Right," we heard Mum reply, sounding reluctant.

Thankfully, Dad came home soon after, and Lois and I felt quite sorry for him. We had to witness Donna fluttering her eyelashes at our dad — who to his absolute credit treated her as if she were some slightly unhinged stranger (which she is) — and Mum looking more and more exhausted.

As we went upstairs to bed, I caught sight of Mum still on the sofa, having her ear bent by the unstoppable Donna. I was shocked to see the edges of my mum were blurry, as if somehow Donna's energy was causing Mum to fade from the outside in.

I made a silent vow to step up our efforts to find the *Book of the Dead* so we could make our mum whole again, before it was too late.

14

BUSTED

The next day, Mum and the awful Donna left very early, and I can't say I was sad to see her go. However, I was fed up that we hadn't had Mum to ourselves. A little seed of fear had lodged itself inside my head; what if Mum preferred being with Donna and her work friends?

The day dragged by with Adi and I exchanging knowing, excited looks until, at last, the bell went and we legged it out of school.

This had to be carefully executed, as Frances was still collecting Lois from the playground and, naturally, thought Adi and I were staying behind for a club.

We snuck out of the school gates as soon as we saw the back of Frances collecting Lois down by the opposite side of the playground. We had to pretend to Miss Hick that I was going to Adi's house for tea — he's allowed to walk home, as he lives so close to the school.

Moments later we were on the bus and on our way to the tunnel entrance. I hadn't really given much thought as to how we would get past Reg, the miserable ticket man in the George's Dock Building, but I guess we'd cross that bridge when we got to it.

Luck was on our side. As we crept into the building, it was empty, with the familiar notice on the ticket booth saying, *"Tour full. Come back in one hour"*.

We high-fived each other and hopped over the barrier, keeping an eye out for any staff. Adi was great at remembering the way we had come before, and we were soon descending the first staircase that led to the door that said *"Extractors"*.

My heart was beating superfast as Adi gently tried the handle to the door, and in we crept. Our ears were once again assaulted by the almighty sound of the fan, which was louder than any aircraft I had ever heard.

"I'll press the button to switch it off, and you jump through first," Adi instructed me confidently.

I pulled a face. "Are you sure about that, Adi? After all, you were really nervous before. I don't mind letting you go first?"

Adi shook his head emphatically. "No, Rosemary, I'm the technician here."

In the end, I decided I was more than happy to let him have his way, and as soon as he had pressed the button to stop the fan, we watched, transfixed, as the numbers started to go down.

We had watched the dial get to 1534 when we suddenly heard voices shouting loudly above the whirring; voices that sounded as if they were coming closer.

I glanced at Adi, whose eyes had widened behind his large black-rimmed glasses, and I looked to the door as it started to open. We both willed the dial onwards, as it was slowing now.

522, 367...

"Adi, we will have to jump together!" I shouted, anxiously.

Just as the dial reached 137, Adi pushed me forwards, and as we flew through the air, I heard a male voice shouting, "Oi, who's there!"

But we had already gone.

I landed softly and moved quickly, so Adi wouldn't land on top of me.

"Did they see us?" I whispered.

Adi shook his head. "No, I'm pretty sure they just saw the tail end of us, maybe?"

"Oh no! Does that mean they'll follow us through?" I asked nervously.

"I wouldn't have thought so," Adi answered. "I mean, by the time they reach the fan, they'll be wondering where we've gone. No one in their right mind would think that anyone would actually jump through the blades, would they?"

"No, I guess not, but let's not hang around, just in case," I added, getting up and walking hastily to the door that led to the corridor.

As we marched along the corridor, past the glass partition, the office seemed quite empty.

Adi tapped me on the shoulder. "Er, Rosemary, one thing though ..."

"What?" I hissed.

"I forgot to turn the fan back on."

"Oh no." I stopped in my tracks. "Should we go

back? We can use the remote control on this side to switch it back on, can't we?"

"I don't think we should risk fiddling with it. What if those guys have already switched it back on? It would cause too much suspicion now. I'm sure it will be fine," Adi spoke confidently.

We reached the end of the corridor, which had widened out into a tunnel and the place where we were presented with seven options to choose from. How funny that, according to Frances, after 6 p.m. there became eight tunnels. I wondered to myself where the eighth led to.

"It's this one," Adi said, pointing to the fifth tunnel.

"Are you sure?" I asked nervously.

To be honest, I had forgotten which tunnel was which, and as we hadn't been told what the order of tunnels was, we were really just stabbing in the dark.

"Look, if it's the wrong one, we'll just head back and try a different one. It's fine, don't worry," Adi reassured me.

So, we ploughed on and chose the fifth tunnel. Before long, thanks to the moving floor, we had reached the end of the tunnel and the precarious ladder above which we could see the porthole out.

I followed Adi up, and all hopes were dashed when I heard his cry of "Oh no!" as he pulled himself out of the porthole.

"What's wrong?" I called out, hearing him do his usual high-pitched noise with hands on his ears.

I guessed we had chosen the wrong tunnel.

"Oh!" I added, equally disappointed.

We weren't in the desert. We were clearly in another part of England. It was similar weather to Liverpool — a bright June day — and the river beside us looked decidedly grey. There was a large building in front of us emblazoned with the words: "*Channel 9's Brightside Bungalows*". But the "Bungalows" part had been crossed out.

I was about to exclaim to Adi that we must be in Birmingham where Mum filmed, when I suddenly cried out in surprise, as I recognised the person who was strolling along the riverside, her gaze fixed on the "Brightside" building.

"Adi, get down. It's Aradia!"

"What? What's she doing here?" he whispered frantically.

"I have no idea, but I think we'd better get back into the tunnel, don't you?" I replied nervously.

Adi nodded his agreement and we crept back down the porthole, my eyes never leaving Aradia until I knew we were safely hidden once again.

"It's the River Tame," Adi stated.

"What?" I asked, my thoughts elsewhere. I was trying to work out what the heck *she'd* been doing by my mum's work.

"If we're in Birmingham, by the studios your mum works at, then this is the River Tame," Adi continued.

"I think I've got it!" I blurted out, interrupting him. "Remember Lois told us that Aradia watched us leaving the British Museum?"

Adi nodded.

"Aradia was sacked last year from her role as

Gatekeeper of the Portal, because she'd been caught moonlighting for the enemy, remember?"

"Moonlighting, as in *helping* the enemy?" Adi asked eagerly.

I nodded. "Yes, and who is the enemy?"

"Mal Vine, of course," Adi said without hesitation.

"Exactly! I think Aradia might be spying on us and then reporting back to Mal Vine."

"But why would he be spying on *us*?" Adi frowned.

"I'm not sure yet, unless he's watching us to see if we discover where he's taken the book? Whatever, it's bound to be trouble ..."

"Talking of trouble, I'd say you were already in it, young lady!" A familiar voice echoed around as we approached the meeting point where all the tunnels merged.

Who should we see marching towards us, looking more than a little angry? Frances and my sister Lois, who, clutching Bea to her chest, was smirking like a cat that had got the cream.

Oh poo, I thought. "It's not what you think, Frances. We do have a good reason for being here," I stated, more confidently than I felt.

"Yes, and I would love to hear it," she replied seriously.

I looked at Adi, and he looked back at me, wide-eyed and unsure what to say.

I took a deep breath. "We thought if we found the Akashic Library—"

"Bless you!" Lois piped up, rather smugly.

I paused and gave her a hard stare. "If we found

the library, we'd be able to look up Mal Vine and
see where he's taken the *Book of the Dead*, and that
way we'd be able to help you find it more easily."

I didn't want to tell her that I also wanted to
look inside it to find these so-called spells that
would help Mum to stop losing parts of herself. For
some reason, I thought Frances might either pretend to me that everything was all right with Mum
or dissuade me from doing this, as it wasn't 'their
kind of magic' but some kind of Ancient Egyptian
form that I felt she might be against. Of course, I
had no real evidence to back this up. None of them
had said anything bad about Ancient Egyptian
magic — but I had a gut instinct that they would
warn me off it.

Frances blinked a few times as if she were
trying to comprehend what I had said, and then she
smiled slowly. "Do you know, Rosie, I think you're
right. And I think this is the reason why we need
you three. This is a brilliant idea!"

Phew, I had got away with telling her fibs about
me and Adi doing a club after school.

"But," her face grew serious, "you should not
have lied to me about this. If we are to help each
other, we must be honest with one another. No
made-up stories, okay?"

Perhaps I hadn't got away with it.

"Okay, sorry Frances," I added in a small voice,
barely able to look at her.

If I'm honest, I wasn't sorry we'd fibbed — I was
sorry we'd got found out. I know that sounds bad,
but I was so anxious to get on with things, and I
knew Frances would make a huge deal of sharing

the idea with Uncle Vic and Phyllis and Mr Foggerty, rather than letting us get on with it.

"Oh, and another wee thing! When Lois and I arrived at the extractor room, there was a kerfuffle going on. Apparently the fan had been switched off and not switched back on, and there were two members of staff saying they thought they'd heard voices down there tampering with it. I take it that was you two?" She looked gravely at Adi and me.

"It's my fault, Frances," Adi mumbled. "We rushed through, and I forgot to turn it back on after we heard people coming into the room."

"How did you get through the fan then?" I asked Frances tentatively.

"We cheated actually." Frances blushed, and I noticed Lois looked extremely smug.

"We came on Frances' broomstick," my sister boasted proudly.

"Aye, well, enough about that, and please keep it to yourselves, as I'm not supposed to use it to carry non-witchy cargo, so to speak. It's NUTS."

"Well, I wouldn't go that far!" Adi exclaimed.

"No, no," Frances added, shaking her head, "NUTS stands for New Underground Tunnel Safety. No broomsticks allowed in the tunnels. I think the ceilings are a little too low for some folk. Mind you, I'm a good driver, so I've never had any bother with keeping low. I can see why we're not supposed to carry non-witchy cargo, but I think in this instance—"

"Frances," I interrupted her before she could ramble on about any more of the boring rules. My mind kept racing back to what she had said before.

"When you said you think this is why you need us three, what did you mean?"

Frances looked puzzled.

"You know, when I said about us going to the Akashic Library to find out where Mal has taken the book?" I repeated slowly, throwing a death stare towards my sister in case she was harbouring thoughts of anymore "bless yous".

Frances nodded.

"And you said you thought that was why you needed the three of us," I continued.

"Oh yes!" Frances replied, her face illuminated with excitement. "I will have to check with Mr Foggerty and Phyllis. They are the brains, really, about all this stuff, but it makes sense, Rosie, as we cannot access the library's records."

Adi looked puzzled now. "Why not?" he asked, pushing his glasses back up his nose.

Frances thought for a moment. "How can I explain this now? Well, you see, we are not 'living' in the same way that youse are 'living'. We are, for want of a better word, magical creatures with special powers and gifts, and you can only get into the library if you ..." She paused as if searching for the right words.

"If you have colours around you?" I stated slowly.

"Aye, that's a good way of explaining it, Rosie."

Lois frowned and piped up. "What are you talking about, Rosie? Will I be able to get in? I want to go, too."

"Listen, pet, you can go, too. Every person living on this Earth now has an energy field of colour surrounding them, and your sister can see these around folk. But Phyllis, Uncle Vic, Mr Foggerty and I, we don't have this colour, because we're from another world really, so that's why we cannae get into the library."

"But Frances, you do have colour. You have yellow on your dress, and I love it. You're like my very own yellow sumbarine."

Frances laughed and ruffled Lois' hair.

"So, what now then, Frances?" I asked impatiently. "Can we go back to the library?"

"No, I must check first with the others. I'll need to grab Vic, and we'll have to try to intercept Phyllis and Mr Foggerty, who are on their way to the Tunnel of Eternal Darkness."

Suddenly, she gasped. "Oh gosh, what's the time? Does anyone have a watch on them?"

Adi quickly glanced at his wrist. "It's 17.58."

"What does that mean?" Frances replied, screwing up her face.

"Two minutes to 6 p.m.," Adi replied slowly, as if he were talking to a child.

"Oh, perfect! So, you three must go to Jonathan in the Tunnel of Eternal Darkness and tell him that Phyllis and Mr Foggerty will be arriving soon. He has to be warned so he can keep them away from the prisoners, as there's no telling whether Mal still has his spies in there. We don't want Mal discovering that Phyllis has gone there."

"Okay, but how do we get to the Tunnel of Eternal Darkness?" I asked, puzzled.

Frances had already started to move off hastily, back towards the George's Dock Building. She turned her head and shouted behind her, "At 6 p.m. precisely, it will appear. Just stay where you are, bairns, and follow that tunnel!"

The three of us remained silent, watching as Frances disappeared into the darkness, all probably wondering what we were supposed to do next. There was a rumble coming from my tummy, which Adi must have heard, for his decided to join in, too.

"I'm starving," I added for good measure.

"Me, too," replied Adi, sounding quite forlorn.

"Oh, Rosie," Lois interrupted, "flying on Frances' broomstick was amazing! I definitely want to get a broomstick when I'm older."

"Yeah, right!" Adi chimed in, suppressing a chuckle.

I think Lois would have replied with some smart comment, but at that very moment we felt a warm breeze blowing towards us, together with a shimmer of dark-blue light. It was a bit like the blast of warm air that hits you as you get off the aeroplane if you ever go on holiday somewhere really hot.

I felt Lois grab my hand and burrow her face into my side. "It's okay, Lois, don't worry. Nothing horrible is happening. Frances would not have left us to deal with anything scary."

I hoped I was speaking the truth.

"Wow!" Adi announced as the blue light faded and, literally from nowhere, another tunnel appeared. "Right, come on, this way then," he continued, starting to walk towards the new opening.

"Are you sure this is the way we're meant to be

going?" I asked nervously as Lois and I took tentative steps to follow him.

"Absolutely!" he called behind to us.

We followed for a moment or two until Adi, possibly feeling his bravery was deserting him, waited for us to catch up.

It had suddenly got colder, damper, and very dark. There was a 'drip, drip' sound coming from the sides of the tunnel, and my insides were prickling with fear. With every step we took, I felt as if we were walking further into a tunnel of doom.

"Let's turn back, Adi," I said anxiously, gripping Lois' hand tighter.

"Yes, let's," Lois agreed.

Adi paused for a minute and looked at the pair of us. "Yeah, you're right," he conceded.

I felt a huge amount of relief as we all turned back to retrace our steps.

We took three steps forward, when there was an almighty creaking sound and a *thump* — and right in front of us a heavy, latticed iron gate shot down from the ceiling, preventing our escape.

We were trapped.

15

THE TUNNEL OF ETERNAL
DARKNESS

"What's happening?" I cried.

We clung on to the latticed gate, our fingers feeling around for any way of releasing it.

"It's no good, Rosemary," Adi sighed. "We are well and truly stuck here. The only way to go is onwards. Maybe we shouldn't have turned back."

"We've got no choice but to carry on, and I've got a bad feeling about this. It just feels so horrible in here." I glanced around the darkness once again.

Though ordinarily being in the dark would be enough to be scared, it was more than that. It felt as if the tunnel contained all the sadness and gloom and evil in the entire world. The energy was heavy and oppressive, and it felt almost impossible to shake it off, but I knew I had to be strong for my little sister.

"I wish Paloma was here," Lois said in a small voice.

I squeezed her hand in a reassuring manner. "Don't worry, Lois, once we get to Jonathan everything will be okay."

"How do we even know Jonathan is here?" Adi said crossly as we started to walk into the depths of the tunnel.

"Well, Frances said he definitely was. She has no reason to tell us lies," I said, more confidently than I felt.

"Hold on!" Adi whispered, stopping suddenly in front of us. "Can you see that?"

"What?" Lois and I said simultaneously.

"Ahead, those flickering orange lights." Adi pointed ahead, and sure enough, very faintly in the distance were some lights glowing gently.

"Yes!" I punched the air triumphantly. "I hope Jonathan is there."

"Me too," whispered Lois.

We increased our pace, and as we grew closer the tunnel widened out somewhat. We soon realised the source of light was coming from candles on either side of the tunnel. Some were flickering steadily and others looked as though they had already blown themselves out.

The eerie feeling increased — as did the feeling of dread.

I noticed there were pools of water on the floor. The walls were made from dark-coloured brick, with rivers of water flowing down them periodically. We automatically clung to each other as we could see the beginnings of bars on either side of the tunnel, bars that meant only one thing: prison cells.

We looked in horror to our right, and Lois gave a small shriek as there, clutching the bars of his cell, stood a terrifying-looking large man in a tight white vest with a shaved head and tattoos all over his muscly torso. He grinned and gave the three of us a little wave, which sent a chill down my spine.

Before we had any time to react further, a piercing siren sounded, and the tunnel was filled with flashing red lights. It was difficult to see what was going on, and for a moment I was filled with fear that maybe one of the prisoners had escaped and we were in mortal danger.

We clung to each other, until, as quickly as it had begun, it stopped, and there standing in front of us was our dear friend Jonathan, the giant tawny owl.

He looked magnificent in a full purple apron that covered both his front and back. On the front it had the words: "*I'm in charge*".

"Jonathan!" I squealed as we all rushed towards him and nearly knocked him flying with our enthusiasm. It was such a relief to see a friendly face. "Thank god you're here."

"Ooooh, Jonathan," murmured Lois, "I'd forgotten how soft your feathers were. You're just sooooo cosy."

Even Adi hugged him, clearly just as relieved as we were to see him.

Jonathan chuckled with delight. "Well, well, what a surprise to see you three. My, how you've grown! But hold on, what the dickens are you doing down here? It's not the place for children, my friends."

"Frances sent us to warn you that Phyllis and Mr Foggerty are on their way down here," I whispered. "She's got to go into hiding in case Mal is coming for her."

"I see," Jonathan replied, looking perplexed. He turned sharply around in response to a low mumble that was coming from the various cells. It looked like the prisoners were all up on their feet trying to see what was going on. "Quiet please, boys!" he hooted crossly, and I noticed as he turned around the back of his apron said: *I can see you.*

"I love your apron, Jonathan," Lois crooned. "*Can* you see me if I'm behind you?"

"I certainly can, dear girl," Jonathan replied. "Watch this."

He turned so he had his back to us, and then twisted his head almost all the way round, so he was looking right at us.

"See?" he said, turning back to face us. "I can turn my head two hundred and seventy degrees. So yes, I do effectively have eyes in the back of my head."

No sooner had he said that, he then swivelled his head round very sharply to the left. "And you, Mickey J, will stop that right now," Jonathan said.

I glanced at Mickey J, who was a small man with round spectacles. He hastily removed his finger from up his nose as he met my eye.

"Come along, chums," Jonathan continued, turning back to us. "Follow me. Time for some introductions, I think."

We followed Jonathan a few paces on and stood in the middle of the tunnel while he addressed all the prisoners with a flowery lilac megaphone.

"Right, you lovely lot, we have some guests. Let's be polite and introduce ourselves, shall we?"

He winked at the three of us and proceeded to give instructions to his charges. "You two first — we'll go alphabetically, like we practised. A one two, a one two three four..."

Jonathan raised his talons in the air as if he were conducting an orchestra, and then the most bizarre thing happened. The extremely large man with bulging muscles and scary face started singing a clapping song, facing his colleague in the adjacent cell. They mimed the clapping, and it went like this:

> *"My name is High Low Jackalow,*
> *Jackalow High Low,*
> *High Low Jackalow,*
> *My name is ..."*

And Jonathan, his claws briefly leaving the ground as he took flight momentarily with excitement, pointed exuberantly to the large man and shouted:

"COLIN."

Colin then grinned at us and gave us a thumbs up. His colleague next door then started singing, and when he got to the bit that went, *"My name is ..."* Jonathan pointed once again, faced us, and shouted:

"DAVE."

The song was then repeated by Fred, Horatio, Kalim, and Mickey, finishing in a flourish with

Trevor and Quentin, who looked particularly fed up with having to do this.

There was a brief silence once they had finished their introductions, then Jonathan looked at us encouragingly and started to clap.

Adi and I glanced at each other and started clapping slowly, whereas my sister was already clapping with gusto and — surprise, surprise! — was already singing the song. I could tell this was going to be an earworm that would be difficult to remove.

Once we had stopped clapping and the prisoners had all bowed, looking pleased with themselves (except Quentin, who was scowling), Jonathan introduced us one by one as his NWC (Non-Witchy Cargo) chums.

I noticed with interest that none of the prisoners had colours around them, so I guessed they must have been from the witchy world, and I wondered to myself what they had all done to be sent to this horrible place. In spite of the good cheer that Jonathan was trying to infuse into everyone, the place had a heavy feeling of dread, which was making me feel quite tired.

Jonathan glanced at the watch he had pinned to his apron, rather like a nurse's watch. "Right, just enough time for a little snackerooni, I think. Let's go to my office, shall we?"

"Oooooh yes, what a good idea!" Lois replied happily, in the knowledge she was going to get food.

My tummy growled again in protest; a snack would be just what the doctor ordered.

We followed Jonathan past the cells, the occupants of which had taken on a more menacing expression in spite of the laughter from only a few moments ago. We came to a sort of T-junction, and in the left-hand corner was a room with a desk, lamp, and fluffy rug. There was a whole heap of magazines opened on various pages featuring different types of rodents in a variety of poses — large black rats swirling their tails and small field mice nibbling on cheese.

"Oh yes, don't mind these," Jonathan said, hastily picking up all the magazines and throwing them in a corner. "I was getting some recipe ideas, that's all."

We all sat down, and Jonathan produced a jug of green liquid from behind him.

"Urghhh, that looks gross!" said my sister, clearly having no filter whatsoever.

"Lois!" I berated, embarrassed on her behalf.

"It's quite all right. Don't be backward in coming forward — my sentiments exactly. But sometimes, friends, things are not always what they seem. Can I dare one of you to take a taste?"

"I will!" Adi said, clearing his throat. "I'm parched!"

Jonathan poured some of the yucky green goo into a glass and passed it to Adi, who took a tentative sip.

"Wow, that's amazing!" he gasped, then collectively our eyes widened as the liquid in his glass turned orange.

"Your favourite drink, perhaps?" Jonathan grinned as Adi nodded in surprise. "Yes, it does tend to turn into whatever your favourite tipple is. I'll show you!" he added, pouring himself a glass.

We watched, transfixed, as Jonathan took a sip of the green drink, which then gradually turned a lovely golden brown. He smacked his lips in appreciation. "Ah, yes, barley wine, my favourite."

Lois and I needed no further encouragement. We both had our glasses filled up, and Lois' turned pink and fizzy.

"Yay! Pink lemonade!" she trilled.

Mine turned creamy and frothy. My absolute favourite treat: vanilla milkshake.

Soon we were enjoying biscuits and tiny little finger sandwiches filled with cucumber and ham and Nutella (not all together, of course), but I couldn't shake off this feeling of anxiety in my tummy, like a heavy rock. I glanced down at my sister who had gone very quiet, and I noticed she looked awfully pale.

"Are you feeling all right, Lois?" I asked her, concerned.

She shook her head, and her eyes started to flicker as if she were fighting off sleep. "I feel so tired, Rosie, and I feel sick and cold."

It wasn't cold in Jonathan's room. There was a fire blazing behind us, and the room was comfortable, but I knew what she meant. Although I was able to resist the feeling, I was aware of it, too. I glanced at Adi, who also looked miserable.

"What's wrong, Ads?" I said, feeling worried by his gloomy expression.

"Feel really, really sad," he whispered, his eyes filling up with tears.

This was freaky. He hadn't even told me off for calling him Ads.

I looked at Jonathan, who was meticulously licking Nutella from his talons. After what seemed an age, he glanced up at me, and then Lois and then Adi.

"Ah," he said, as if some great revelation had dawned on him. "Of course, it's time for you to leave."

"What's happening, Jonathan?" I asked anxiously, wondering why he suddenly looked so concerned.

"NWCs like yourselves cannot spend very long here in the Tunnel of Eternal Darkness. It seeps inside of you like an insidious mist, wrapping its tendrils around your happiness until all you feel is deep, dark, depressing dread."

At that moment, Lois closed her eyes and slumped forward onto Adi, who started crying silent tears. They were running down his face, and he looked completely terrified.

"Jonathan," I begged, "please get us out of here NOW!"

16

A TOUCH OF THE DARKNESS

Jonathan scrambled to his feet and fussed around us, gently picking Lois up in his feathery arms. "Are you two able to walk?" he asked anxiously, as he led the way out of his office and into the dark tunnels once more.

"I'm fine," I answered, glancing at Adi, who really wasn't himself at all. His head had drooped, and his glasses were almost falling off his nose. "Adi," I asked gently, "can you walk for a bit, so we can get out of here?"

He nodded miserably and even let me take his arm, which surprised me, as even though he's shorter than me, he always likes to make a point of being "small and mighty".

"Is Lois going to be all right, Jonathan?" I was so worried about her, and for the first time, I wondered whether Mum had been right about us not getting involved in any more magic.

"Yes, yes, my dears, of course she will be. It's precisely why I said this is no place for children. The dark energies here are too much for your little bodies and too elaborate for you to be able to shake off." Jonathan was puffing slightly. He was walking so fast that Adi and I had trouble keeping up with him.

"Jonathan!" I called ahead to him. "Isn't there any way we could fly out of here on your back? You know, you've carried us all before."

"I wish I could, but unfortunately these tunnel ceilings are just too low for me to carry cargo — more's the pity. The main prison does have higher ceilings, but that really is a no-go area for you all."

"Do you mean there's more cells than those back there that we've seen?" I was astonished.

"Oh yes, those cells house the petty criminals, in for things like illegal shape shifting, broom raiding, tampering with magical codes, that sort of stuff. But the real, hardened crims, like the Mal Vines of the world, all reside in a different section of tunnel where there are three floors of prisoners. We really are rather overrun, I'm afraid. We need to build more rooms of light, where we can put the tricky customers."

"Rooms of light?" I asked.

"Yes," Jonathan continued, "we give the real nasty prisoners a dose every few days in a room of light. It helps burn away the darkness, otherwise they'd have no chance of rehabilitation." He wrinkled his beak up and down in an agitated movement.

"What's the matter?" I asked, still dragging poor Adi along beside me.

"You couldn't just scratch my nose for me, could you? Only my arms are rather full of this little lady, who, I must say, may look like a feather but actually feels like a rock."

"Yes, of course," I answered, reaching up to scratch Jonathan's beak.

"Much better, thank you, dear. Now, where was I? Oh yes, telling you how overcrowded we are," he continued. "There seems to be more badness in the world than ever. Your witchy chums were all sent out to Egypt as Mal Vine had been spotted hanging around over there, you see. So they went to keep an eye on him."

"So why did Hecate post Mr Foggerty and Phyllis at the British Museum? Did she know the *Book of the Dead* was in danger from Mal Vine? Wasn't that putting Phyllis directly in the line of danger? After all, he still hasn't taken his revenge on her, has he?"

Jonathan hummed and hawed. "Yes, you're quite right. Something doesn't fit, does it? All I can say is Hecate really does know what she is doing. I'm guessing she knows more than she lets on."

"I wish she'd just tell us, then, what we're supposed to be doing to help. Instead of us having to second guess all the time," grumbled Adi.

"Adi, you're speaking!" I gasped. "Are you feeling better?"

"Tiny bit," he replied.

I had to admit, I did agree with him. Why hadn't we been told exactly what we were supposed to be doing?

"Jonathan, where is Hecate? Do you think we should be going to see her to ask what our involvement in this should be?"

Jonathan shrugged his feathery shoulders. "I dare say I would recommend it, but no one knows where Hecate is right now. And I really ought to be one of the first to know, being her assistant and all that. The last I heard, she was dealing with some personal problems."

How funny, I thought, that a shapeshifter and goddess like Hecate should have "personal problems".

At last, I noticed we had come to the end of the dark, gloomy tunnel, and there was a chink of light coming through a crack in the wall. Jonathan tapped his beak firmly on the wall, and lo and behold, a door within the wall swung open to a dazzling room.

And who should be standing at the doorway squinting at us cautiously?

"Uncle Vic!" I cried out in relief. "What are you doing here?"

"I should ask you the same thing, young lady, but I have just got back from being accosted by Frances, who relayed everything to me. I'm surprised you haven't passed Phyllis and Mr Foggerty on your travels. They should be with you by now, Jonathan."

"Oh gosh! Oh golly!" Jonathan replied, hastily handing over a still unconscious Lois to Uncle Vic. "I'd better go quickly before Phyllis gets into a conversation with Colin and upsets him. He's not a fan of music. Well, unless he's making it, and you know how she loves to sing."

Jonathan started to rush off and turned quickly, waving his feathery arms about. "Lois will be okay.

She's got a *touch of the darkness*, as has Adi, only not as bad. Just give them some TT."

And with that, Jonathan had gone.

Uncle Vic ushered us into the bright room and pushed the heavy walled door shut. I felt myself shiver with relief that we were out of that awful place, and now I knew why Phyllis was so worried about going there. She had been miserable enough in the Room of Free Will, where we had found her last year, so this place would really be the end for her. Surely there had to be another solution to keep her safe from Mal Vine?

"Right, missy, let's get her laid down for a minute or two." Uncle Vic placed Lois down on a squishy couch and motioned for Adi and I to sit on the floor, which was covered in a thick-pile cream carpet. He pressed his finger to his lips by way of motioning us to be quiet.

"The door is locked," he whispered, "but I don't want Reg getting suspicious. I'm meant to have clocked off, so let me put some music on to camouflage the noise."

He leant over and flicked a small innocuous radio that immediately started playing an Abba song. I recognised it, as my mum liked them.

"It's 'Eagle' from *The Album*," he whispered to me, blushing slightly. "Don't let on to Jonathan, will you?"

Then Uncle Vic took a large white feather from the back of the sofa and started tickling Lois' feet with it.

I stared, astounded. I looked to Adi, who was just staring into space again — thankfully he had stopped crying, though. I didn't know whether Uncle Vic was performing some kind of elaborate ritual with the feather or not, but in the end, as he wasn't getting any kind of reaction from the sleeping Lois, I decided to intervene.

"What are you doing, Uncle Vic?"

"Tickle Therapy. Cannot understand why it's not working though. Very strange." He scratched his head and paused.

I screwed up my face and thought hard. "She's not got tickly feet," I stated, not knowing whether this was a helpful thing to say or not.

"Well, where is she ticklish then?" he asked.

"Her armpits, I think," I replied, still slightly confused.

So Uncle Vic proceeded to gently lift Lois' arms and tickle her armpit and sides. As soon as the feather touched her, she started to wriggle like a worm. She opened her eyes as if she'd just awoken from the longest, deepest sleep, and a burble of pure giggle came out right from the very pit of her tummy. It bubbled and frothed until she was writhing about on the couch begging for mercy.

"Lois!" I cried once Uncle Vic had stopped. "Are you feeling better?"

She was red in the face with the exertion of laughing. She sat up, stretched her arms out (she was miraculously still holding Bea), and stated, "I'm starving! When is it teatime?"

"I think you've already had your tea. Frances gave it to you before you came out after us," I replied, smiling in spite of her annoying habit of always being hungry.

"That was ages ago. Oh! And I never want to go in those tunnels again. They were horrid. Especially that one where Jonathan was. Why is he doing that job? The walls were full of creepy crawlies, for a start. And the smell was terrible."

I didn't want to tell her that I hadn't seen any creepy crawlies, nor had I smelt any terrible smell there, but my thoughts were interrupted by a great, guttural noise.

When I turned around, I realised it was coming from Adi, whose feet were being attacked by Uncle Vic with the white feather. It was the most bizarre sight I have ever seen. A rotund, grown man bouncing around like a clown tickling someone's feet.

Adi's glasses had disappeared, and he was holding his head in his hands, moving from side to side, making a noise that I can only imagine was laughter.

"Please stop!" he shouted. "I can't bear anymore. I feel like I'm going to explode!"

"Better, young man?" Uncle Vic shouted back over the Abba song.

Adi nodded and gave me the thumbs up.

Uncle Vic held the feather out towards me, but I shook my head. I felt absolutely fine, so I guess maybe I didn't need it. He switched the radio off and went back to whispering. "Right, we need to get you all home now, okay?"

"We'd better hurry then, as my dad will be back from work soon, I think," I added anxiously, desperate for some proper food and then my bed.

SAMANTHA GILES

Suddenly, we all jumped, as there was a gentle tap at the door.

Uncle Vic looked like he had been poked in the ear with a sharp stick, and he motioned for us all to be quiet.

"Who's that knocking on my door?" he sang with fake jollity.

"Vic, it's me, Frances," came the whispered reply.

We collectively exhaled in a huge sigh of relief as Uncle Vic unlocked the door and ushered Frances in.

"Thank goodness you are all here!" she wheezed, clutching her chest dramatically. "I was on my way back to your house when I suddenly realised I had forgotten all about taking you three with me! I think all this rushing about has addled my brain."

"I've been poorly, Frances," my sister stated, cuddling up to Frances. "The smelly old tunnel made me sleepy, but I'm okay now."

"We're going to have to break some rules, I'm afraid," Uncle Vic stated solemnly to Frances. "NWC, it's the only way to get them back quickly and will attract the least attention."

Frances nodded sagely. "You'll have to take young Adi, and I'll take the girls. My old broom won't allow me to take more than three. She'll play dead if I try that trick on her." She opened the door and swiftly reappeared inside the room holding her broomstick.

Uncle Vic retrieved his broomstick from underneath the couch, and the three of us looked stunned as he cocked his leg over it and motioned to Adi.

"Come on, young man," he said. "I'll drop you home, and Frances can take the girls."

I think the last words we heard him shout as he literally disappeared in front of our very eyes were, "Don't have your music too loud, Frances."

17

IT'S A KIND OF MAGIC

"Shut your mouths, girls, a fish might pop in," Frances said, gathering her skirts and placing the broomstick underneath her bottom.

"Oh goody!" Lois said gleefully, placing one leg over the broomstick. "I get to have another ride. Brilliant!"

"This is highly illegal," Frances whispered, "but never mind. Needs must. Otherwise your father will wonder where on earth we are. Rosie, get on behind Lois and hold on tight to the broomstick itself. If you want to make friends with her, just stroke her gently. She stays calm that way. Now, this first bit getting out of here is going to feel strange, but don't worry, we'll soon be outside, so just count to five, and it will all be over."

With that, the broomstick began to hover and some loud music blasted out. I recognised it as Queen, Frances' favourite band, with the track "It's a Kind of Magic".

"Oh goodness, Vic said not to have it too loud. Wendy, turn it down please!"

"Who's Wendy?" Lois shouted above the din.

"My broomstick!" replied Frances, decreasing her shout to a normal voice as the volume of the music grew quieter.

As if in agreement with Frances, Wendy shot up and down in a quick movement, which nearly flung us all off.

"Hold tight!" Frances cried as we raced upwards towards the ceiling, and I honestly thought I was going to die.

What happened next was one of the most unpleasant experiences I have ever had. The only way I can describe it is as if we were pushing through a great wall of firmly set jelly. The ceiling somehow gave way as the broom rose, and I felt totally squashed and couldn't breathe properly. I tried not to panic and counted to five in my head, which was what Frances had instructed us to do.

Just as I thought I could no longer bear the pressure on my head and back, we were free and flying high up in the sky.

It was still light, and the sky had a beautiful pink tint to it. There was a warm breeze blowing through my hair, and the sensation of being high up in the sky flying on a broomstick was indescribable.

I felt a moment of sadness that my mum wasn't here doing this with us. She had always wanted to fly a broomstick.

I gazed down in awe as we passed The Three Graces where the Liver Birds resided. The River Mersey painted an outline around the city and onwards towards Wales, the Wirral, and far, far beyond. No one except us knew how all these other wonderful rivers around the world were so accessible from the tunnels. I felt lucky to be living in such a great city, with so many secrets that only my little family knew about.

For once, Lois was quiet on the ride home. In fact, I think we were both just speechless, taking in the enormity of what we had been lucky enough to experience.

We landed with a slight bump and an expletive from Frances in the back of our garden, right next to where Maggie was having a wee. She nearly jumped out of her skin and looked most put out to be disturbed.

"I'll just leave this here, girls," Frances added, propping Wendy up against the wall as we crept round the side to get into the house via the front door.

We had just finished our food, and Lois was in the bathroom with Frances, when I heard the key in the lock signalling not Dad's, but Mum's arrival home.

"Mum!" I cried, giving her a hug just as she entered the kitchen. I noticed she looked really exhausted, and I pulled away sharply as I saw a green mist swirling around her head area. "I didn't think you were home until tomorrow night," I said carefully.

"I was supposed to be, darling, but luckily I finished a bit early. It means tomorrow I will be staying in Birmingham, unfortunately. Ooooh," she sighed, throwing herself into the rocking chair. "I am shattered."

She tipped her head back and closed her eyes for a moment, and my eyes widened in disbelief.

There was a huge hole in Mum's throat. This time I couldn't see through it to the back of the chair — this hole was somehow more sinister, as it swirled around in an ever-decreasing circle, like the colours in a kaleidoscope, except it was completely black.

I swallowed nervously and touched my own throat. What was going on with Mum? She now had a hole by her wrist, in her tummy, and one black one in her throat.

This was getting more serious. We really needed to find the *Book of the Dead* and, hopefully, a way of curing her.

Suddenly, Mum's nose wrinkled up, and she opened her eyes quickly and sat up with a start.

"That smell ..." she said sharply.

"Yes, sorry, probably Lois. She's had beans again," I said apologetically.

She shook her head emphatically. "No, Rosie, it's magic. I smell magic."

My tummy did a little wobble of fear, as I have to admit, I had never seen Mum quite like this before. It was as if someone had taken my mum and replaced her with a mad clone of Donna. It just wasn't her. She was snappy and sad and tired, and now she was saying she could *smell* magic.

I laughed nervously. "Mum, what are you talking about?"

"What has Frances been doing with you, Rosie? And where is she?" She heaved herself up out of the rocking chair and made to go upstairs.

Obviously, I didn't need to tell her that Frances was upstairs with Lois in the bathroom, as we could hear the two of them singing, "My name is High Low Jackalow, Jackalow High Low", as per the song of the prisoners.

I inwardly cringed. *Please don't let Mum realise we'd been in the Tunnel of Eternal Darkness.*

I heard Mum's voice from where I was in the kitchen as she reached the bathroom. "Frances, what's going on? Why can I smell *that smell*?" She sounded very cross.

"Hi Mummy," Lois called, presumably still in the bath. "It wasn't me. It was Bea, and anyway, I'm having a bath, so I'm all clean now."

Mum ignored Lois, and I heard a low rumble of incomprehensible Scottish words from Frances followed by Mum shouting.

"You know exactly what I'm talking about, and I've already warned you about it," she said. "I will not tolerate it in my house!"

It was quite terrifying hearing Mum behave like this towards Frances.

Thank god for Dad, who must have got home during the middle of the shouting, for I heard him say quite clearly, "Won't tolerate what, Rae? What on earth's happened?"

I dashed out to the hallway and Dad was there, looking confused. He gave me a thumbs up as if to say *are you all right?* and I nodded and watched him run up the stairs two at a time.

I hid down by the bottom of the stairs and listened.

"What's happened, Rae? Is everything okay with Lois?" I heard Dad say.

"Yes, fine," Mum replied, sounding sightly flustered. "It's all fine. I was just telling Lois off for being naughty."

By now, with all the shouting, Lois was crying, so the sounds of her sobs were like the backing vocals to the louder noise that my parents were making. Frances kept unusually quiet.

"For goodness' sake, Rae, that was a lot of shouting. What on earth has she done?" Dad asked reasonably.

"You know, just being cheeky and answering back." Mum faltered slightly as Lois screamed.

"I haven't done anything wrong," she said. "I only had baked beans. Frances, tell Daddy!"

It was all quite horrid to hear, and then, to top it all, the doorbell went.

Who would dare ring our doorbell in the middle of a crisis like this?

I tentatively opened the door and then very quickly wished I hadn't bothered.

Who was standing there with a tear-stained face and pinched lips like a cat's bum?

Donna. That's who.

"Hello, er, thingy, is Mummy there?" Donna murmured while dabbing her eyes and barely looking at me.

"And who the heck is that?" my dad shouted, completely silencing the din upstairs.

I looked at Donna with a smug expression on my face. She had the grace to pale slightly and then pushed past me and stepped into the house.

"Hello! Jonny!" she cried out softly. "Is Rae here?"

"It's John, not Jonny," Dad stated crossly, still from the top of the stairs.

I took this moment to swerve around Donna and hot foot up the stairs myself. I didn't want to be stuck down there in the hallway with *her*.

As I got halfway up, I saw Mum had started to descend. She looked totally washed out. She glanced at me, paused, and I just knew what she was thinking. We NEVER cross each other on the stairs in our house — it's a magical superstition that it's bad luck to do that.

I stared at her defiantly. I wasn't going to budge.

She hesitated and then retreated back to let me pass before she continued with her own descent.

Yes! I thought. *So, she hasn't really turned her back on magic then, has she?*

Dad disappeared into their bedroom, and poor Lois was still in the bath, crying.

I went in to quieten her down and speak to Frances, but she must have slipped out the back way once the doorbell had gone. While I was trying my best to make Lois laugh and get her dry, I could hear snippets of Mum's conversation with Donna.

"Harriet shouted at me because I was late! Can you believe it?"

After that not much else happened, as I could hear Donna faking some noisy tears.

Dad emerged from the bedroom as I was helping Lois get into her nightie.

"Has Miss Fitherfuddle gone, Rosie?"

"Er, yeah," I replied, haltingly at first. "I think she left just after Donna arrived." Not really a fib.

"Well, I'm not surprised. I wish I'd joined her," he joked. Except I knew it wasn't a joke.

Lois was so upset with Mum that she didn't even want cuddles from her when she went to bed, which was just as well in some ways, as Mum was trapped in the lounge with Donna, who was pouring her heart out.

Although I was cross with Mum for (a) pretending she was angry at Lois and therefore confusing her, and (b) shouting at Frances for using magic (none of which she had any proof of, by the way), I also felt a teeny bit sorry for her. Donna was the most selfish person I had ever met, and, hearing how often Mum said she was late on set, I didn't blame Harriet for shouting at her.

Later that night, I overheard my parents doing one of their whispering rows that didn't happen very often but left us all feeling rather uncomfortable until they had made up.

"I'm sorry, Rae, but we can't have that self-absorbed woman staying with us anymore. Tonight is it. I really mean it. She's trying to take you over."

"She's worried Harriet's trying to get her sacked, John. I can't just ignore her."

"That woman was a complete cow to you when you did the play, and she's done nothing except undermine you in this job, and you're still letting her call the shots."

"I'm just trying to be kind, that's all," Mum sniffled.

"How about being kind to your family, Rae?" Dad replied with feeling.

After that I didn't hear anymore. Actually, I got under the covers and put my hands over my ears, not wanting to know anything else that they were saying to each other.

The truth was, Mum was disappearing, not only in a physical way in terms of her body, but emotionally, too. She was so far from the mum we knew and loved, and I just couldn't understand how she could be sacrificing all those things she held so true just for a stupid job with people who weren't even being nice to her.

I was glad she was going to be staying in Birmingham for a few nights.

I decided I'd get us to the Akashic Library tomorrow, if it was the last thing I did.

18

A SENSE OF URGENCY

The next day we tiptoed around each other. Donna seemed to have recovered from the upset of last night.

"Can I help you with your school tie, Lois?" she smarmed to my sister, who, to my utter joy, shook her head and wiped her nose with Bea.

"You know you can get some awful germs from using cuddly toys as handkerchiefs," Donna said nastily as my sister just eyeballed her and repeated the action with more gusto.

I studied Donna thoughtfully. For someone who had been 'bullied and betrayed' last night, she looked okay to me. I glanced at Mum's tired-looking face. It was almost as if Donna had sucked Mum's happiness out of her and replaced it with her own misery.

"Thank you so much for letting me stay, John. I do appreciate it." Donna smiled girlishly at my dad.

"As a *one off*, it's no problem," Dad said gruffly, which really made me laugh, as what he actually

SAMANTHA GILES

meant was, *we had no choice, but it's not happening
again* ...

Donna smiled and batted her eyelids. I'm not
sure she knew how to take Dad's simple delivery.
For once, I was glad that Dad wasn't such a
smoothie with words.

Being dropped off at school by Mum was a relief in
some ways. At least we could escape the sickly-
sweet Donna, who was taking over our mum. We
wouldn't see Mum for a few days now, but it meant
we could concentrate on finding the *Book of the
Dead*.

Frances hadn't had a chance to tell us what her
discussions with Mr Foggerty and Phyllis had been,
but I felt sure that they would be in agreement with
us gaining access to the library if it was in order to
find the book. We just needed to somehow look inside it, find those spells for Mum, and get it back to
Mr Foggerty in London. Simple.

My tummy flipped over. It seemed like an enormous task, and we weren't even sure that this is
what we were meant to be doing. If Mal Vine had
also been spotted in Egypt, was he planning on
hiding the book there?

I confided in Adi at break time.

"Why do you think Mal Vine was spotted in
Egypt, Adi?" I asked him as we walked round the
playground enjoying the sunshine.

"I don't know, Rosemary. It's weird."

"Do you think he was checking the place out

for somewhere to hide the book once he'd stolen it? Where *would* you hide a book if you'd stolen it?"

"Oh yes!" Adi jumped up and down in excitement. "Of course!"

"What?" I asked him, smiling at his enthusiasm. "Tell me quickly before the bell goes."

"A library!"

I stared at him, his brown eyes widening, his nostrils flaring slightly, as he attempted to stop his glasses from sliding down his nose.

"Where would you hide a book?" he garbled excitedly. "You'd hide a book in a library, wouldn't you? It's full of books, so it's the least likely place anyone would look!"

Suddenly, I twigged. "So, are you saying that Mal might have hidden the book in the Akashic Library then?"

Adi nodded, looking very pleased with himself.

"You're a genius!" I said, patting him on the back. "We've got to go there after school. If we get into the library and find we don't even have to look up where the book is, because it's already there, that will be a result."

I lifted my hand to high-five him, grinning with anticipation for 3.30 p.m. to come round quickly.

As soon as the bell rang to signal end of school, Adi and I rushed out of the classroom and into the playground. I scanned the waiting parents briefly — there was no sign of Frances. Surely she hadn't forgotten us again, had she?

I looked down to the other side of the playground where Lois usually came out and couldn't see anyone there either. Suddenly my heart sank, as I saw the rotund figure of Uncle Vic hurrying down the walkway, puffing, his cheeks red with exertion. He waved enthusiastically at me and pointed over to Lois' classroom area to show me he was collecting her first.

"Adi, looks like Uncle Vic will be taking us down to the tunnels," I remarked gloomily. "I wonder where Frances is? She'll have to turn up later when Dad gets home, otherwise he'll wonder who has been looking after us."

"As long as he gives us the okay to go to the Library then," Adi said, gesturing to Uncle Vic with a worried expression on his face.

We watched Uncle Vic and Lois saunter over to us. I could see my little sister was chatting away to him, and he had that glazed expression on his face, but at least he had brought her crisps so he would be in her good books.

As we three left the playground, I could sense Adi was a bit anxious about whether it was okay or not to accompany us.

"Uncle Vic," I whispered, taking him to one side, "we were planning on going to the Akashic Library today, so we can find out where Mal Vine has taken the *Book of the Dead*. Did Frances tell you? Is she okay?"

"Goodness me, young lady, questions, questions ..." Uncle Vic quickened his pace so we could hop on the bus that was approaching. "Frances has had to go and see Phyllis. Being such a sensitive soul, she's finding it a bit tricky being in the Tunnel of Eternal Darkness, as you can imagine, and poor old Foggy isn't sure what to say or do to comfort her."

After a few strange looks from the bus driver, we boarded the bus and heaved ourselves upstairs. I guess Uncle Vic did look a bit wacky with his lemon-check short-sleeved shirt and brown trousers, particularly as the trousers were of a cropped variety, which made him look even shorter than he already was.

"Yes, she did tell me about your plans, very good, very good," he whispered, perching on the edge of a seat next to a frightened-looking school-boy. "I will hang about and wait for you, so to speak, as you know we can't get in, don't you?" he continued, tapping his nose.

I wanted to laugh. The boy he had squeezed next to looked terrified.

Lois was unabashedly singing THAT song from the prison again, and Adi was doing a sudoku puzzle. I couldn't help thinking what a peculiar group we were.

At last we got into town and were soon walking towards the George's Dock Building.

For once, the waiting area was empty, aside from the familiar sign, which never failed to amuse me — *"Tour full. Come back in one hour"* — and we were able to go down the steps and enter the room where the giant fan was housed.

Uncle Vic was extremely breathless as we descended the steps down to the fan, and he haltingly ushered us forward.

"Right, what we'll do is you lot will go into the

Library, and I'll wait at the base of the Sphinx, okay? Come on, let's hurry!" he said, glancing at his watch.

Once again, we watched as the numbers started to slow down on the counter as we waited for the mystical number 137. I had no idea why that was the number that we had to wait for, but as it hit its target, I heard Uncle Vic shout, "Go, go, go" and Adi flew through first, followed by Lois with a whoop.

Just as I was preparing myself to jump through, I heard the door creak open, and Uncle Vic say, "Ah Reg! Yes, just checking this pesky fan ..."

I didn't wait to hear anything else — I jumped through as if my life depended on it, knowing that Uncle Vic would have re-started the fan and it would shortly resume its original speed.

Lois and Adi had already brushed themselves down when I came flying through and landed on the cushions.

"Reg has just come in the room, so I don't think Vic will be able to follow us right away," I said. "We'd better get going quickly, in case anything happens." I didn't know why, but something was making me feel uneasy.

We walked briskly out of the room and down the corridor, past the glass-windowed office. As I glanced through, I wondered whether it was a one-way mirror. We could see into it, but no one seemed to be able to see us, or even ever to glance our way.

When we came to the tunnel splitting off, we left it to Lois to tell us which way.

I didn't really understand this strange relation-
ship she had with Paloma — how Paloma could tell
her things without any of us seeing her — but
whenever I questioned her about it, she always said,
"Just because you can't see her, doesn't mean she's
not there", which I thought was a fair enough answer. After all, people believe in lots of things they
can't see.

We climbed the ladder and lifted up the porthole lid. I breathed a sigh of relief as I felt the heavy
heat of the desert and felt grateful that we had
brought my little sister, even though she could be a
windy old moaner.

"Can we go home in a minute?" she whined,
having been practically pushed up the ladder
by me.

"Lois, we've only just got here, silly! All we've
got to do is get to the Library, find where the book
is, and that's it really," I said, hoping that it was
going to be that simple.

"This way!" Adi said, striding ahead, taking
charge.

"How do you know this is the right way, Ads?" I
called after him.

"Don't call me Ads, please."

"Soz."

"Look behind you, Rosemary," Adi said. "We
can't go that way — the river is in our way — so it
has to be straight ahead."

I looked behind at the flowing Nile. It was
much wider than you would imagine and had long
reeds either side of it. I wished we had time to go

and take a dip. It was so hot that all I wanted to do was jump into a nice, cold swimming pool. Luckily, we had brought water with us, so instead I passed my bottle to my sister, which stopped her moaning momentarily.

We seemed to have been walking for ages, and I was wondering if we had got this horribly wrong, when all of a sudden, Adi cried out.

"Look, everyone!"

The three of us stopped. One minute there had been nothing, and then it was almost as if we had passed through some kind of invisible curtain, for suddenly there they were: the Great Pyramids of Giza and the Sphinx, splendid and magnificent. We stood in silence, in awe of their majesty. There was a stillness in the desert and a sense of peace and power that seemed to come from the limestone Sphinx. It was a huge monument with the body of a lion and the head of a pharaoh.

"Wow!" exhaled Adi quietly.

"That is amazing," I gasped.

"I need a wee," Lois stated.

I rolled my eyes at her terrible timing and pointed to an area of shade. "You'll have to squat down over there, Lois. We need to climb up this beast somehow, as the entrance is apparently by its ear."

"Its ear?" she asked.

"Yes, now do you want me to stand in front of you in case someone comes?" I asked patiently.

"Yes, please," she answered. Then, after having the quickest wee in the world, she was up on her feet running over to the lion's foot.

"Come on, guys!" she called with the enthusiasm she usually reserved for digestive biscuits. "Let's go!"

Adi and I exchanged a glance — part fear, part excitement — as we started our climb.

19

THE GREAT SPHINX OF GIZA

The Sphinx was huge — its paws alone were about five feet high. Once we had climbed up the feet, there was another long stretch to the shoulder and then its ear. It looked impossible, and I felt a wave of defeat wash over me.

Lois' initial enthusiasm of climbing had quickly vanished, after she had slipped down each time she'd tried to get a grip on the grainy, limestone paw. Eventually, she sat down, leaning up against the foot of the Sphinx sucking on one of those sweet lollies — the kind that take forever to eat.

"Trickier than it looks, isn't it?" remarked Adi, pushing his glasses up his nose and flaring his nostrils as he squinted into the sun.

"That lolly is going to make you so thirsty!" I warned my sister, knowing we only had one bottle of water between us. I don't know why I didn't think to bring more.

"Can't finish it. Here you are," she said, passing it to me, and getting sticky lolly all over her hands.

"Lois!" I moaned, thinking that I didn't want to

waste our water on washing our hands. "I don't want it. I don't even like these lollies."

I passed it to Adi, who, without even thinking, stuck it into his mouth and continued gazing up at the pharaoh's face.

Urgh, did he realise he'd just put a load of Lois' gob in his mouth?

"Now my hands are all sticky, too. That's really annoying!" I continued.

Suddenly, I opened my mouth in shock. My sister was now at the top of the lion's paw. She stood triumphantly with her hands on her hips, doing a little wiggle of her bottom as a victory dance.

"I got to the to-op, I got to the top!" she sang cheerfully.

"How did you do that?" Adi asked before I could even form a sentence.

"With these sticky hands!" Lois did jazz hands at us. Fingers outstretched, she waved them around as if she were cleaning windows. She ran over to the next bit of climbing, which was not quite as smooth as the paw had been. "Look!" she shouted, as she grabbed hold of the stone and hoicked herself up to the next bit that jutted out with ease.

"That's amazing! Well done! So, the sticky lolly is helping you to climb up without slipping?" I shouted. "Come on, Adi, get some of that lolly on your hands and let's go for it."

I placed my hands hesitantly on the smooth paw and, sure enough, they stuck firmly to the stone as I lifted myself up to the next level. It was tricky when there was nothing to put your feet on, but my hands were so gluey that I was easily able to move one further up and successfully climb to the top.

The rest of the Sphinx should be much easier, I thought, as it had more uneven pieces of stonework that stuck out and would provide better footholds.

Soon Adi had wiped lolly over his hands and joined us at the top of the paw.

It seemed strange following Lois up the outside of the Sphinx — usually it was me or Adi in front. But here she was in her new-found position of leader, without a mention of food or drink.

Once we had reached the top of the shoulder, we took a breather and had some of the water, which was quickly disappearing.

"I hope someone might let us refill our water bottle when we get inside the Library," Adi said hopefully, as he wiped his mouth with the back of his hand.

"Yeah, I could just down the rest of this," I added, my mouth still parched from the heat of the sun.

"I'm getting a bit hungry," said Lois, who did look tired, now the thrill of being Spiderwoman had worn off.

"Come on," I soothed, "not much further to go till we get to the ear. Then once we're inside, it will be easy."

Suddenly my eyes caught the figure of a man and woman in the distance, walking towards the Great Sphinx.

"Who is that?" I said quietly, almost to myself.

"What? Where?" Adi asked, standing up and leaning over the edge of the pharaoh's shoulder.

"Adi, get down!" I whispered nervously, still squinting my eyes to see who it was, though the knot in my stomach told me it wasn't Uncle Vic.

We all jumped as we heard the loud "Caw! Caw!" of a bird flying overhead.

I listened with dread to the delight in my sister's voice as she announced, "It's Paloma!" and started jumping around dangerously.

"Lois, be careful!" I said, grabbing hold of the skirt of her school dress. "Listen to me. If that's Paloma, who do you think those people are coming towards us now?"

Lois soon shut up as Adi said the words I'd hoped never to hear: "It's Mal Vine and Aradia."

I could feel myself panicking. "What are we going to do?"

"But Paloma's my friend," Lois stated, lifting her head up from the ground, where I had pulled her down.

"I know that, Lois, but she's currently with Aradia and Mal Vine, who are not, I repeat, NOT our friends. So we'd better get up this pharaoh's face and into the secret opening before he spots us."

"Are you sure you don't just want to lie low?" Adi whispered. I could hear the fear in his voice.

"No, Paloma says don't worry, keep moving," Lois stated confidently.

"Right, well, I'm thrilled that's all sorted then, Lois. If Paloma says don't worry, then let's not worry," I said sarcastically.

"If you're going to be mean to me, Rosie, I'm

not going to tell you what Paloma is saying to me."
She sulked.

"Look, I suggest we stop arguing and just keep
going!" Adi hissed. "Uh-oh!"

"What?" Lois and I said at the same time.

"They've spotted us. They're running — come
on, let's hurry!" Adi got to his feet and lifted Lois
up first to tackle the next leg of the journey to
the ear.

"Lois, go on, just don't look down," I said as I
glanced down and nearly lost my balance. We were
an awfully long way off the ground.

I threw a quick look at the two figures who were
gaining on us. Aradia looked like a cartoon character in a long black dress, with her dark hair tum-
bling around her. She must have been soooo hot
dressed all in black in the blazing sun.

Mal Vine was as skinny in the flesh as he had
always looked — I realised I'd only ever seen him in
my dreams and on the TV screen. Even though
they were still a good distance away from us, I could
feel his eyes boring into me and sense his voice
whispering in my ear: *Where is it? Give me the
book.*

I concentrated on the climb and forced my
mind not to think of him and his voice and his flinty
brown eyes. We had to get to the top.

I could see Lois was flagging — she was
moaning as Adi threw her words of
encouragement.

"Come on, Lois, just a bit further. You can do
this!" he shouted to her.

I didn't dare look down, even when I heard

Mal's voice call up to us, and my stomach rose to meet my throat.

"No need to rush, ladies and gent, certainly not on our account. In fact, why don't you hang on, and we can all go in together?" He chuckled joylessly.

"Ignore him," Adi whispered to me.

"Hey, Rosie! Can you hear me, kid? I'm so glad we've bumped into each other. We've been hoping you'd show us to the entrance of the Akashic Library. Isn't it lucky we found you?"

"You know exactly where the Library is, you liar!" I couldn't help myself. I had to answer him.

I heard Adi tut and sigh. "Don't engage with him, Rosemary," he whispered crossly. "Come on, we're nearly there."

My heart was beating like a drum as I focused all the energy I could on heaving myself up the last few feet until we were all standing on a kind of windowsill edge just below the ear of the pharaoh. We couldn't see the ground from where we were standing, so we had no idea whether Mal and Aradia were already climbing up or not.

"Aradia knew it was in the Sphinx, but we didn't know where the secret entrance was. Why would we?" called the sinister voice of Mal Vine again. This time he sounded impatient.

I looked at Adi who put his finger to my lips and shook his head.

"How do we get in?" whispered Lois, who was hopping from leg to leg.

"Please don't tell me you need another wee?"

She glared at me. "No, but I'm very thirsty and hungry now."

I rolled my eyes.

Mal spoke again, more vehemently. "I said, how would I know about the secret entrance? Answer me!"

I tried not to listen to him. The three of us cast our eyes over the stone, hoping we would see a door.

We pushed, we gently traced our fingers over the rock's surface, and we knocked. Nothing. Absolutely nothing.

Again, Mal's evil voice boomed out, as if he were speaking through some kind of megaphone.

"Answer me now! I demand to know how I would know about the secret entrance to the library!"

Before we knew what was happening, Lois took a deep breath and shouted back at him, "Because you took the book, you stupid man!"

Suddenly, the stone in front of us disappeared and revealed a tall man standing in a doorway — at least, I think it was a man. He had a man's body and muscular brown skin and he was wearing a chunky gold collar, like a necklace, with a skirt tied in a knot around his waist. But his head was that of a wild dog.

He stared at the three of us for a moment.

"He didn't take the *Book of the Dead*," he said. "I did."

20

ANUBIS

The three of us gazed back at him, speechless. I didn't know whether to look at his face, which was scary enough, or the tall spear he was holding.

Any moment now, I thought, *he's going to push us over the edge with the spike of that spear.*

"Are you a dog or a man?" my sister asked boldly.

Adi and I glanced at each other. I could tell he was thinking what I was thinking: *shut up, Lois!*

I felt like I was holding my breath, until the man spoke again.

"I am Anubis, the Egyptian god of the afterlife, sometimes known as the god of the dead. What do you want with me, children?"

"Can we come in, please, and can I go to the toilet and get something to drink and eat? It's really hot out here," Lois continued, casually, as if she were addressing a dinner lady and not an Egyptian god.

"We really would like to come in quickly, if that's okay?" I asked in the politest voice I could, considering my nervousness. "You see, we are trying to find the *Book of the Dead*. We think Mal Vine has stolen it and hidden it here."

Anubis stared at us with unflinching brown eyes and then threw his head back and laughed loudly. It was the most peculiar sound, coming from a man with a dog's head — a sort of cross between a bark and a deep, throaty laugh.

"Please, sir, we don't mean to offend you," Adi offered up in a small voice, which I thought was rather brave of him.

Anubis gathered himself and spoke once more. "Like I said to you a few moments ago, Mal Vine did not steal the *Book of the Dead*. I did. Or rather, I took back what is ours. I knew he was after the book, and so I brought it back here, back to Egypt, where it belongs. And as for him thinking he can chase you and gain access to the Akashic Library—"

"Bless you!" giggled Lois.

Adi and I gave her a hard stare.

Anubis ignored her, thankfully, and continued, "Well, there's no way he can get in here. My light-workers won't allow it."

Suddenly Anubis turned, interrupted by the voice of someone who sounded very familiar.

"Aren't you going to let them in, Anubis, please? The heat is starting to melt us all. For good-ness' sake, shut the door and let them in!"

Anubis stood aside and bowed his head slightly, allowing us to pass by him and into the Library.

As we stepped into the room, which was mas-sive, I was struck by how cool and light the air felt. I looked down and realised, with a shock, that we were floating. Every one of us. The floor of the room was a good four feet below us.

Where was the gravity?

From floor to ceiling were layer upon layer of bookshelves, bursting at the seams with books — some fat, some thin, some coloured, some white, but all shimmering as if they were sprinkled with glitter.

Floating around, in various places of the huge room, were completely see-through beings cloaked in shimmering white and purple robes. They had long flowing hair and were neither men nor women. They moved towards us with their hands outstretched as if they were going to help us down, until Anubis gestured for them to leave us be.

I knew that these were the lightworkers that Anubis had mentioned. Perhaps they were librarians, who guarded the books and helped people find what they were looking for.

As I looked down, I was greeted by the familiar voice once again. "Welcome, children. We've been expecting you."

The three of us landed gently on the floor, and Lois cried out, "Hecate!"

"Hecate?" Adi and I said at the same time, completely shocked by the sight of her.

She was in her pretty-lady attire of a long floaty dress and soft blonde hair, which fell about her face in gentle waves. She held her arms out to us. Her eyes and hands always reminded me of my mother's, with short nails and eyes so blue that they seemed to reflect yourself in them. I was relieved she wasn't in her old-crone disguise, as I remember being quite scared by how she looked that time.

"What are you doing here?" I asked without thinking. "Sorry," I corrected myself. "I didn't mean to sound rude. It's just that our Aunty Frances said no one of her kind could access this place."

"It's perfectly fine, Rosie. You're not being rude, simply curious, which is completely allowed," Hecate said. "Yes, it's true that usually magical people, like us, cannot access the records, but I am an exception." She threw a glance to Anubis, who had by now joined us on the ground. "Because Anubis is my husband."

Anubis turned to her and gave a brief growl or bark in response. I'm not sure what he meant, but it certainly wasn't well received.

Hecate turned to him and hissed. "They are only here because you chose to mess with my plans. It was always supposed to have been Mal Vine who took the book."

As she spoke, her face started to change into that of the old crone. She became lined and snarly, and her fingers, which were jabbing in an accusing fashion at Anubis, were gnarled and bent.

"I am not going to apologise for taking something back that belongs to us," Anubis said. "Now it is where it should always have been — it is home. You more than anyone should know how important it is to be true to your own beliefs, even if others don't agree with you." Anubis' voice came out in barks, which, though mesmerising, was also quite scary.

Hecate gave him what I'd call a death stare, and

Anubis retreated back to stand by what I can only describe as a round hole in the room, like a well. I couldn't see what was down the well, but as he stood there, his body seemed to shudder, and I saw right before my eyes he had become a gold statue and no longer a living, breathing being.

Hecate turned back to us and motioned us to follow her. "Come, children, let us have something to eat and drink, and poor Lois needs the ladies' room, too."

"No, it's okay. I just need the toilet, not the ladies' room," Lois said in her most polite voice.

"It's the same thing!" I whispered to her, smirking.

I flicked a supportive look at Adi, who seemed to be more than a little nervous. He kept wrinkling up his nose repeatedly, so I took his hand and gave it a squeeze.

We followed Hecate along one of the many corridors of books and came to a stop by a little area that was decorated with soft rugs and refreshments.

"The toilet is just to the left, Lois. Do you want your sister to go with you?" Hecate motioned to me to accompany Lois, which I did.

Soon we were back on the floor, joining Adi who had already eaten one or two cakes, judging by the crumbs around his mouth.

Hecate poured cool glasses of refreshing, ice-cold water and passed around fairy cakes and carrot sticks with hummus — just what we needed to restore us after our mammoth climb.

Once we had finished eating and drinking, she began to speak.

"I am sorry, children, that you had to witness that little exchange between my husband and I."

I was still processing the fact that Hecate was married. Not only that, but her husband was Anubis, the Egyptian god of the afterlife! I don't know why it seemed so strange; perhaps it was because their backgrounds were so very different.

It was as if she could read my mind. She smiled at me gently. "Sometimes it is very difficult being married to someone from such different magic than myself. Ancient Egypt magic abides by some terribly outmoded rules and regulations, and I'm afraid the gods and goddesses are a little bit 'devil may care'."

"What does that mean?" Lois asked with her mouth full.

"It means they do whatever they wish, I'm afraid. Which sometimes means that Anubis and I disagree on how things should be handled," Hecate answered. "I knew Mal Vine would be looking to take the book so that he could unleash the demons inside it. That is why I sent Phyllis, Frances, and the others to Egypt, to keep watch on him. Whether he was here to research the ancient artefact, or to attempt to use Egyptian magic to gain access to the book is unknown. However, my problem is that we cannot send him back to the Tunnel of Eternal Darkness unless he is actually caught *doing* something horrific. So now that Anubis has taken the book, it has rather spoilt my plans."

"So that *was* his intention then?" Adi asked, looking very serious. "To unleash the demons."

"Oh yes, I'm pretty sure it was, and probably

still is." Hecate sighed, looking far off into the distance. "It does mean, of course, thanks to Anubis bringing the book back here, Mal is more than likely going to resort to all number of other ghastly things to get to the book. All of which I'm very confident you'll be able to handle." She smiled at us all.

"What do you mean, we'll be able to handle?" I asked slowly, sipping my water.

"Rosie, my dear," Hecate addressed me, her dark blue eyes boring into mine, "you have a special connection with Mal Vine, don't you?"

I nodded nervously, my heart sinking a little. "I suppose so, only in that I can see him in dreams, and I've seen him appear on the TV talking to me once or twice."

"So, you see, it only makes sense that, if the three of you have access to the book, Mal will follow you, take the book, try to release the demons, and then we'll be able to arrest him," she said.

"Is that why he was outside following us?" I asked carefully. "Because he thinks we already have the book?"

"Yes, I believe so." Hecate paused, looking troubled. "I need to speak to Anubis first, so that he will help the three of you on the journey ahead. We must have his blessing for you all to take the book back to the British Museum, before Mal Vine finds some way of getting to it first."

"What about Phyllis?" Adi asked. "He's her brother. Surely she might be able to talk to him and dissuade him from doing anything horrible again."

"I fear it may be too late for that, Adi," Hecate said gravely. "Mal is so twisted and caught up in how he feels his sister wronged him, that he wants to punish not just her, but the whole world."

"Sounds like he just needs a proper telling off and then maybe a cuddle," suggested Lois, reaching out for yet another cake. "Mmm, these are yummy. Although I don't normally like icing, do I, Rosie?" She licked her lips.

Hecate smiled and took my hand in hers. "Rosie, Adi, Lois, join hands with me, please." She placed her hand on the floor and each of us placed a hand on top and carried on until we had all piled our hands on top of each other in the centre of the floor. "Anubis wants the book kept here, but he must realise that if he doesn't cooperate, and Mal Vine gets his wish, the book itself will be destroyed if the demons were to be released."

She paused for a moment, as if checking that we understood the magnitude of this.

"The only option is to help you three take the journey inside the book and find your way to Osiris, who resides in the Hall of Two Truths. Once you have successfully reached him, he will allow you to take the book. And hopefully, with Mal Vine following you, we will be able to arrest him before he puts his evil plan into action. But — and this is a big but — there are some challenges on the way. However, with the blessing of Anubis, I know you can overcome these — all three of you."

"Get *inside* the book?" Adi asked, looking confused.

Hecate nodded. "It's the only way — to take the journey the deceased would have taken to find their way to Osiris. Don't worry," she smiled at us supportively, "it's easier than it sounds."

"And what about Mal Vine?" I asked shakily, not enjoying the fact we might be bait for him.

"Don't worry about Mal. All you need to do is focus on meeting the challenges in the book and getting it back to London. Leave Mal to me and Anubis."

I wanted to believe her, I truly did. Her blue eyes were so trustworthy, and she had a way of almost hypnotising you when she spoke, but I must admit, I was really afraid.

"We can do this, m'lady. Have no fear. We will do as you command," spoke Adi, sounding like a knight from the realm or something.

I noted, with fondness, that every now and then Adi liked to think he was a superhero in an episode of *Star Trek* — or was it *Star Wars*?

I suddenly realised, if Adi was prepared to do this for no personal gain, then it should be easy for me. How lucky was I to have such a brave friend who was willing to help me and my family?

I reminded myself that this was something I had to do for my mum. Find the book, find the spells that help make a person whole again, and my job would be done.

I looked round at Lois, who had nodded off, and felt my determination strengthen.

"When should we start the journey into the book then, Hecate? We aren't really prepared now. We just thought we were coming here to find out where the book was."

Hecate smiled and released our hands. "I

would love to say now, but I think you ought to go home, gather the things you think you'll need, and return fresh tomorrow."

I opened my mouth to ask her what things we ought to bring, but she silenced me with her hand.

"Bring what feels right," she said. "Now go, and I will talk to Anubis."

"But what about Frances? I don't think she'll be too keen on us coming without her," I managed to garble.

"Leave the witches to me, my dear girl. They will have other things to deal with," she replied as she started to lead us round the corner, back to the main entrance.

I glanced over to Anubis, who was still in statue form, guarding the well, as we floated back up to the Library's doorway.

"What about Mal Vine and Aradia? Are they still outside?" Adi croaked nervously as the doorway opened to let us out, and a wave of heat hit us.

Hecate shook her head. "Close your eyes."

I heard her click her fingers and mutter something under her breath, and I could feel a coldness.

"Has anyone opened their eyes yet?" I said out loud.

"No, have you?" Adi replied.

"I have," Lois said. "We're back at the tunnel crossroads."

And we were, and who should be trundling towards us puffing like a steam train?

Uncle Vic.

21

AN ADVENTURER PREPARES

"Sorry about the delay, kids. That Reg is a right old nosey parker, you know," Uncle Vic said as he made his way through the tunnel towards us. "To be honest, I think he's jealous of me. He's been working here twenty-odd years, and he's never had the promotion I've just had. Mind you, of course, he doesn't realise a bit of magic's been involved in that ... And who knows, this time next year I could be working for London Zoo or summat, feeding the lions!" He finally paused to take a breath and chuckled to himself as if he'd cracked the funniest joke ever.

"Is Frances still with Phyllis?" I asked, wondering whether Uncle Vic was ever going to ask us how we got on at the Library.

"No, no, she's waiting for you at home. So come on, gang, let's get you to the Library."

"We've already been," Lois replied smugly.

"Oh!" Uncle Vic looked surprised and tapped his wristwatch.

"Aren't you going to ask us how we got on?" I

couldn't believe he was more interested in checking the time on his ancient-looking watch.

"Oh yes! Well, obviously you haven't got the book, have you?" He turned briefly round to look at us, as if he were double checking we weren't carrying it or something. "It's been a bit busy here, you know. A bit of trouble going on in the Tunnel of Eternal Darkness, so we've been trying to help Jonathan sort all that out."

We passed the window where the office was, and there was a real hive of activity inside. Six people were gathered round the large map on the screen, pointing and gesticulating. Uncle Vic barely gave it a second glance as we reached the point that led back to the extractor room.

"I'm afraid we can't go back that way — too dangerous with Reg on the prowl — so I'll see if I can find the short cut, eh? Would you like that, young lady?" he said jokingly, ruffling Lois' hair.

"What I'd like is a piece of Madeira cake, please, Uncle Vic. Can you magic that up for me?" Lois asked earnestly.

Uncle Vic chuckled. He obviously didn't realise Lois wasn't joking.

Her face dropped, and I could see she was going to cry.

"Come on, Lois, we'll be home soon, and I bet Frances is already making our tea, so you'll be able to have it as soon as we get in, okay?" I said in my best soothing voice.

"Okay," she replied miserably.

I had to admit, I did feel quite sorry for my little sister. She probably didn't have that much idea about what we were potentially getting involved in, and I was none too happy that Uncle Vic seemed more concerned with whatever was going on in the Tunnel of Eternal Darkness, rather than our battle to retrieve the *Book of the Dead*.

"What's he doing?" Adi whispered to me. He pointed subtly to Uncle Vic, who we were all gathered behind, while he seemed to be prodding and poking at the wall.

I shrugged, feeling a little careworn. I just wanted to get home and think about what we might possibly need to take tomorrow.

I wished we didn't have to go to school. By the time we got back down here, it would be gone four o'clock. We'd be tired and not really up for a whole adventure in Egypt.

"Right, gotcha, you little rascal!" cried Uncle Vic as he pushed an area of wall with his foot, which then gave way to reveal a round entrance from which a ladder was hanging. "Follow me up this ladder. By rights, this should bring us out just round the corner from your house, if I've got my geography right!" He chortled, extremely pleased with himself.

Adi and I exchanged a look which said something along the lines of, *I have no idea what Uncle Vic is up to, but we've got no choice but to just go with it.*

Lois was complaining that her tummy was rumbling. I let her go in front of me to follow Uncle Vic up the ladder.

It was a bit of a squeeze to get through the hole and then negotiate the narrow ladder, so I'd no idea how he managed it. I did hear lots of puffing and panting and expressions like "cripes" and "stone the crows", which made me smile.

At last I could see daylight as Uncle Vic pushed up one of those portholes — rather like the ones we found at the end of the tunnels that led out to London, Birmingham, and Egypt — and lo and behold, we were opposite the wasteland on Thingwall Road, just a street away from our house.

"How did you do that, Uncle Vic?" asked Lois curiously, watching him intently with her head leaning to one side.

"Ahhhh!" he replied, tapping his nose. "That's magic, that. Come on, it's teatime, ladies and gent."

We arrived back at our house to some wonderful smells coming from the oven. "Do you want to stay for tea, Adi?" I asked, feeling bad that he must be starving, too, and here we were about to sit down and tuck in.

"If that's okay?" Adi said shyly. "But I just need to phone my mum and tell her."

"You go right ahead, young man," replied Frances, looking flushed, as if she had been rushing. "Are you staying, Vic?"

"No, no, dear, got to get back. I promised Jonathan."

Frances nodded as he left, and once she had dished up our tea, she threw herself into the rocking chair and exhaled a deep sigh.

"Are you okay, Frances?" I asked, with my mouth full of creamy mashed potato. "How was Phyllis, and what's going on in the Tunnel of Eternal Darkness?"

"You know that saying, it never rains but it pours?" she said. "Well, that is so true, poor wee Phyllis. It's no' going well in there. The darkness is getting to her, much more than it usually does for our kind. I feel pretty exhausted trying to cheer her up. There's a leak in the prison, you see, from the Category A prison area, through the walls and into the area where the less dangerous criminals are kept and where, of course, Phyllis is."

"Is that the bit that Jonathan showed us?" Adi asked.

"Aye, that's right," Frances said. "So this leak is sending everyone a wee bit bonkers."

"Can't they just get a good plumber in?" Adi asked as if it were the most obvious answer.

Frances chuckled. "It's not that kind of leak, Adi." This caught my attention, and I wanted to ask her what sort of leak it was then, but she had already waved away our curious faces with her hands. "And to top it all, Hecate is nowhere to be seen."

"We've seen her!" Lois said innocently, and I wondered just then whether that was the right thing to say or not.

Frances stopped suddenly. "You've seen Hecate?" she asked, astonished.

Lois nodded, her mouth full of beans. "She was in Egypt, in the library, with her husband."

"Oh!" Frances said, her mouth forming a perfect circle.

"She told us to gather what we thought we might need and then go back for the book tomorrow ..." I hesitated. I didn't want to worry Frances, but I also knew I had to tell her what we'd been told to do. "She wants us to get into the book and lure Mal Vine into it, too, so that they can arrest him once he tries to unleash the demons in the book."

"Rosie, what are you talking about?" Frances looked totally confused. "I thought Mal Vine *had* the book?"

Adi butted in confidently. "No, apparently Anubis took the book back to Egypt, and Hecate is cross with him because she wanted Mal to take the book so they could then arrest him, but now we've got to act as bait to get him to follow us so he can try to carry out his plan ..."

"Well, I never did. I was convinced Mal had taken that book." Frances sounded downright annoyed that Mal Vine *hadn't* taken it.

"Mmm, sometimes one and one do make eleven," Adi mused wisely.

"What?" interrupted Lois. "One and one make two, Adi, not eleven. Huh! And we thought you were a maths genius."

I smiled to myself. I did like Adi's sayings, even if Lois got them totally wrong.

"So, let me get this right." Frances closed her eyes in concentration. "Hecate wants you to go back to Egypt, get inside the book, hopefully Mal will follow youse, so then he can be caught doing something bad?"

"That's right." I added, checking with Adi that it was correct.

"And we're doing it tomorrow," Adi said, screwing his nose up with concentration.

"Well, we'll see about that. I am not happy at all

about you doing this alone. I know *we* cannot get into the library, but I can certainly be outside waiting for you, with my broomstick, if necessary." Frances looked terribly worried. "I promised your mother I'd not do magic with you, and here I am practically condoning this trip that sounds fool-hardy to me."

"Please don't worry, Frances. Paloma will look after us. She is my friend; she will tell us if we need to worry about anything," Lois added, sidling over to Frances and cuddling her.

"I'm not sure how true that is, Lois," I said gently, trying not to hurt her feelings. "Paloma might have been there today, but she didn't exactly stop Mal and Aradia from trying to chase us into the Library, did she?"

"You don't know her like I do. She won't put us in danger." Lois pouted. "I'm going to get my things for tomorrow." And off she trotted upstairs.

I was a little bit stunned.

I thought the last thing she would want to do is think about, never mind prepare for, a trip back to Egypt after school tomorrow. Would she have enough room in her school rucksack for the millions of snacks she'd need, plus Bea?

"I'd better go, too," Adi said, taking his plate out to the sink.

"Thank you, young man, you're very polite." Frances smiled at him.

"I don't think I need to bring much, but I'll have a think," he said, supportively squeezing my arm.

Just after Adi left the house, we heard the sound of my dad's key in the door.

"Good evening, all!" Dad shouted. "Everything all right, Miss Fudgy Finger?"

I closed my eyes in exasperation. Would Dad ever get Frances' name right?

I crept upstairs and packed a few things in my school bag that I thought I would need for tomorrow. I don't know why, but I poured some lemonade into a flask, as well as grabbing a couple of bottles of water and snacks. I also rummaged through Mum's dried ingredients that she used for spells, which were now taped up in a box in Dad's office, and found some liquorice root. I remembered the Summoning Spell by heart and thought, if we got into any danger, maybe I could summon the witches, or Hecate?

Dad was alone in the lounge, once Lois had gone to bed, with Bob draped over him. I peered round the door.

"Can I give Mum a quick ring, please, before I go to bed?" I asked.

"Sure, she normally rings about now anyway. Let me speak to her after, won't you?"

I nodded and hesitated. "Dad?"

"Mmm?"

"Do you think Mum's changed since she's been doing this job?" I asked tentatively, thinking about the holes that had appeared in her.

"In what way?" he answered slowly.

"Well, you know she just seems a bit like she's trying to be someone else, and as if she thinks they won't like her if she's herself."

"Mmm, I know what you mean, love," Dad responded. "Your mum's a worrier; she doesn't realise that it doesn't matter what people think. It's more important to just be yourself. As long as you're true to your own beliefs, then stuff everyone else! It's not an easy thing to do, though."

"Are you yourself when you're at work?" I asked, curious.

Dad pushed his hands through his hair and looked a bit puzzled to have been asked this. "Well, good question. I think I am, but I expect Mum would say I'm a 'larger than life' version of myself, perhaps."

"Well, I think Mum's a smaller version of herself lately," I said. "She seems to be disappearing." I mumbled the last bit to myself.

"It's only another month or so before it all ends," Dad said reassuringly as he went back to playing his video game.

I dialled Mum's number, and she picked up at once. "Hi Mum, miss you," I said.

"Hello. Sorry, who is this?" came the stilted reply.

"Mum, it's me, Rosie," I said, a bubble of anxiety rising up from my tummy. "Are you all right?" She didn't sound at all like herself.

"Oh yes! Rosie. Yes, I'm here." She paused. "Isn't this weather awful today? Looks like rain. Shame for June, really." There was another long pause before she continued, "Tell her I love her, won't you? And John. Goodnight, darling."

And before I had a chance to hand the phone to Dad, she was gone.

22

THE WANDERING WARBLER

The next day I made sure that Lois and I had filled our rucksacks with all the things I thought we would need and instructed her firmly to leave behind anything unnecessary at school.

"But what if I forget, Rosie?" she whined.

"Well, then you'll have a very heavy rucksack to carry, won't you?"

She glared at me, and I could see she was trying to think of a suitable reply.

Throughout the day I kept getting little nervous fizzing sensations in my tummy as I thought about what we were planning to do. I was excited, too, but somewhere deep inside I felt that everything would be okay — rather foolishly, maybe.

As soon as the bell went for the end of the day, we dashed outside and met Frances who had her determined face on her. I could tell she was in a "no nonsense" mood, as she, too, was wearing a rucksack — which she never wore — and she had a sort of practical denim pinafore dress on, under which was a yellow vest, with her black Doc Martens. I guessed she was dressing for the desert, which I suppose was sensible, even though there was a slight cool breeze here in Liverpool, in spite of it being June.

"Right, come along, all. Let's go, pronto. Lois, no dawdling, please. We've a journey ahead of us!" chimed Frances as she strode off, giving Mr Bobbin a wide smile as she passed him.

Once we'd got on the bus, Frances passed around a flask of something she had made earlier. It smelt like Parma Violets and was bright orange.

"What's this?" I asked before I dared take a sip.

"It's a little pick me up, dear. It will give you all a shot of energy, like having a good sleep or energising meal." Frances took it from me, wiped the mouth of the flask and chugged back a large swig. "Come on, your turn, Rosie, then pass it to Lois and Adi."

I nervously raised it to my mouth and allowed a small amount to pass my lips. I was surprised — it didn't taste of violets, it tasted of sunshine and green fields and summer. It was delicious!

I took another large gulp and then giggled, nearly choking, as Frances emitted an enormous loud burp.

"Ooooh, pardon me, vicar!" she said loudly, placing her hand over her mouth in surprise.

Lois took a long drink from the flask and smacked her lips in appreciation. "Delicious. Just need a nice piece of Madeira cake to go with that." She grinned at me, suddenly revitalised, and I grinned back. Her smile was infectious.

Adi took cautious little sips, which kind of

summed up his personality, really. Once he was sure he wasn't going to drop down dead any minute, he relaxed and allowed the liquid to trickle down his throat.

"Wow, that's different," he said, wiping his mouth with his hand. "Kind of fizzy but creamy, too. A bit like a combination of Lucozade and strawberry milkshake."

I pulled a face. "That sounds gross! Glad I wasn't drinking what you were drinking."

Soon we were getting off the bus and making our way to the George's Dock Building once again. This time, to my surprise there was quite a queue of people, handing tickets in and being ushered through to the first room before their tour started.

We spotted Uncle Vic stamping tickets and uttering the same thing to every person. "Thank you kindly, my friend. Just follow the arrows round to the left, and my colleague Reg will let you choose from his illustrious collection of neon jackets, and then you will begin the tour shortly. Enjoy! Next please."

Frances whispered to us to look "inconspicuous". I didn't know what that meant, but it sounded important.

"She means don't stand out," Adi mouthed to us.

"Well, why didn't she say that then?" asked Lois, who had popped Bea into her rucksack so she was peering out and had a great view of the room.

The three of us pretended to look at the pictures on the wall, which were actually quite boring, old black-and-white enlarged prints of tunnels and men digging. The tunnels we had discovered were much more interesting.

I could see Frances out of the corner of my eye bouncing around, trying to get Uncle Vic's attention. What was she doing? She told us to blend in, and there she was jigging about and clearing her throat loudly.

Uncle Vic was doing his best to ignore her, but I also knew he had seen her — his left eye had started to twitch as if something in his periphery was irritating him.

Once the queue of people had gone through, he turned to Frances, his face red, clamping his hand over his twitchy eye. "Thank you, Frances, I can see you, and you've brought my twitch back, for goodness' sake. Couldn't you hear me sending you a message to say I'd seen you and just hang on quietly?" He shook his head. "Honestly, all I ask is that my colleagues melt into the background here, so we are less likely to be noticed," he hissed. "But no, I telepathically send you messages, and you ignore me."

"There's engineering work being done on the line," Frances said, equally cross.

"What are you talking about?" Uncle Vic looked baffled.

"My telepathic phone line is down," Frances said.

"I don't think it's ever been up and running, if memory serves," Uncle Vic replied sharply.

"I will choose to ignore that, thank you, Vic."

Frances flared her nostrils, and her eyes flashed. She had never looked so cross. "We have a job to do, and I have these children to protect. If you don't mind letting us through ..."

"We have to be more careful than ever, Frances. The Tunnel of Eternal Darkness is in chaos right now. Bad feeling and misery is leaking furiously into the area where Phyllis is, and we can't find the source of the leak. It's all hands to the deck." Uncle Vic scratched his head.

So that was the leak that Frances had mentioned. Not a water leak, as I had imagined, but a leak of sadness and gloom.

I thought of Phyllis and how she had been bullied by everyone to go and hide there in the tunnels, and it seemed crazy to me that she was there. If Mal Vine was after the book, then surely Phyllis would be safe to come out of there, right?

I touched Frances' arm gently.

"Frances, if Mal is in Egypt, following us, why can't Phyllis get out of the Tunnel of Eternal Darkness and go and hide somewhere less depressing? I think she's probably safe from Mal Vine, don't you?" I asked.

"Listen, pet, I cannae think right now of what my own name is, let alone how we'd get Phyllis out and safe somewhere else, unless you can think of somewhere or someone she could go with who had no link to her at all?"

"And another thing to remember," stated Uncle Vic, as we followed him down the stairs to the extractor room, "the tunnel entrance to the prison is appearing all day now and not just after 6 p.m., which is yet another security worry. So, take that into account when you go and come back, won't you? Don't wander into it by accident. It's too dangerous right now."

Frances smiled half-heartedly at us and rolled her eyes at Uncle Vic's bossiness. I had never seen him quite so stressed before.

We walked down the stairs and arrived at the fan where Uncle Vic pressed the stop button in order for it to slow down. He gave us all a brusque half-smile as we waited patiently for it to reach number 137.

"What's so special about that number, Adi?" I whispered, knowing that if there was anything to know about it, being mathematical, he would know the answers.

"It's supposed to be the most perfect, pure, magical number," Adi whispered back, not taking his eyes off the dial. "You see, the fine structure constant is equal to 137."

"What's the fine structure constant?" I asked, my brain feeling as if it was being fried.

"I'm not totally sure," Adi replied, looking a bit sheepish. "It's quite complicated, but basically, it's to do with the electrical charge going on between electrons. All atoms, which are electrons and neutrons ... well, they make up all the stuff in the world — all energy, all space, and time — and it all relates to the number 137. It's a pure number, too, which means that it is dimensionless. It can't be defined, because I guess you can't really see it."

Adi really was a maths genius (even though I didn't have a clue what he was on about). Suddenly, I was more concerned about jumping through the fan, which had just reached the magic number.

"Go!" Uncle Vic shouted, ushering Frances and Lois through first. I watched Lois jump with glee, followed by Frances, who still had a red "Sale" sticker on the bottom of her Doc Martens boots.

Adi motioned to me to go first, which I did, rather than waste time arguing with him, and I landed in a heap next to my sister, who was chatting to Bea about what to expect when we arrived in Egypt.

"Come along, folks, let's hurry now, important to get this over with," Frances called to us, marching towards the door.

The room with the maps was empty, which I must admit I found a little strange. There were two red lights flashing on the world map, but we were going too quickly for me to figure out where in the world appeared to be on red alert. Plus, I thought, sometimes it was better not knowing these things. We just needed to focus on the job in hand, get into the book, get to Osiris, and then we would, according to the witches, have the power to move it back to the British Museum.

We reached the tunnel divide once more, and we all looked toward Frances to tell us which of the eight tunnels we should choose from.

Frances smiled nervously and closed her eyes in concentration.

"This is ridiculous," Adi hissed in my ear.

"They must have a system, even if it changes regularly. We are wasting precious time here."

Suddenly we heard the faint warble of a familiar voice coming from the fifth tunnel. We all froze, and Frances looked to the three of us with her eyes wide.

"Don't tell me that is who I think it is coming towards us!" she whispered, leaning forwards as if she were straining her eyes.

"Let's go and find out," stated Lois, moving off down the tunnel confidently.

Adi and I looked at each other, and then at Frances, and knew we had no choice but to follow Lois towards the mournful sounds that were coming from a female form ahead of us.

"Have any of you seen my Wolfie? We were meant to meet at noon, but I can't. I can't leave my little brother. I'll have to let Wolfie go. My brother needs me ..."

"Phyllis!" Lois shouted, throwing herself at the tall skinny lady in front of us. "What are you doing wandering out here? Would you like a biscuit?"

Adi and I exchanged a look of fear with Frances.

First, how had Phyllis got out of her hiding place in the Tunnel of Eternal Darkness, and second, why was she talking nonsense?

"Phyllis!" Frances spoke loudly and slowly to her as if she were deaf. "It's me, Frances. You're here in the tunnels with us girls and Adi. Can you hear me, hen? What are you going on about?"

In spite of the seriousness of the situation, I

wanted to giggle at Frances who was waving her arms about as if she were directing traffic.

But then Phyllis answered her, and suddenly a chill came over me.

"My brother needs me. Mal needs me. Mal Vine. Tell him I'm coming."

23

THE RIDDLE OF THE SPHINX

There was silence as Frances' mouth dropped open. Adi and I exchanged a look of helplessness, and even Lois backed away from Phyllis.

No one dared say a word, until my little sister — not one to enjoy silences — opened her mouth.

"Phyllis, Mal Vine is your EVIL brother. Why would you want to go to him? We are trying to keep you safe from him." She tugged at Phyllis' arm as if trying to jolt her out of her strange ramblings.

To our horror, Phyllis slumped down on the wet floor of the tunnel and hugged her knees up to her chest.

Frances looked frantic. "I cannae get down there with you, hen. I'll never get up again," she said breathlessly.

"It's all right, Frances, I'll sit with her," Lois said confidently, taking charge and handing Phyllis one of her precious digestive biscuits. "Eat this, Phyllis. You'll definitely feel better afterwards."

"What do you think is wrong with her?" Adi

whispered to Frances and me nervously. "You don't think Mal has got to her, do you?"

I shook my head thoughtfully. "It might be the darkness affecting her. What do you think, Frances?"

"Aye," Frances agreed, sounding relieved. "I think you're right, hen. It sounds to me like her brain has gone back in time to when she was only eighteen and she left her little brother Mal in order to be with Mr Foggerty. The darkness can do strange things to people."

"Hello there, everyone," Phyllis spoke suddenly. "I'm sorry to have troubled you all. I don't know what I'm doing here." She sounded so forlorn and confused that my heart went out to her.

With Lois on one side and me on the other, we helped her stand again and hugged her tightly.

"It's okay, Phyllis, you're with us. You're safe. Are you feeling like yourself again?" I asked.

She nodded slowly, nibbling on the rest of the biscuit Lois had given her.

"You gave us quite a fright there for a minute," Frances said, rummaging around in her bag for the flask she had given us all earlier on the bus. "We thought you were off to join the No-Laws or something! Here, take a swig of this, lady. You'll feel a wee bit better then."

Phyllis took the flask and drank from it deeply. "Oh lovely, a nice cup of tea, how perfect."

Adi and I grinned at each other, thinking how funny it was that it tasted different to everyone.

"You know, this place is rather horrid. I think I was asleep and having a peculiar dream. I felt I was eighteen again, back at home, packing up, ready to leave to be with Wolfie. Of course, you already know how devastated my little brother was about me leaving. It was almost as if he were right there beside me. The next thing I knew, I was wandering these tunnels being found by you. What a silly old fool I am."

"Oh, Phyllis," I said, hugging her again, "you're not a fool."

"The Tunnel of Eternal Darkness is a scary place though, Phyllis, so I don't blame you for trying to get away from it." Lois helped herself to another biscuit.

Frances looked serious. "But you know what I'm going to say, don't you, Phyl?"

Phyllis nodded, looking utterly miserable.

"I'm afraid I've got to take you back there. Mal could be coming for you any time now. We need to keep you safe, and we all agreed it's the last place he would look for you."

"Is there really nowhere else that Phyllis could go into hiding?" Adi asked earnestly.

Frances paused and looked from Adi to me, to Lois, to Phyllis and then sighed. "I don't know, Adi. Look," she continued briskly, "we cannae stand around here waiting for the floods. Let me take Phyllis back and speak to Jonathan. This is no good if the leak in the tunnel is making you feel worse, but we can't start making decisions willy-nilly."

Lois looked worried. "When are the floods coming, Frances?"

Adi and I started to giggle, and even Phyllis looked amused.

"It's just a saying, Lois," I explained. "You know, like 'watching paint dry' means something is boring."

"Why would anyone want to watch paint dry?" she repeated with disgust.

"Exactly!" I replied, still trying to hold back my amusement.

"Right, so," continued Frances, "are we all agreed then? I will take Phyllis back immediately while youse carry on to Egypt, and I'll follow you as soon as I can."

"Agreed!" Adi and I said in unison, followed by Lois and then the small voice of Phyllis, who looked as if she was just putting a brave face on it all.

We all hugged her and watched as they gradually disappeared from view on their journey back to the Tunnel of Eternal Darkness.

"Okay, everyone," I said, sounding more confident than I felt, "let's hurry. Frances will meet us by the Great Sphinx as soon as she can, so we'll know if we get into any trouble that she's only outside. She will help us."

We continued our journey down the tunnel until we reached the metal ladder. Adi led the way, followed by Lois, with me bringing up the rear.

As Adi lifted the porthole at the top, I was filled with relief as the burning sun hit us. Sure enough, as we climbed out, it was all as before: the Nile in all its splendour behind us, slightly hidden by thick reeds and papyrus, and then nothing but desert ahead.

We all paused to take a good slurp of water.

"Right, ready for a little walk?" Adi said, smiling.

Lois and I nodded, and off we went. It seemed to take ages this time before we saw anything ahead of us, and then, as before, all of a sudden, they were there: the pyramids and the Great Sphinx, glorious against the pure-blue Egyptian sky.

I started to look around nervously, wondering if at any moment we were going to see Mal Vine and Aradia waiting for us again.

"Have you seen or heard from Paloma?" I asked my sister cautiously.

She shook her head, still cramming the last of her cake into her mouth. I didn't know whether that was a good or bad thing. Although my sister was sure that Paloma was on our (well, her) side, I wasn't quite so convinced about that bird. But I was, however, slightly relieved that she hadn't appeared so far today. That meant Mal and Aradia couldn't be here.

We hurried on towards the Great Sphinx and stopped at the base of its huge paw for refreshment again. It was so hot we were dripping with sweat.

Suddenly Adi put his hands over his ears and did his high-pitched "uhhhhhhhhhhhh" noise.

"What's wrong, Adi?" I gasped, wondering what could have happened to make him react in this way.

"How are we going to climb up? No one's got a sticky lolly!" he cried, anxiously.

"Adi," I said calmly, reaching into my rucksack, "I brought my mum's glue stick. We can put that all over our hands and climb up that way."

"Oh," he replied in a small voice, removing his hands from his ears.

So, we wiped a good dollop of glue stick all over our hands and started our climb. Soon we were up by the shoulder, and we took a breather there just to survey the land.

Confident there was no one around except us (I must admit, I could hardly believe our luck), we continued upwards until we reached the ear of the Sphinx where we knew the entrance to the Akashic Library was.

But how were we going to get in?

"Shall I knock on the door then?" Lois asked eagerly.

"I can't remember how it opened before," I said slowly, thinking back to what had happened the other day.

"I think Lois shouted and then it just opened. Probably a bit of a fluke," Adi suggested rather unhelpfully.

"Shall I shout again then?" Lois said, beaming.

"No," I replied quickly. "We don't want to draw attention to ourselves, just in case Mal or anyone else we don't want to be seen by is around. Let's just try knocking and see what happens."

We knocked, we whispered, we did all the things we had done before — nothing worked.

We were just about to give up hope, when suddenly some writing appeared on the stone.

The Riddle of the Sphinx

What goes on four feet in the morning,

two feet at noon, and three feet in the evening?

Speak your answer clearly.

"Oh no!" I cried out, disappointed. "There's a riddle to solve before we can go in."

"Is it a spider?" Lois suggested boldly.

"A spider? A spider has eight legs, silly!" I couldn't believe she could be so daft. "No, it's not a spider, Lois. Try again."

I repeated the riddle quietly to myself. I hated these kinds of things; they were never my strong point at school.

"I've got it!" Lois shouted excitedly. "It's a chair."

"What? Lois!" I sniggered. "Just be quiet if you can't think of anything sensible to say."

"Why couldn't it be a chair?" she asked. "It has four legs, then someone could be swinging on it at lunchtime, so it would only have two, then in the evening they might be on a three-legged stool at a breakfast bar."

Suddenly Adi gripped both our arms tightly.

We looked at him anxiously, wondering if he was okay.

"I've got it!" His eyes were sparkling. He cleared his throat and spoke confidently. "The answer is: man."

The door opened, and we stepped inside.

"I don't get it!" Lois was still saying as we found ourselves floating once more above the great Akashic Library.

"For goodness' sake, Lois!" I whispered, trying to shush her. Though to be honest, I didn't get it either.

"It's simple once you know the answer!" came the booming voice of Anubis, who was waiting for us on the ground, standing astride with his great spear pointing upwards. "Man begins his journey of life as a baby as he crawls on four legs; at the noon of life, as an adult, he walks on two legs; then as one reaches the twilight hours of life, he walks with a stick, hence three legs."

"But what if you're old, and you don't want to use a stick?" added Lois earnestly. "My grandma refuses to use a walking stick, doesn't she, Rosie?"

I nodded briefly.

"So, to what do I owe the pleasure again to-day?" Anubis asked. He gazed steadily at me, though I could have sworn I saw a little twinkle of amusement in his eye.

I squeezed Lois' hand tightly. I wasn't sure whether or not to say we were going into the book.

Thank goodness, at that moment Hecate appeared, looking again like her beautiful self.

"Ah, my friends have arrived, how lovely. Have you told them of our plans, Anubis?" I watched in amazement as she stroked the top of his doggy nose and he shook his head, snuffling, as if reluctantly accepting her affection.

Anubis strode back over to the well that he had been guarding last time, and we all followed him and Hecate. She looked intently at her husband, and we waited for him to speak.

"I give you all my blessing to enter the book and make your way to Osiris and the Hall of Two Truths," Anubis said. "I will help you if I can, but I'm afraid the journey is yours alone to make."

We all looked from him to Hecate, who was gazing at him adoringly. I wasn't desperately thrilled at the "blessing" he was giving us. In my mind what he was actually saying was, *"Feel free to get into the book, make the journey, and I'll pretend that I'll help you if I can, though in truth, I can't."*

I didn't feel particularly reassured, put it that way.

"So, friends," Hecate beamed at us, "you may jump."

"Jump?" Adi repeated nervously.

Hecate nodded. "Yes, jump from this well down into the book."

Adi and I looked at each other, horrified. This sounded like a very dangerous thing to do.

"How far is the jump?" Lois asked seriously.

"Don't worry about that, just jump. Let's call it a leap of faith, shall we?" Hecate giggled to herself, which I must admit I thought was a bit unfair, given it was us and not her doing the jumping.

"Like Anubis, I will try to help you wherever I can, but remember I will only be able to if all else has failed," Hecate said as she started to fade from view.

"No, wait!" I cried out, knowing deep down it was too late.

Anubis smiled at us serenely and then seemed to shudder as he became a gold statue once more, his spear upright, guarding the well.

We were on our own.

"Come on then," I said to Adi and my sister as I looked down into the circular depths of the well.

It looked like the deepest one I had ever seen. There was just a tiny shimmer of something gold in the distance, which I guess had to be the book. I couldn't believe Hecate and Anubis were expecting us to jump in with no ropes and no magic potions to help us.

"There is no way I am doing this," Adi stated, his hands shaking slightly.

Every bone in my body was saying, *nooooooo*.

Lois, however, stepped up on to the brick structure of the well, turned to us, grinning wickedly, and said, "See you in a minute, scaredy cats."

In the next moment, she was gone, whooping as she fell, down, down, down into the well.

I almost burst into tears, I was so scared. I climbed up to where she had been standing.

I had no choice but to follow her.

"Rosemary, are you sure this is the right thing to do?" Adi whispered, his eyes full of tears.

I couldn't speak. I nodded, feeling saltwater running down my cheeks.

Then, I jumped.

All I could remember was an overwhelming desire not to let my sister be alone and scared. I had to be with her, and if that meant jumping into the unknown, then so be it.

After what seemed like an age, I heard a distant splash, and I suddenly found myself being catapulted down into water. I tried not to panic as I held my breath and gravity brought me up to the surface, where I gasped for oxygen.

There was another loud splash right next to me, which I was praying was Adi. I managed to tread water for a few moments until his familiar black hair bobbed up to the surface.

But where was Lois?

"Lois!" I screamed, looking round frantically in the dusky light.

On the horizon was a huge orange sun, which was gradually setting in a clear sky, and we seemed to be in a lake or river. There were no waves; the water was incredibly still.

"Lois!" I cried again, and then I heard her.

"Over here, Rosie!"

Her voice was coming from behind me, so I turned around, and it was a relief to see her little figure clinging on to the edge of a rowing boat.

"Lois, don't move!" I called anxiously, swimming over to her. "Come on, Adi, this way," I shouted to the dark-haired person bobbing about in the water.

She was grinning from ear to ear, as if she was having the greatest adventure ever. "I'm fine! I just need to check Bea is okay. Can we get in the boat?"

I thanked God that my little sister was a bit of a water baby. She had always been able to swim well and loved going underwater, which is more than could be said for me. I had learnt to swim under pressure from my parents and hated getting my hair wet, so this introduction to getting into the book was not a good start to this adventure.

"You're very quiet, Adi,"" I called out to my friend, who was staring into space.

"That is something I never want to repeat, Rosemary," Adi murmured, still sounding as if he was in shock. "It was not fun at all."

After a bit of jostling, we finally managed to clamber into the boat.

"Whoa, what am I sitting on?" Adi asked.

He rummaged around underneath him and brought out a gold-leafed hardback book, a little like a leather-bound family bible.

"Is that it?" I said in surprise.

"Is that what?" repeated Lois, looking puzzled.

"The book. The *Book of the Dead!*" I said, as if it were obvious.

"I thought we had jumped into the book," Lois said slowly. "So how can that be the book if we are in it?"

"Maybe we're not in it. Maybe this is it, and we

have to find a way to get into it," I said, sighing deeply.

"We'd have to shrink, and I can't see how we'd be able to do that," Adi replied hopelessly. "It's definitely the book," he added, showing us the front page, which was embossed in gold lettering.

The Book Of The Dead

"Oh, this is a joke. Go to page one, Adi, and tell us what it says," I said, reaching into my rucksack for a packet of crisps.

"Okay," Adi said. He sounded defeated. "Welcome, explorers," he read, "you begin your journey following the setting sun. You will trace the sun god Re's journey under the Earth and back to the east — but beware the creatures of the night."

"Okay, bit weird, but I guess that means we row towards the setting sun then. Do you think we're in the book, Adi?" I asked, chomping crisps and trying to row with the other hand.

"Don't know," he said thoughtfully. "Look, there's a picture of people in a boat going towards the setting sun." He showed the book to me and Lois, and then took the other oar and helped me row.

Lois seemed to be studying the picture.

"Oh wow!" she cried out in amazement. "The boat in the picture is moving. And it's got three people in it."

"Don't be daft, Lois. Let me see." I grabbed the book back off her and studied the picture. It did look as if the boat was moving, and there were definitely three people in it, though the detail of them was unclear.

"Look!" I said, laughing. "One of the figures is raising their arms in the air."

I looked up and felt slightly nauseated as my sister was indeed waving her arms in the air, and as she lowered them, the character in the picture also lowered its arms.

"Okay, I think we can safely say we're in the book," stated Adi confidently.

"What happens on the next page?" I asked nervously.

"I've already tried turning the page, but it won't let me," said Lois, unwrapping a piece of Madeira cake.

"Right, let's just row and see what happens," I said.

As I uttered those words, I wondered whether it would have been different if I hadn't said anything at all. For the water beneath us started to get choppy, and the skies darkened. The sun was almost at the water level, and ahead it looked like we were approaching a gigantic waterfall, over which our little boat was about to tumble.

"Hold on tight!" Adi shouted.

The boat tipped, and as we were flung over the edge, we were indeed in the middle of a giant waterfall.

I lost an oar, but Adi luckily had the foresight to throw his into the boat as we clung on for dear life.

Water was flying into the boat from all angles. I could feel everything getting wet. I closed my eyes and prayed it would stop and we would be safe.

At last it was silent. I opened my eyes a crack, and I could see we were on still water. The sun was behind us, and miraculously there was no water in the boat, nor on our clothes.

"This is freaky. I think I want to go home now," said Lois quietly.

"I know," I said, gently gripping her hand. "We have to get to Osiris, I think, before we can take the book back with us. Hopefully not much further."

"Oh!" Adi shouted triumphantly. "I can turn the page. I think once you've dealt with an obstacle it lets you move on to the next page. Yaaaa—"

Then he stopped. His mouth was wide open in the 'yay' position, but there was no sound coming out of it.

"What's wrong?" I said, my tummy feeling as if it were full of tickly insects.

"Rosemary, just row!" Adi commanded, grabbing his oar and firmly closing the book.

But I couldn't row. I'd lost my oar. So I tried putting my hands in the water and scooping it along.

"Keep your hand in the boat!" Adi screeched, shocking me into pulling both hands out quickly.

Just as I did, a crocodile's jaws missed my fingers by about a millimetre. It was a huge green slimy-looking croc with cold, hard eyes and teeth like piano keys — only they were brown and dirty-looking.

Lois and I screamed. The crocodile continued to grind its teeth together, flicking its tail up in the air, so it made our little boat wobble.

"What are we gonna do, Adi?" I shouted, terrified.

"I don't know. Just don't look at it. Keep focusing on moving forward. We are strong. We can do this," Adi chanted.

I don't know where we would have been without his focus, for I was ready to close my eyes, cuddle my sister, and pray for Hecate to come and save us. But instead, I held onto Lois, so she was in front of me with my arms around her, and I knew she was holding Bea in the same position.

We looked forward, and I trembled inside, knowing that surrounding us there were now not one, but several huge crocs thrashing around in the water trying to overturn the boat.

Suddenly, there was an almighty wave up ahead of us.

I thought it might be some sort of tsunami, and my throat tightened with dread. But as I squinted my eyes to look closer, I could see what I can only describe as a giant serpent riding through the water, creating an enormous wake either side of it.

The creature reached our boat and dive-bombed around us, snapping up every single crocodile in its mouth, shaking them and swallowing them whole.

The three of us watched the battle, half fearfully, half in awe.

"These must be the creatures of the night that the book mentioned," I whispered to Adi and Lois.

When the serpent had swallowed the last remaining crocodile, it gently disappeared from sight under the water, and we all stared at each other wide-eyed.

"We need to get out of here while we can," Adi whispered.

Lois and I nodded and scanned the horizon for any land that we could head for. It was not going to be easy rowing with only one oar.

We were just starting to make shaky progress, with Adi and I taking it in turns to use the oar, when quietly in front of us, the serpent raised a large ugly head from the depths of the water.

Its huge scaly cheeks were pulled back, and its head flattened like a cobra about to attack its prey. Its teeth were shiny and looked like giant needles, and its tongue flickered in and out of its mouth.

It pulled its face back from us, as if readying itself to strike, and the three of us let out almighty screams of terror.

"Silence!" the serpent cried, turning its head to survey us from another angle. "Who goes here and with whose permission?"

"We have Hecate's permission to come and seek Osiris," I said as loudly as I could, even though my voice felt very wobbly.

"And who is this Hecate?" the serpent asked, snarling and snapping its teeth at us.

"She's married to Anubis, and they both told us we could come here. Please don't hurt us. We don't want any trouble," I continued.

I could tell my sister was terrified, for she had snuggled into me, clutching Bea. Adi was silent and still, probably trying to work out what he could say to outwit the serpent.

"Ah, Anubissss," the serpent said, elongating the "ssss" sound at the end of his name. "Why didn't you say so? Perhapssss you know who *I* am?" The serpent's face came closer, so that we could smell its breath, which wasn't unlike one of Lois' meaty farts.

We shook our heads, too terrified to speak.

"I, ssssweet children, am Apep, the serpent queen of these waters, and it is my job to eradicate any threat to my offspring. How would you like to die?" she continued silkily.

I was stunned — had we heard her correctly?

Thank goodness Adi seemed to have regained his sense of self, and he answered her rather courageously.

"Queen Apep, we do not wish to die at all," he said. "We wish you and your offspring no harm. We just need to cross this water and take the next steps on our journey."

Throughout his speech, my sister had slid off my lap and reached for the book. I had no idea why, as I certainly didn't fancy turning the page and seeing the three of us being eaten by a huge serpent.

Apep brought her head back even further and lunged forward suddenly. A huge amount of yellow spittle erupted from her mouth and narrowly missed our boat.

She roared once more. "You see that?!"

I wondered whether to answer or not. We all turned our heads to see how the yellow liquid was fizzing and smoking up from the water that it had come into contact with.

"That is my venom, my sssspittle, you might call it," Apep continued. "And let me assure you, it is deadly."

I thought I'd better try to see if I could succeed in reasoning with her. "Please, Apep, please spare us. We mean you no harm. We have food, if you are hungry."

I saw my sister cast me a dirty look from the corner of my eye as I held up some of her favourite biscuits.

"Sssspare me your nonssssense, girl! Perhapssss you would prefer to be sssstrangled?" We watched, horrified, as Apep then took a dive down into the water and lifted her tail high up into the air.

With one swift move, she had it curled around our little boat and was raising us up into the sky.

Adi and I screamed.

I looked at Lois, who was holding the book in front of her, concentrating. She started to speak loudly and slowly, carefully pronouncing all the difficult words phonetically.

"I will not be inert for you." Adi and I looked at each other, wondering what she was doing. Lois continued, "I will not be weak for you."

Suddenly, Apep lifted her head up from the depths of the water and stared, horrified, at Lois.

"Your poison shall not enter my members," Lois continued.

"Nooooooo," Apep screamed, starting to shake furiously.

But still, Lois calmly continued, "For my members are the members of Atum."

Adi and I looked at each other again and exchanged an idea, as if we were reading each other's mind. We leaned over either side of Lois and repeated with her what she was reading from the book.

"I will not be inert for you," we all said as the

boat was gently placed back down on the water. "I will not be weak for you." Apep started to move away from us, still shaking. "Your poison shall not enter my members, for my members are the members of Atum."

Apep sunk down into the water. A soft mist seemed to rise up from where she had disappeared, and the river glinted as if renewed.

She was gone.

"What was that?" Adi stated slowly, looking around nervously.

"I don't know, Ads, but she was scary," I said. "Well done, Lois, you got rid of her!"

"Don't call me Ads, Rosemary," Adi said automatically.

I smiled to myself and ruffled my sister's hair, who was grinning broadly.

"I just looked in the book, and after the scary picture of Apep it had these instructions — look." She showed us the top of the page, which read:

In order to defeat the advances of the serpent Apep, who will defend her waters until her death, you must say the following words:

And there were the words Lois had read out that had miraculously vanquished Apep.

"Of course!" Adi said suddenly, as if it was all glaringly obvious. "The *Book of the Dead* contains instructions for the deceased to navigate their way through all these obstacles in order to get to Osiris for the final part, which is the weighing of the heart, to see whether they go to heaven or hell. We need to use the instructions in the book to help us get there!"

"So where now?" Lois asked, hugging Bea to her. "Now we've got rid of her, shall I try turning the page?"

Adi and I grinned at each other.

"Go for it, kiddo," Adi said in an American accent.

Lois grinned back cheekily and turned the page.

At once everything went bright white and very windy — and I don't mean Lois' bottom wind, though that might have been preferable at that moment. It was as if we were being swirled around in the eye of a tornado. We spun in circles and eventually had to hold on to each other, with our heads bowed so the wind didn't get into our eyes and ears.

After what seemed like ages, it stopped, and I could feel the sun on my back once more. I opened my eyes.

"We're on land!" I cried, feeling such relief that we were no longer navigating the water.

We all took a moment to look at the shore we had landed on, still within our little boat. The water was behind us, and though it wasn't the sea, it was the biggest river or lake I had ever seen.

Apart from the grassy bank we were situated on, you could see no other sign of land anywhere. There were tall palm trees in front of us, so it was clear that was the only way we could go.

"Come on then, let's just go for it," Adi suggested bravely, gathering up his rucksack.

"I need a wee and something else to eat," murmured Lois, cuddling Bea to her chest.

"Right, come on, Lois, you'll have to wee behind one of those trees," I said, pointing to one with a nice thick trunk that she could hide herself behind. I rummaged through her ever-decreasing supplies of food and found a banana. "Why don't you have this? It will keep you going for longer."

She looked at me with a sulky expression. "I'd rather have another biscuit."

"I'm sure you would but eating too much junk like that makes you hungrier. If you have the banana, you'll feel more satisfied and fuller for longer."

She snatched the banana from my hands and peeled it hastily, while walking over to the tree.

"Oooooooh," I gasped, suddenly remembering that Lois had turned the page of the book just when the wind came. "Did you get a chance to see what the next page of the book showed us?" I asked her, intrigued.

"No, it was windy," she replied crossly.

"It's okay," Adi shouted back to us from the boat. "I'll look at it now, and we can see what we have to do in a minute."

Once Lois had finished, we rejoined Adi and studied the book.

There was a picture of a rough, walled building with a large gate barring its entrance. Underneath this image was a bird's-eye view drawing of a labyrinth, which just looked like someone had scribbled a series of swirls and right angles on a piece of paper. It made no sense at all, apart from the fact we could see the outer wall and gates with three figures standing outside ...

"Come on, we'd better go and see if we can find this peculiar maze and get through it," I said, taking charge. "Adi, does it say what the next challenge is?"

He shook his head, still attempting to turn the page, which was firmly stuck down. "It just shows these drawings and that's it, no instructions, nothing. Guess we need to find this walled building first."

I nervously took the lead through the palm trees, cautiously looking down to make sure I wasn't stepping on any snakes or spiders or anything equally scary. It was cooler in the shade of the trees, and we only needed to stop briefly to have a good glug of water.

"Look!" shouted Lois, who had skipped on ahead, seemingly unworried by any potential danger. "There's a building with a gate like the picture!"

Sure enough, we had arrived at a large iron gate and a rough wall that looked as if it was made from earth and sticks.

"Probably animal dung and straw has kept that all together," Adi said, running his hands over the wall.

"Urgghhh," Lois said, pulling a face. "You've just touched poo, Adi. Don't come near me."

"Waaaaahhhh," Adi shouted, lunging his hand

towards Lois, who screamed excitedly and then collapsed into giggles.

"I am an Egyptian mummy, and I have poo on my hands and am going to spread it all over your face, Lois." Adi continued with the daft game, doing a slow robotic voice and walking over to Lois like a zombie.

She was screaming with laughter and fear in equal measure, and I wouldn't have minded ordinarily, but they were both missing the action that, sadly, I had to witness on my own.

I stood looking through the gates, mesmerised, as a mummified creature — which is the only way I can describe it — had begun to walk slowly towards us. I was so scared I couldn't move.

The mummy's bandages weren't white; they were a pale brown colour, tinged with black on the edges, as if they had been burnt. The figure walked stiffly towards the gates, as you would if you were covered in tight bandages. But what was scary was its eyes, which were dark pools of nothingness that seemed to reflect back to me my own fear.

"Guys!" I hissed for about the fifth time. "Guys, I need you to shut up and help me. There's a mummy coming towards us."

They continued to ignore me, so I did the only thing I could think of. I grabbed Bea from Lois' arms and threw her through the gates.

Now I had their attention.

Lois shrieked, the chase with Adi completely forgotten. "That's Bea! What have you done with her, Rosie?"

She went very quiet when she saw the mummy

stumbling towards the gate, and even Adi drew his breath in sharply and whispered, "Oh my. I hope I haven't caused this ..."

"What should we do?" I whispered frantically.

"Get Bea back now!" Lois moaned, starting to cry uncontrollably. She reached her hand through the gates in desperation, but I had thrown Bea too far away for her to reach. "I hate you, Rosie, I hate you!" she cried.

I felt terrible. It was fear that had made me do it, and the fact that I couldn't think of any other way to get their attention.

"I'm sorry, Lois," I sobbed. "I was scared. I needed you both to stop and see what was going on. We'll get her back, I promise."

The mummy paused, looked down at Bea, and my worst nightmare happened. It picked Bea up and cuddled her. Then it came right up to the gates and, with one sharp pull on the latch, opened them.

Lois, fear aside, marched straight up to the mummy and demanded Bea. "You have my rabbit. Please may I have her back?"

Full marks for her politeness, and her nerve. I'm not sure I would have had the courage to do that.

The mummy stared at her as if it didn't know what she was and just turned and walked away down a slope into the building.

Lois chased after it, jumping and crying as she tried to reach Bea.

I couldn't bear it. "Please, Adi, do something. She'll be devastated if she loses Bea."

Adi looked at me with a helpless expression on his face and dashed after Lois. I watched with fear as he tapped the mummy on the back and asked for Lois' rabbit.

The mummy turned, gave a huge roar, dropped Bea on the floor as it took a sharp left turn, and simply disappeared down a corridor.

We all exhaled a huge sigh of relief as Lois bent down and gathered her bunny into her arms.

But our relief turned to horror once more, as Bea literally disintegrated into sand and slipped through her fingers and onto the dusty floor.

Bea had vanished.

26

THE RIDDLE OF THE LABYRINTH

"Okay, okay, don't panic, Lois. We can sort this, can't we, Adi?" I looked up at Adi pleadingly. We had enough on our plate right now without dealing with the disappearance of Bea.

"Yeah, shall I go and see where the mummy went?" Adi asked cautiously.

"No, it's not a good idea. Let's see if the book has got any of those spells in it for putting missing pieces back together or something. That's one of the reasons I wanted it — to try to repair Mum."

"Is Mummy ill?" Lois lifted her tear-stained face up to me. She was still collapsed on the ground, as if too full of sadness for her lost Bea to be able to get up.

I shook my head quickly. "No, she's not, Lois, don't worry. Adi, look in the book quick."

"She's ill, isn't she? I wish Mummy was here. She'd know what to do. She'd find Bea, she always finds Bea," Lois wailed.

"Look, Lois," I said, trying to hide my rising panic, "Mum isn't here. This is down to just us.

We've got to get through this next bit of the journey. I think we'll find Bea, don't worry."

I turned away from my little sister, desperately hoping Adi would have some answers. We huddled together, our backs to Lois. I didn't want to alarm her.

"What's wrong with your mum?" Adi whispered.

"She's started getting all these holes appearing in her body. It's almost as if she's losing herself. The witches told me the book contained spells to stop someone losing parts of themselves. Maybe we can use one to find Bea, too."

Adi showed me the page of the book. In bold print, it said:

Labyrinth

At each set of gates, you will recite some text or answer a question. The correct answer will open the gates, and you shall continue your journey. The incorrect answer may leave you rotting in the depths of the labyrinth for eternity.

"This is a nightmare, Adi," I cried, fearfully. "A labyrinth is a kind of maze, isn't it? How are we going to get through this?"

I waited for Adi to answer me with some wisdom or other, but his face had fallen, and he looked fearful.

"What now?" I whispered.

Adi turned me slowly round to where my sister was sitting on the floor, mourning Bea.

She had gone.

"Lois!" I screamed. "Where are you?"

I ran to the corridor on the left, where the mummy had disappeared, and leading off it were two other corridors that opened out into large rooms full of Egyptian statues. I briefly noticed that the walls were covered with bright paintings of Egyptian scenes.

I called Lois' name, I don't know how many times.

"Adi, you go straight on," I instructed, once I'd returned to where we had started. There was another corridor on the right, too, which seemed to lead down some stairs. "This is crazy. Which way would she have gone? Why isn't she answering us?" I was starting to panic.

"Keep calm," Adi said, taking my face in his hands. "Go down the stairs and call her. I'll go straight on and look for her. Listen hard once you've called her name, in case she's further away than we think and her voice is faint."

I nodded, frantic with worry. Losing my sister was not part of the plan.

I dashed down the stairs, surprised to find a dead end of empty wall at the bottom. I called her name loudly and waited. Silence.

I ran up the stairs and went back the way the mummy had gone, this time entering each room and calling out Lois' name loudly. In the second room, I finally heard her.

"Lois," I repeated. "Can you hear me? Where are you?"

"I'm in a room with a stone bed and there's pictures on the walls," she responded.

Her voice sounded faint, and I couldn't be sure which direction it was coming from.

"Right, I'm going to walk round this room," I said. "Can you sing or something, so I can work out where you might be?"

I started pacing round the room. It had another set of gates at one end of it, which I hoped might be a good sign. Maybe she was the other side of the gates?

I could hear my sister singing that blasted song, "My name is High Low Jackalow, Jackalow High Low ..." but I just gritted my teeth and focused on where the sound was coming from. It was peculiar, as it didn't seem to be coming from anywhere other than far, far below me.

"Lois," I shouted, "just stop singing a minute and try to remember which way you went."

"I followed the mummy, and then I saw bits of Bea on the floor, so I picked them up and then I got to a gate that I couldn't open. A lady appeared and dragged me through the wall."

"What?" I gasped. "A lady? Is she there now?"

"No, she's not here now. She had a funny name, but I can't remember it. This is her room. She told me to wait here." Lois sounded so alone.

"Are you okay, Lois?" I asked softly. "I'm so sorry about Bea."

I heard a few distant sobs and then her voice again. "Rosie, I just want Mummy. Please get

Mummy here. I want my mummy. I need my mummy."

It was absolutely heart-breaking, and I could feel the tears running down my own face.

Suddenly it occurred to me: the summoning spell. We would have to summon Mum, and we needed to do it NOW. She would know what to do, and any reluctance to use magic would just have to go out the window — we had to rescue Lois.

I turned back the way I had come and bumped straight into Adi, who was running into the room where I was.

"Rosemary, you were supposed to meet back at the start," he said. "You had me worried for a minute. Feel my heart." Adi grabbed my hand and placed it on his chest. It was beating very fast.

"Sorry, Adi, I was talking to my sister."

"Where is she?" he asked, looking round the room.

"She's somewhere near here," I said. "I can hear her, but just can't work out where she is. She's really upset now and wants Mum. Some lady dragged her into a room and said she'd be back."

"Was she a scary lady?" Adi asked, his eyes wide.

"I don't think so, but we've got to use the summoning spell and get my mum."

Adi looked serious. "Wouldn't it be better to use it to get one of the witches or Hecate? Surely they'd be able to help us?"

"I don't know if the witches would be able to get in here," I said. "Remember Frances said only people with colour around them could get into the Akashic Library."

"But this is the book, not the Library," Adi replied.

I gazed at him, pleadingly. "But Lois is crying for Mum. I just can't use it on anyone else. It has to be Mum."

He nodded in his understanding way and squeezed my arm. "When you are in the water, you swim," he said quietly.

I gave a small smile of gratitude, pulled my rucksack off my back, and reached into it, about to take out the small bottle of lemonade and the liquorice root, when suddenly we heard footsteps coming from afar.

We looked at each other nervously.

"Let's just get through this gate, like the book says to do, quickly," Adi suggested, leading me towards it.

There were a set of instructions on the wall next to it.

I am what most people fear. I can strike without warning, for I cannot be stopped. Even though I can hurt, celebrating me will set you free. What am I?

"Not another riddle," I groaned, closing my eyes. "Adi, thank god you're here."

Adi flared his nostrils and lifted his head up

slightly, gazing at the riddle. "I am what most people fear?"

"Death?" I asked quizzically.

"No, don't think so," he dismissed me, shaking his head. "Because not all death strikes without warning. Erm, I can hurt ..." he said quietly to himself. "What can hurt?" He scratched the bridge of his nose.

"Er, I dunno. To tell you the truth, I have no idea when it comes to solving riddles," I replied at a loss.

"Exactly!" he grinned, clapping his hands. "You said it. Brilliant!"

"So what's the answer then?" I asked, even more confused than before.

"The answer has to be 'truth'. People fear the truth, it strikes without warning ..."

I turned round at a low growl coming from behind us.

Standing on four stubby legs, with long brown hair all over its body, was a fierce-looking goat with huge horns and snarling teeth. I had never thought until now that something resembling a goat could be scary.

"Adi," I whispered, "can I tell you what else might be about to strike without warning?"

"Yeah, hang on," he muttered, repeating the rest of the riddle. "The truth hurts and the truth can set you free!" he shouted with glee. "Yes, the answer is Truth!"

At that moment, the gates swung open, and the hairy goat charged.

"Come on!" I shouted, pulling Adi by his T-shirt through the gates and ramming them shut, just as the hairy goat reached them.

"Next time!" the goat growled, dripping grey saliva all over the floor and narrowly missing my shoes.

"Oh, my goodness!" Adi exclaimed, almost losing his glasses in the chaos. "Why didn't you tell me that was stalking us?"

"I'll tell you one thing," I said seriously.

Adi looked at me quizzically.

"That riddle was a sign. Who's the one person I feel most uncomfortable about not having told the truth to? Someone who also isn't being true to themselves by turning their back on their witch family and beliefs? My mum."

"Okay," Adi nodded. "Let's do it. Let's summon your mum."

27

BE CAREFUL WHAT YOU WISH FOR

"Can you remember what we have to do for the spell?" Adi asked me, wrinkling his nose up.

"Yeah, I think so," I replied, "but I'm not sure what moon phase it was supposed to be done in and all that."

"Well, let's just try," Adi said. "We've got nothing to lose, and if this fails, are we agreed we need to call out for Hecate to come and help us?"

I nodded, silently wondering how she would even know if we needed her. I put the lemonade and liquorice on the ground, together with the box of matches, as I remembered we had to burn some of the liquorice root.

"Okay," I said bravely, "we each drink half of this lemonade. I mean really gulp it, as we've got to burp. Once the burps start, we have to say Mum's name as we burp. So you'll say 'Rae Pellow', and I'll obviously say 'Mum'."

Adi nodded. "Right, okay, are you going to start? And I'll light the liquorice, shall I?"

"No, don't light the liquorice until we've drunk

the lemonade. I think that's right," I said, racking my brain and wishing I'd torn the page out of the book and brought it with us.

Adi grasped my hand. "Rosemary, don't worry, we can do this," he said gently. "It will be fine. Have faith."

I felt so comforted having my best friend with me, even though he was a boy and could be annoying and didn't blow his nose often enough.

I took the lid off the lemonade bottle and knocked back as much as I could, as quickly as I could. Almost breathless, I passed it to Adi.

"Your turn, and then let's light the liquorice root. Bleugh," I burped, covering my mouth. "Pardon me."

They'd already started. As I could feel the next one brewing, I got ready to say Mum's name.

"Muuuuuum," I burped, giggling at how funny it sounded.

Then Adi lit the root and joined me with his burps.

It was so funny, me saying Mum and him saying Rae, which is all he could manage. More often than not, our burp-talking didn't sound anything like the names we were trying to say, but I guess the intention was there, which I think is all that matters when you're casting a spell.

Finally, we had finished the lemonade and burped so much that I felt kind of shaky and a bit sick.

"I think the spell says you have to lie down for a short time," I said, lowering my body down on the cold stone floor.

"What should I do with this root?" Adi asked me.

"I don't know, is it still burning?" I peered at it.

"Sort of. I'll stamp on it now we've finished."

No sooner had Adi stamped on the root, we heard a voice coming from the corridor ahead of us.

"Hellooooo!"

It was a woman's voice.

Adi and I looked at each other, not daring to hope ... Could it be? Had it really worked?

"Is anyone there? Where am I?" said the voice.

I sat up and tentatively called out. "Mum, is that you?"

"Rosie?" the voice replied.

I could hardly believe it!

"Mum, we're here," I called out. "Follow my voice. We're in a labyrinth, and we've got to get out."

"Where's the book, Rosie?" came Mum's voice.

I pulled a face at Adi. *How weird!* I thought. *Why is she asking about the book? How does she know about it?*

Adi instinctively placed the book behind his back.

"We're *in* the book, Mum," I said. "Look, I'll explain when I see you."

She finally appeared, and I tried to look joyful and excited to see her, but in truth I was shocked.

It had only been a few days since we'd seen our mum, but she looked terrible. Her hair was dirty-looking, when usually it was thick and glossy. She looked full, and I mean FULL, of holes, from her throat to one ginormous void down the left side of her face, to her tummy. Her lips looked dry, her eyes were sunken, and she had dark circles around them. Every now and then, I'd catch a glimpse of five o'clock shadow on the holey cheek and have to blink my eyes to make it go away. It was truly awful. However, I gathered myself together quickly and drew her into a hug.

"Mum, it's so good to see you. We've missed you so much," I said, snuggling into her. Her body felt weird, a bit bony and sinewy, not soft and cuddly as it usually was.

"I've missed you too, kid," she replied, kissing the top of my head.

A little alarm bell rang in my head. *Kid.* She never called me kid.

"You're not cross we summoned you, are you?" I asked nervously, wondering how we were going to explain all of this to her.

She shook her head and smiled strangely at me. "You did the right thing, so don't worry. Come on, let's go quickly. There's not much time to lose."

Adi was staring at me like a madman and seemed to be motioning with his eyes at something.

I mouthed *what?* to him, and he looked like he'd had an electric shock as Mum eyeballed him as though she'd never seen him before.

"It's Adi, Mum. You know, from school." I paused for a moment, slightly thrown.

"Come on, Rosie, let's go. Where's the book?" she said robotically.

"Don't you think we should be getting Lois first, Mum?" I questioned.

"Of course, yes, but just tell me where the book is, and then we'll get Lois," she insisted.

"Why are you so interested in finding the book, Mrs Pellow?" Adi asked quietly, still holding it behind his back.

Mum turned quickly, and her eyes focused on Adi. They looked brown and cruel, not blue and smiley. "We're all after the book, Adi, aren't we? So why don't you just tell me where it is?"

"Mum, you're being really weird. I told you, we are in the book, and though Adi has got a copy of the book, it's not really the—"

I wasn't able to finish my sentence before she jumped with excitement and flung herself on Adi.

"I knew it!" she said, grabbing at Adi's arms so he was forced to drop the book behind him. "This is what I need!" She held the book above her triumphantly. We watched in horror as her skin seemed to peel away from her body, like a banana. As Mum's outer body collapsed on the floor, I gasped with shock.

For what emerged from the shell of my mother was the grinning figure of Mal Vine.

"How did you get here?" I cried with anguish. "You're not supposed to be able to get in here."

Mal threw his head back and laughed spitefully. His thin fingers clutched the book, and he jabbed at it with a bony finger.

"How did I get in?" he said. "With thanks to your dear old mum. Easy to slip in through those holes. Not much left of her now, is there? Surprised you didn't recognise me when you were on the phone to her last night. I'd just got comfy. I thought one of you whingers would soon be crying for your mummy and how right I was! Nice knowing ya."

And with that, he took off, turning right down the corridor that led out from the room.

"And good riddance to you!" shouted Adi. I had never seen him so angry. "You'll get your comeuppance. You've no idea how to use that book and no idea what's coming either, you big, skinny, horrible ..." Adi seemed to falter, as if he were trying his hardest to think of the nastiest words to describe him, "evil, old goat."

"I think that's an insult to goats," I said shakily, attempting a joke.

"Are you okay, Rosemary?" Adi asked me, his fists clenched, as if he was about to launch into a fight scene from a James Bond film or something.

I nodded, still shaken up. "I knew she wasn't right when she arrived. I just knew it wasn't my mum," I repeated, feeling utterly stupid that we had been taken in so easily. "What are we going to do?" I started to cry, looking down at her crumpled body. "How can we help her now he's taken the book?"

"Look, Rosemary, don't worry. Let's concentrate on getting your mum to wake up, and then we can find Lois and get out of this labyrinth. He can't take the book out of here, remember? You have to meet Osiris before you get to take the book, and somehow I don't think Mal will have bargained for the power of the god of the dead."

"I thought Anubis was the god of the dead?" I sniffled.

"Well, technically speaking, they both are."

"Oh!" I said, looking quizzically at Adi, who blushed.

"I've been doing some research," he continued. "Osiris is Anubis' uncle, so he is the one who weighs the heart before deciding whether you can enter the heavenly afterlife or not. Osiris is a kind of governor of the afterlife, whereas Anubis, who is also known as the god of the dead or the underworld, leads the deceased to his uncle for the weighing of the heart ceremony."

"So, do you think between them they will be able to stop Mal from unleashing the demons?" I asked anxiously, feeling completely overwhelmed by all this information on which god did what.

Adi nodded and used one finger to slide his glasses further up his nose with a flourish. "Absolutely no problem for them."

"Okay," I whispered, my attention now on my mum, who looked like she'd been run over by a tractor. "She is breathing, isn't she?" I asked, kneeling down and putting my face to her nose.

"Of course she is, Rosemary. Look at her chest moving up and down." Adi pointed to the low rise and fall of Mum's chest, so though she still had her eyes closed, she was alive.

She still looked very pale and I could still see plenty of holes in her body. How could Mal Vine have jumped inside her? I thought back to our weird phone call last night. It had been the first time she'd sounded completely unlike herself, as if she were talking through someone else. That must have been when Mal had first got into her body. I hoped that he hadn't done anything to jeopardise her job for her.

"Mum," I nudged her gently and kissed her cheek (the one that was still whole).

She opened her eyes and looked confused.

"Rosie? Where am I? What's going on?" She sat up and put a hand to her throat. "Ooooh, I don't feel well at all. I feel sick and a bit dizzy."

"Let me handle this," commanded Adi, kneeling down on the floor to join us. "You may not like what you are about to hear, I'm afraid, Mrs Pellow."

"Rae, please, Adi. I think we've known each other long enough," Mum smiled weakly.

"Yes, Rae, sorry," Adi cleared his throat. "You remember the *Book of the Dead* was stolen from the British Museum?"

Mum nodded.

"Well, we are in it right now."

"The British Museum?" Mum asked, screwing her face up.

"No, the *Book of the Dead*." Adi stopped and glanced at me.

"What Adi is trying to say is—" I started, but Adi raised his hand and continued.

"I know you've turned your back on magic and all that, but we needed to help your witch family find the book. Mal Vine is planning to release the demons inside it into the world. We have to get through this labyrinth to the Hall of Two Truths and speak with Osiris about reclaiming the book and putting it back where it belongs."

"Hold on," Mum said slowly. "Surely the *Book*

of the Dead belongs in Egypt, doesn't it? And what does all this have to do with the witches?"

"Phyllis and Mr Foggerty were working at the British Museum," I said, finally able to have my turn. "And Hecate, well, we've seen her in the Akashic Library, and she said it was down to us to retrieve the book and lure Mal Vine here so that he could attempt to unleash the demons. They can't arrest him unless he actually tries to do something bad, even though they know he has the intention. Hopefully we'll be able to stop him before he does actually succeed."

"This is an awful lot to take in," Mum said softly. "Are you saying Mal Vine is already here, or are we waiting for him to arrive?"

Oh, she doesn't know, I thought.

I caught Adi staring at me as if wondering which of us should tell her.

"Mum," I said hesitantly. "He hitched a ride in your body. We did a summoning spell to get you here, as Lois needs you, and once he'd taken the book off Adi, he jumped out of you and disappeared into the labyrinth."

"What?" Mum looked completely shocked. "He used my body as a vehicle to get here, into the book, to take the journey through the obstacles to meet with Osiris?"

"Oh, you know about the journey of the book then?" Adi said, impressed with my mother's knowledge.

She nodded. "No wonder I feel weird. And Lois? Where is she?"

"She's somewhere here below us. A lady took

her to a chamber, and she's trapped there waiting for us," I said with tears in my eyes.

"She's somewhere below us?" Mum repeated, standing up shakily.

As if she had been quietly waiting for the right moment, we suddenly heard Lois' voice, mournful and tear ridden.

"Mummy, is that you?" she said. "Please come and get me. I haven't even got Bea." And then she was silent.

"Oh, my god, Lois!" Mum cried in response. "Where are you? I'm here, darling. Mummy's here, and we're going to find you and get you home. Can you hear me, Lois? I'm coming."

Adi and I took an arm each and tried to guide my mum out of the room in an attempt to follow Lois' voice, but as we moved towards where we thought her voice was coming from, it suddenly changed direction.

One minute we were wanting to turn right, then her voice would appear to be coming from the left.

We must have looked as if we were doing some kind of mad dance, until suddenly her voice sounded clearly behind us.

"Where are you? I'm right here," she cried.

We turned, all together, readying ourselves to grab her if necessary, when there was a loud bang of a door slamming, and there in front of us appeared a black wall, barring our way.

28

SEKHMET'S TEMPLE

"This is pointless," Adi stated calmly, looking at the dead end that had appeared in front of us. "The direction of her voice is misleading. Let's just move forward. We'll find a way."

I looked at Mum, who was clearly only just holding it together and was glad Adi was taking charge of the decision making here. We had no choice but to move on.

We took a right-hand turn down the corridor, and I placed a gentle kiss on my mum's arm.

"I'm sorry, Mum. You told us not to get involved in any magic, and we ignored you. Frances said it would be okay. She said she'd be waiting for us by the Sphinx when we came out."

"It's all right, Rosie," Mum answered softly. She stopped and held my face in her hands in that way she always did to show me she wasn't cross. "I should never have turned my back on my beliefs. It was stupid of me and selfish, as well." She smiled sadly. "You should never have to pretend to be something or someone else, just because you think you might not fit in."

"*I* don't fit in," Adi stated, sniffing loudly.

"Darling Adi, you fit right in with us," Mum answered, striding forwards once more, and I grinned as I saw Adi go bright red.

"At the end of the day, it doesn't matter what other people think of you. Just be true to yourself, my darlings. How boring would the world be if we were all the same? We need to celebrate our differences and be proud of who we are." Suddenly she stopped in her tracks and pulled the strangest face. "Good god, what is that smell?"

Adi and I looked like two crazy rabbits, scrunching our noses up and down in earnest until the smell reached our nostrils, too.

"Oh! Oh no!" Adi cried, looking as if he was going to be sick.

"I'm afraid I recognise that smell," I said, smiling widely.

"Me, too," grinned Mum, winking at me.

"Well, I'm glad you two do!" Adi replied, his arm covering his nose. "Is it an Ancient Egyptian toilet or a burial ground for rotten meat?"

We shook our heads. "It's definitely a not-so-ancient stinky bum, and we know who owns one of those, don't we, Mum?" I added, laughing.

"We most certainly do. It's Lois, for sure. Bless her. I say we follow that smell. What do you think, guys?" Mum said, waiting for our approval.

I nodded and laughed, tickled by the expression on Adi's face. I don't think he would ever get used to my sister's windy bottom.

We followed the smell along the corridor, which twisted and turned and seemed to get narrower. There were still amazingly bright coloured pictures of people in Egyptian dress all the way along the whitewashed walls, but thankfully we didn't come across any more gates asking us to answer riddles.

Finally, there was a set of smooth sandstone steps that led down. There was no other choice but to follow them. We all looked at each other nervously, and Mum courageously led the way.

"I don't think I've ever had quite an adventure like this, aside from my times going through the portal, of course," she said.

I was surprised she spoke of that, as Mum never tended to talk about what her role had been when she was the Guardian of the Portal. I was eager to know more.

"Did you ever get to ride on a broomstick, Mum?" I asked excitedly.

Mum shook her head and briefly turned back to glance at us as she continued to descend the steps. "Never. I think part of it was I never truly believed I could do it. Do you know what I mean, Rosie?" she asked. "So much of magic is about belief, and while I believed there were many things I *could* do with my rituals and spells, flying the broomstick was something I never really had faith in for myself." She paused and looked quite sad for a moment. "Silly, isn't it? And probably too late now for me. My chance has gone. The headquarters have moved. I'm no longer as involved as I once was."

"At least it means you can get on with your own

life now though, Rae," Adi said. "You know, with your acting work and all that."

"Mmm," Mum said dreamily. "True. Although that's not as simple as it should be." She sighed. "I've finally realised there are too many people like Donna around — out for what they can achieve themselves, rather than for the greater good. Determined to drain other people's energy to make themselves feel better."

I was glad to hear that Mum had seen Donna's true colours at last.

Finally, we reached the bottom of the stairs, where the smell was so strong we all had to cover our noses and mouths. I racked my brain to think of what my sister must have been eating to produce such a terrible stench.

There was a huge dark grey stone door at the left of the stairs, so Mum knocked loudly and called out, "Lois, are you in here, darling? Open up if you are."

She gave me and Adi the crossed-fingers sign, and we waited.

All of a sudden, the door swung open, and there sitting on a stone bed — I suppose you could call it that — was my little sister, casually swinging her legs.

"Mummy!" she screeched, jumping down and rushing over to us. "You found me! How did you find me?"

Mum looked at me, half-smiling, as if wondering whether to tell her we followed the smell of her farts. There didn't seem any point saying this once we had entered the chamber, though, as the smell had completely disappeared, which was weird.

Now Lois had Mum's total attention, she was able to start up the waterworks again. "I've lost Bea though, Mummy. This person dressed in bandages took her, and now I've only got a few bits of her." She held up Bea's tail and an arm and leg, which was all she had of her precious bunny.

I must admit, even I felt like crying then. I didn't take my teddies around with me or anything, but I still liked to sleep with Jell and Ted, even though I wouldn't have dreamt of telling anyone that, of course.

I noticed Adi out the corner of my eye was trying to get my attention. I turned away from Mum and Lois, who were still hugging and chatting quietly, and looked towards Adi.

"*Over there,*" he mouthed to me, looking scared.

Oh no, not again, I thought, wishing this journey was done and dusted. I could really do with having a nice, hot dinner and watching some TV.

I carefully turned to where Adi was motioning and nearly fell over with surprise.

Standing in the corner was a lady — well, I think it was a lady. She had the face of a lioness. Her brown skin was dotted with freckles, yet her nose and head were definitely of the cat variety, and she had long whiskers protruding from either side of her face as if half-human, half-cat. She was wearing a long red robe and had the most beautiful snake cuff high up on her right arm, which glinted not only gold but green, too, as it had a large emerald stone for its head. Her face was kind, and though she held a tall spear, like Anubis, I didn't feel she was a threat.

"Mum!" I said in a low voice, not taking my eyes off the lion lady. "Mum!" I gave it more urgency this time.

"What is it, Rosie?" Mum finally turned her head and stopped in her tracks as she also saw the lady. "Ah ..."

"That's the lady that brought me here," Lois pointed out fearlessly.

The lady came forward out of the corner of the room and addressed us all with a small bow of her head. "My name is Sekhmet, and this is my chamber. I am known as the warrior goddess as well as the goddess of healing, and I have brought you here for some healing before you continue on with your journey."

"Is this normal then?" Adi piped up. "I mean, does everyone get the healing treatment on their way to the Hall of Two Truths for judgement?"

Oh, Adi, I thought nervously. I was worried the goddess might get annoyed at him asking too many things.

"Absolutely not," Sekhmet said, dusting down her red gown. "Your companion needs putting back together, doesn't she?" She addressed Lois, who nodded vehemently. Then she turned to my mum. "And you, dear lady, need putting back together, too, before you lose any more of yourself."

"I told you the book had spells to help prevent you from losing parts of yourself," I whispered to Adi.

Sekhmet must have had superhero hearing, for she looked at me and responded quickly, "Yes, the book has special spells for those deceased who may be losing limbs, so they can repair themselves before they reach the judgement hall. But you no longer have your instruction book. It's been taken from you, hasn't it?"

We nodded. "Yes, Mal Vine took it," I said glumly.

Sekhmet shrugged. "You can't use the spells once you're out of the book anyway. They are useless. So now is the time to act."

Thank goodness we had been lucky enough to meet Sekhmet, otherwise I had no idea what we would have done to help Mum.

"Bea first," Sekhmet ordered as she took the few remaining parts of Lois' rabbit and laid them on the stone bed. "If you could all just go and sit down in the corner, and please be as quiet as you can while I perform this ritual."

We all nodded, in awe of this beautiful lion goddess, and we sat down, relieved to finally be able to rest.

Sekhmet cast her hands over the few bits of Bea and chanted something that none of us could properly hear or understand. She moved her hands up and down, and from them exuded the most beautiful, mesmerising white light.

I had to blink a few times, as when I looked again there appeared to be hundreds of real bunnies surrounding the stone bed.

I glanced at Lois, who was open-mouthed. So she had seen them, too.

The bunnies were hopping and sniffing and munching on carrots and generally causing chaos on and around the bed. The room then momentarily went dark, and when the lights came back on, all the real rabbits had gone — but Bea was back, revitalised and sparkling, though still with her "loved-off" nose.

"Bea!" Lois shouted, choking back sobs. She ran over to the bed at Sekhmet's nod and flung her arms around her beloved rabbit, kissing and hugging her tightly. "Thank you!" Lois said, pulling Sekhmet into the cuddle.

I glanced at Mum, who looked approving, due to the fact that Lois had remembered her manners, which wasn't always a given.

"And now Mum, please." Sekhmet motioned to our mum.

Adi put his hand up, and I looked at him in confusion. We weren't at school!

"Please, miss, who were all the other rabbits we saw around the bed when you did the healing?" he asked.

Sekhmet smiled. "Those, my friend, were all of Bea's ancestors from hundreds of years back. They were rabbits that started life as toys but were given real life by their owners." She looked at Lois. "Bea is real to you, isn't she?"

Lois nodded eagerly. "She's my best friend."

"Well, there you are then." Sekhmet turned her attention to Mum. "Right, Mummy, on the bed. Close your eyes and relax."

We all sat back down in the corner and watched with anticipation.

Again, Sekhmet cast her hands up and down Mum's body, bright white light flowing from them. There were shadowy figures beginning to appear around the bed, and the three of us gasped and exchanged looks of wonder.

"It's Gran-Gran Joyce!" Lois whispered loudly to me as we noticed a round-faced, smiling woman wearing a homemade yellow dress on one side of Mum's head.

"How do *you* know?" I whispered back. "You were a baby when she died. *I* remember her."

"So do I!" Lois answered sharply, waving at her.

None of the figures seemed to notice us though. We didn't recognise anyone else around the bed. There were a few eccentric-looking figures — a woman with a long black dress on and flowing black hair with a twisted band around her forehead, a man with a long white beard, and a very small boy dressed in rags.

Eventually, the room darkened again, and when the darkness lifted, our guests had all disappeared, and Mum sat up from the bed looking revived, relaxed, and, most importantly, whole again! I was so happy to see she no longer had pieces missing from her.

"Gosh, that felt wonderful. Thank you, Sekhmet." Mum took the goddess' hand, and I noticed a current of purple light travel from Sekhmet's forearm to Mum's, as if she were giving Mum some kind of extra power.

"You are welcome. You need some protection, something you used to have?" Sekhmet asked questioningly.

Mum put her hand up to her throat sadly. "Yes, my necklace. I took it off, and perhaps if I hadn't, Mal Vine would never have been able to jump into my body."

"You need to go now. Someone is waiting for you." Sekhmet motioned us to leave her room, and I must admit I felt a real sadness as we left the peace of her healing chamber.

The stairs were no longer there. Instead there was another iron gate, but this time, it had a gate-keeper on the other side of it.

Anubis.

29

THE LAST CHALLENGE

"Anubis!" Lois cried out, as if she were greeting a long-lost friend. I guess she would have been pleased to see anyone right then, having been trapped in that chamber for what must have seemed like forever.

Anubis gave us a low bow. "I am impressed with your resourcefulness, children. So I am here to accompany you onward to the Hall of Two Truths. Here you will confess your sins, and Osiris will meet with you for the weighing of the heart."

My tummy gave a little flutter of fear. I hadn't given it much thought before, but now the weighing of the heart suddenly seemed very real and filled me with dread.

Anubis always seemed to look so scary, even though he had clearly come to help us. The trouble with having a dog's head was that even if he was smiling, it would have looked like he was baring his teeth.

"I'm Rae, the girls' mum," Mum said loudly, extending a hand towards Anubis, which he looked at briefly but didn't take. "I seem to have found myself here as an unwilling vehicle for a certain—"

"Mal Vine," came a voice, interrupting her.

Mum looked shocked to see a rather beautiful-looking Hecate, who just appeared out of the blue, standing next to Anubis. She was dressed in what looked like Ancient Egyptian clothing, with a wide gold and aqua necklace and a soft green robe with gold belt. On her arm was a similar cuff to the one Sekhmet had on, but Hecate's was an owl with a ruby for an eye. Her long blonde hair was sleek and framed her face, and she looked kindly on my mum.

"Hecate!" I murmured, surprised to see her.

"I'm so sorry, Hecate," my mum spoke softly. "I didn't recognise you. Forgive me. I think we only ever met when you were dressed as THE STRANGER."

"You may be right, Rae. My work takes me far and wide, and I am often in disguise for ease of passage. However, I have joined my husband briefly today, as there is something I need to give you." Hecate reached into a deep pocket in her robe, pulled out a necklace, and handed it to Mum. "I believe this is yours, Rae."

Mum held it up to the light — it was her pentagram necklace that Frances and Phyllis had given her years ago!

"Thank you," she said, sounding choked up. "I took it off, and I'm sorry, I never should have ..."

Hecate raised her hands as if brushing off Mum's worries. "No matter. What's important now is that you have rediscovered your faith." Hecate turned her head, as if she was listening to some voice beside her. "I must go, my dears. I am needed at the Tunnel of Eternal Darkness."

Anubis gave a low snuffling sound, which she smiled at, and she turned to go.

"Oh, by the way," she added, turning back to us and speaking quickly as her image began to fade. "Mr Vine has found himself in several skirmishes, in spite of having the instruction book to take him through the labyrinth, so you will soon be seeing him at the Hall of Two Truths, where hopefully his journey will be ending."

With that she was gone.

We all stood for a moment, taking in what Hecate had said. Mum fastened her necklace and it seemed to sparkle extra brightly, as if it were pleased to be back there. Lois was cuddling Bea and sucking her thumb, and Adi was gazing up toward the ceiling with his usual flared-nostril look.

"Come along then. Nothing to see here," barked Anubis as he opened the gate and let us through.

We followed him along several winding pas- sageways. It was nerve-wracking hearing all sorts of animal noises in the distance — hisses, wails, roars — and I wondered where all the animals were, and whether they were beasts of the labyrinth that Anubis was helping us avoid.

"Sir!" Adi called, running after him. "Where are you taking us and what are all those scary sounds?"

"You talk too much. Ask too many questions," Anubis retorted. Then after a pause, he answered less gruffly. "I'm taking a shortcut, so you can avoid the rest of the gates of the labyrinth. We will get to the Hall of Two Truths before Mal Vine."

Suddenly, he stopped, and we all backed up behind him. Mum was clasping Lois' hand, who I could tell by now was pretty tired.

We found ourselves at the banks of a narrow river. Behind us, you could see the walls of the labyrinth stretched far beyond. Across the water was a series of white pillars in a triangular format, and a building beyond that.

"Here I will leave you with your final challenge: to cross the river. I will see you inside the Hall of Two Truths," Anubis said, preparing to walk away from us.

"How do we get across?" Adi asked anxiously.

Like him, I could see all manner of large fins bobbing up and down on the surface of the river.

"You'll see, just by the stile over there." Anubis pointed downriver slightly.

We all turned to look, seeing an ordinary-looking wooden stile in the distance, and when we turned back, Anubis had gone.

"Don't panic!" I stated, more confidently than I felt. "I'm sure we will work this out, no problem."

"Mummy, are those sharks in that river?" Lois questioned nervously.

Mum and I exchanged a look, knowing full well their fins suggested they had to be sharks. They weren't likely to be friendly bottle-nosed dolphins, were they?

"No, darling, I think they are just large, erm, dogfish or something," Mum said very unconvincingly.

"What are dogfish?" Lois asked, wrinkling up her eyebrows in confusion.

"A type of shark," Adi answered casually, to our horror.

Lois' face crumpled, and she started to cry.

"Now look what you've done, Adi!" I whispered to him. "How are we going to get her across the river if she thinks there's sharks there?"

Adi looked confused. "But there are sharks there, Rosemary. There's no point pretending. 'Danger should be feared when distant and braved when present.' So, we need to know the facts and just get on with braving this."

I felt like making up my own Indian saying, but I thought, seeing as Adi would probably be helping us get safely across the river, I'd better be quiet.

"Come on, Lois. I'm here," soothed my mum. "We'll get over this river no problem."

We reached the stile, and there was an envelope with a set of instructions inside. Adi read them out loud.

"I am one of these,
So, I can be divided by the greatest mystery.
I am whole.
I am the power of this.
I am the last wonder of the world.
What number am I?"

"Oh dear, riddles aren't my strong point," Mum said, defeated.

"Hey Mum, look!" I cried. Out of the water appeared some stepping-stones with numbers on.

There was a choice of four stones to choose from, then another row of four followed by another row of four, which then, presumably, allowed you to jump onto the bank on the other side.

"Oh, so I suppose we have a twenty-five percent chance of picking the right stone to step on," Mum added gloomily.

"That's correct, mathematically," Adi breezed. "However, we will work this puzzle out, and we will choose the right steps each time. It's not going to be a guess."

"What will happen if we choose the wrong step?" Lois asked, clutching Bea tightly.

"This," said Adi, throwing a stone onto a random step.

As the stone hit the step, which was marked with a number nine, it rapidly sank and three huge-looking sharks appeared, their ugly jaws snapping viciously.

Mum, Lois, and I screeched and clung to each other.

"Don't worry, it's not going to happen." Adi smiled, scratched his head, and continued to study the instructions.

"Okay, gang," Adi said after a few moments. "What is whole?"

"Why are you asking us?" Lois said suspiciously.

"I think I know the answer, I'm just making sure I'm on the right track. So, what is whole?" Adi said, in schoolteacher mode.

"A digestive biscuit?" Lois suggested, a look of longing on her face.

Adi shook his head.

"A Madeira cake before I've had a slice?" she tried again.

"No, Lois," I berated. "Stop thinking about food. We're here to get across the river."

"What about the number one?" Mum said, unsure. "That's a whole, isn't it?"

"Absolutely," Adi replied, excitedly. "So, if the first number is one, what is the second? I am the power of?"

"The power of three?" I suggested. "In magic, three is always used as the power number."

"Exactly!" Adi grinned. "Now we know there are only three numbers, as there's only three rows to get across, so if we do one, then three, then what's the next number? The clue is, 'I am the last wonder of the world'."

"Ooooooh, tricky. Would it be the pyramids, as we're in Egypt?" Mum suggested. "Or is it something like the Great Wall of China?"

"I don't think they're looking for us to name the seven wonders of the world, Mum. I think they just want to know a number." I racked my brain. Suddenly it clicked. "Of course, seven! Is seven the answer, Adi? The Seven Wonders of the World, so the last wonder is the seventh!"

"I think so, yes. So, the number would be 137. Does that ring any bells to you, Rosemary?" Adi asked.

I nodded and so did Lois. "It's the number the fan has to get to before we can jump through!" Lois said.

Mum looked at us questioningly.

"I'll explain all that later, Mum," I said.

"And," Adi said, smiling like the Cheshire Cat, "137 is a prime number, so I think that relates to the beginning of the clue. Prime numbers can be divided only by themselves, and 137 is known as the number that holds the greatest mystery."

"Wow!" Mum said, looking impressed. "You are a clever old stick, Adi. I'll go first."

Adi opened his mouth to protest, but Mum was already in front, cocking her legs over the stile. "I'm the grown-up here, so it's only right I lead the way. I have my necklace on now, don't I?" she said proudly, fingering it. "That will protect me. Come on, Lois, you next."

She lifted Lois over the stile as she shrank back, terrified now she knew there were all number of sharks circling the stones.

I think I was holding my breath as Mum took her first steps onto the number one stone, but thankfully it stayed put, and no sharks seemed to be able to get near it.

"So, it's definitely number three next, isn't it?" Mum called out. "As there's also a number six and a five and two."

"Definitely number three," Adi said loudly.

We watched as Mum successfully landed on stone three and then motioned for Lois to step onto the first stone.

"Then its number seven," Adi called to her.

"Don't leave me, Mummy. I'm scared," Lois said between tears.

"It's okay, Lois. I'll be right behind you, and Mum's right in front," I said, not taking my eyes off

Mum as she landed on stone seven and then hopped to safety on the other side of the bank.

"Hurray!" we all cheered — even Lois, who was still standing motionless on the first stone.

"Go on, Lois. Step onto the next stone with the number three on it," I coaxed, knowing that once she was safely across, Adi and I would be able to get over quickly.

We all exhaled with relief once Lois had jumped onto the last stone and then into the safety of Mum's arms on the bank.

I followed, with Adi planning to bring up the rear.

I was halfway across when my mum's and Lois' faces suddenly dropped.

"What's the matter?" I cried, wobbling slightly as I tried to turn round.

"Don't look back, Rosie!" Mum shouted.

"Why? What's wrong?" Fear gripped me; I wondered if Adi had fallen in and been devoured by a hungry shark. "Is Adi okay?" I called, shaking and barely able to jump over to the last stone.

"I'm fine," Adi's voice replied, only it didn't sound quite like him.

I got to the bank and turned round, anxious to see for myself.

All the blood felt like it had drained from my body.

Adi was being held tightly in a ferocious grip, by none other than a ragged-looking Mal Vine.

30

THE HALL OF TWO TRUTHS

"Adi!" I screamed, starting to move my body to step onto the stones again so I could reach him.

"Rosie, no!" Mum shouted, pulling me back into her arms. "Can't you see what's following him?"

My blood ran cold.

Not only was Mal Vine holding Adi in a tight grip, but behind him, and following the long length of the riverbank as far as the eye could see, were all manner of terrifying-looking beasts.

They ranged from scary goats, to crocodiles, to dragons, to three-eyed toads, all snarling and dripping with green and yellow saliva that burnt on contact with the earth. The growls and barks and shrieks coming from their jaws sent shivers down my spine.

Mal Vine really was gathering an army of beasts of the underworld.

"Let him go, you bully!" I shouted at Mal, who

looked like he had been involved in several fights of his own. His clothes were torn, he had a ragged piece of skin flapping from the cheek that bore the scar, and his lip was bleeding.

Mal Vine sneered at me. "Time to say goodbye to your friend, Rosie. And once I've unleashed these monsters into the world, I'll be able to get rid of those snivelling witches, too." He turned his attention to my mum and winked at her. "Nice to see you looking a little more like yourself, Rae. I did enjoy our time together though. We were a nice fit, don't you think?"

There was no stopping Mum. She pushed me and Lois behind her and puffed herself up to her tallest. "How dare you speak to me like that, you nasty little man? Let go of Adi immediately, or I will come and take him off you. You can't hurt me now. Look!" She grasped her necklace and held it towards Mal.

I think Lois, Adi, and I were hoping it would act like garlic to a vampire and that Mal would shrivel up and die, but unfortunately, he just laughed his nasty, throaty chuckle.

"You want me to let go of Adi immediately?" he replied. "Consider it done!"

And he promptly dropped Adi into the river below.

"Noooooo!" Lois and I screamed.

Lois turned her head and started sobbing into Bea, and I went hoarse with shouting.

"Adi, swim, swim!" I yelled.

The water was crawling with sharks, and though it wasn't far to swim across, it was far

enough when being pursued by several large preda-
tors. I could see Adi swimming for his life.

Time seemed to slow down as one shark
nudged away all other competitors and was gaining
on him. The tip of its nose reached Adi, and it
seemed to dive down in the water — probably about
to toss Adi into the air so it could watch him drop
helplessly into its jaws — when suddenly a loud
booming voice from behind us shouted, "*Qaf!*"

I turned in surprise to see Anubis, standing
with his hands on his hips, looking fearsome.

Whatever he said clearly had an effect on the
shark. We watched, open-mouthed, as it paused,
seemingly listening to Anubis, and then gently
nudged Adi's terrified body onto the top of its snout
and carried him safely across the water, waiting patiently while he shakily clambered onto the bank.

I was the first to hug him, followed by my sister,
as Mum talked quietly with Anubis.

I thought Adi was so brave. He didn't cry, but
he was shaking; his glasses kept steaming up, and
his teeth were chattering.

"Adi, you're so brave!" stated Lois proudly.
"What did the shark smell like?" she continued, as
if interviewing him.

"Lois!" I said crossly. "What a thing to ask
someone who's narrowly escaped death. What do
you *think* it smelled like?"

"Fish?" she pondered, her head to one side.

"To be honest, Lois, I don't remember any
smells. I just hope *I* didn't let myself down," Adi
said, half-grinning, half-embarrassed.

"I'm sure your underpants are clean, Adi," I

said with a supportive smile on my face. "You've been really brave. You're a hero."

I felt a tear trickle down my own cheek. I was so bowled over by Adi and his courage. He swam with a shark chasing him! He was amazing!

"I've always wanted to be a hero," Adi replied, grinning sheepishly. He turned his attention back to Mal Vine, who looked furious, standing on the middle stone of the river. "What's going to happen with him now?" Adi whispered to us.

I shrugged my shoulders. "No idea, but I reckon he'll have to come with us to the Hall of Two Truths."

"What about all the creatures?" Lois whispered dramatically.

"Watch," I replied, my eyes focused on Anubis, who was holding both his arms outstretched above his head, with his hands in prayer position.

"*Imshi!*" he commanded, bringing his hands down to his heart.

A warm wind started to blow. Slowly at first, then it gathered momentum until it was practically a tornado. The funny thing was that it only seemed to be happening on the other side of the river, the side where all the creatures were.

It whirled and howled around them, scattering them far and wide: some back into the labyrinth, some into the river, and some took flight, disappearing into the sky.

At last the wind died down and Mal was left on his stone, looking rather pathetic.

"Come!" Anubis spoke gruffly to all of us, as we

made our way through the triangular shaped pillars into a great hall.

The hall was dazzling white, its floors and walls made from marble that was both cool and luxurious looking. A balcony stretched all around the room, upon which there were many men and women, each dressed in full Egyptian clothing and holding a piece of papyrus.

Ahead of us, standing on a kind of altar, was a very tall man wearing a long white robe, which was partially wrapped around some of his body, rather like the mummified bandages. He wore a tall white hat and had a fierce expression in his brown eyes. In front of him was a large pair of gold scales, one side of which held a long white feather.

He studied us all thoughtfully and then spoke.

"Welcome. I now invite you one by one to stand before our forty-two judges. As each one addresses you, please answer them clearly with an affirmative or denial, repeating their question in your answer."

"What's an aperitive?" Lois hissed under her breath.

"Affirmative or denial," I corrected her. "It means say yes or no." I was as clueless as her as to what was about to happen.

I noticed Mum looked highly anxious and kept fiddling with her necklace. I really hoped it was going to protect us, as we were getting serious now. We didn't want to go to the afterlife, we just needed to take the book from Osiris and return it to the British Museum.

What followed was a long, drawn-out process

where each judge would read a question out from their papyrus until we had each answered forty-two different questions. They ranged from, "have you slain people?" to "have you stolen from people?", with us answering "no, I have not slain people" and "no, I have not stolen from people."

Some of the questions I didn't really understand, like "have you carried out grain-profiteering?" And some I felt a little blush of red creep up on my cheeks, like when I answered, "No, I have not been impatient.".

I guess we were just thankful they didn't ask Lois anything like, *have you wilfully passed wind on your sister*? as she had done this a copious number of times.

These were the forty-two sins that they had to check you were free from, before your heart could be weighed.

We watched, our faces creased with disbelief as Mal Vine denied all charges.

I exchanged a nervous look with Mum, who was clearly wondering when he was going to get his comeuppance, if at all. And then Osiris spoke.

"It is now time for the weighing of the heart. If your heart is heavier than this ostrich feather, you will be condemned and unable to enter into the Gates of Paradise."

Stitch that, I thought. All I want is to take the book back to London, never mind the Gates of Paradise. And how was he intending to weigh our hearts? We weren't mummified, deceased people whose organs had been removed as part of the process.

I think Adi shared my anxiety, as the look of fear in his brown eyes seemed to mirror my thoughts exactly.

"Don't worry, Rosemary. I'm sure this won't hurt," he whispered to me, rather unconvincingly.

"Silence!" boomed the voice of Osiris. "You, first!" He pointed at poor Adi.

What happened next was bizarre. Osiris swung a small bag of something highly perfumed back and forth, close to Adi's face, and Adi seemed to go very relaxed. Then Osiris reached very gently to his chest and brought out this thing, which I'm guessing was his heart. It looked like a large piece of cotton wool, only gold coloured, and Adi didn't seem to be in any pain whatsoever. Osiris placed it on the empty scale, and we watched, holding our breath, as the scale tipped down showing that the feather was heavier than his heart.

Hooray! For the first time, Osiris smiled widely, gently placed the gold cotton-wool heart back into Adi's chest and turned him around. He then smacked him on the shoulder, and Adi opened his eyes.

"*Are you okay?*" I mouthed, scared one of us would be shouted at again. Adi nodded, still looking a bit dazed.

Then it was Lois' turn. She looked terrified, and Mum held her hand as she stood in front of Osiris. We needn't have worried, as he did the same thing with her. Lois stayed quiet and still, clearly in a trance as Osiris removed a pale pink cotton wool heart from her chest. This was repeated, with

Mum, whose heart was purple, and then mine, which apparently was aquamarine.

But every one of us had passed the test — our hearts were lighter than the feather.

Osiris addressed the four of us, beaming. "Welcome to paradise, my friends. You may take whatever you wish into the Field of Reeds now."

I looked at Mum, who nodded her head slightly as if to say, *go on, you know why you're here.*

"Please, sir, we would like to take the *Book of the Dead* back to the British Museum, if that's okay?" I said.

Osiris smiled and nodded at Anubis, who handed us a gold and red leather-bound book. The *Book of the Dead.* I passed it carefully round to my mum, Adi, and Lois.

I couldn't believe it was that easy! We'd finally got it.

I was about to ask Adi how we were going to get home, when Osiris turned his attention to Mal Vine, who was brought up, slightly staggering, to the scales by Anubis.

His flinty brown eyes glinted at me, and I swear I could hear his thoughts. "*All right, kid? You and me, eh? We go long back. We'll meet again. Be sure of that. It ain't over till the fat lady sings, and that Frances ain't about to start.*"

I shuddered and forced myself to look away, trying to ignore his nastiness.

Osiris swung the bag of herbs and Mal's eyes closed. He placed his hand on his bony chest and brought out a large sticky black mass. It looked like a torn loaf of bread that had been dipped in tar.

He placed it on the scales and at once they sank down, forcing the feather to fly high in the air.

His heart was heavier than the feather.

We collectively gasped. I looked at Mum. She had her fingers clasped on her necklace and the other hand over her mouth. Lois was turned away into Bea, too scared to watch. Adi, like me, was wide-eyed with shock.

What was going to happen now?

Stony-faced, Osiris replaced Mal's heart and gave his chest a big thud with his hand. Mal's eyes opened, bloodshot and watery.

"You have sinned greatly. I will not feed your heart to the crocodile as I would normally. You will receive the fate worse than death: non-existence." Osiris placed his foot on Mal's chest and pushed until he fell backwards on the floor. "You have never existed."

There was a roar of anger and disbelief from Mal's mouth as he started to disintegrate until all that was left was a single gold tooth.

Before we'd had time to process what had just happened, there was a great clap of thunder from the skies, and the room grew dark. It felt as if the roof had disappeared from this great hall, along with all the judges who had been on the balcony.

As the lightning started to flash, we gazed up to see Hecate floating above us, her arms and legs out-stretched, her face contorted with anger.

"How dare you defy me, Anubis?" she yelled. "Mal Vine was ours to deal with. I told you we would be arresting him, and instead you ignored me and brought him to be judged here."

Osiris started to slowly make his way backwards, until a few moments later, during another flash of lightning, I noticed he'd completely disappeared.

Anubis, however, seemed to grow in stature. His ears went back, and his dog eyes narrowed; he snarled and bared his teeth. "You are in *our* lands now, Hecate. We live by *our* rules here. Your criminal chose to defy our rules by gaining access to the book via another soul's body, which is forbidden, and by bewitching the beasts of the underworld to follow him, clearly with malicious intent, so he received our punishment. You have no jurisdiction here."

Suddenly — as if things were not weird enough — Hecate's body lengthened and changed until she had morphed into a large pure white cat with the bluest of eyes.

Anubis barked loudly at the cat and then leapt up into the skies to chase her. The sound of caterwauling and barking echoed all around us as the two of them fought.

I remembered being told before that Hecate was a shapeshifter, and I wondered why she would have chosen to turn into a cat of all things, seeing as Anubis had the head of a dog.

As if reading my thoughts, Adi whispered to me. "She's not completely daft. He won't kill her. The Egyptians loved cats, you know."

I raised my eyebrows, hoping he was right. There was one final crash of thunder and lightning, and then suddenly the light returned to normal and there was silence.

Poor Lois, who had closed her eyes in fear, slowly opened them and, still clinging to Mum, said, "Has it finished? Are we home yet? I'm starving."

I saw Adi wrinkle up his nose in disgust.

"She hasn't, has she?" I asked, sighing, wondering if things could get any worse. Adi nodded, embarrassed. "Lois!" I moaned. "Can you just keep your wind to yourself, please?"

"It wasn't me," she pouted.

"Darling, it wasn't any of us, was it?" Mum said gently.

"Well, I never felt it come out my bottom," Lois stated, as if that somehow meant it hadn't happened.

"I suppose it doesn't count then, does it?" Mum reluctantly agreed.

"Hang on!" Adi said with panic in his voice. "Where is everyone?"

We all scanned the great hall — it was empty. Gone were the judges. Osiris and his scales had disappeared. Anubis and Hecate were no longer fighting.

I scoured the area to find the last remaining piece of Mal Vine — his gold tooth — but that had mysteriously vanished, too.

Mum ran outside to see if anyone was there, and we followed, hoping that there might be someone who would tell us how to get back home. The river was silent. There were no stepping-stones, no sign of sharks, and no boats.

"Oh no!" Mum cried, exasperated. "What are we going to do now?"

I had a lightbulb moment and grinned. "Let me just grab something out of my rucksack, and I can get us out of here."

I reached deep into my bag and, feeling incredibly smug, pulled out a white candle.

31

DREAMS DO COME TRUE

"A candle?" Mum said in surprise. "Oh, Rosie, how is that going to help us?"

"Do you remember, guys," I said slowly to Lois and Adi, "when we were on our adventure to find Phyllis, we had three candles, and Adi and I used ours?"

"Yeah, I used mine to go to India and see my cousin, and we used yours on the way to the wormholes, didn't we?" Adi remembered.

"It's mine!" Lois said excitedly. "I never used mine! Yay!" Then her face fell. "I can't remember what I wished for though ..."

"I can." I smiled and whispered to her.

Lois grinned from ear to ear and started doing a little dance with Bea.

Mum looked completely puzzled. "Will someone fill me in, please? I'd really like to get out of here. I'm gasping for a cup of tea."

"Okay, if we light this candle, it will make Lois' wish come true — I hope, anyway — which was to fly on Frances' broomstick. So with any luck, that means Frances will appear with her broomstick and get us home." I passed the candle to Lois, who took it solemnly, as if I had just handed her the Nobel Peace Prize. I noticed a faint look of confusion cross Adi's face.

"I know the witches can't gain access to the Akashic Library, but we're not summoning her there, we're summoning her to the book," I said.

Adi looked doubtful, but I hoped I was right as I fumbled once again in the rucksack for the box of matches and carefully lit the candle's wick.

I think we collectively held our breath. I saw Adi had closed his eyes, bless him. My sister looked excited, Mum anxious, and I waited calmly, though my heart was racing.

All of a sudden, we heard a faint rock-guitar solo coming from somewhere in the sky. When we all looked heavenwards, it increased in volume. We squinted our eyes, until finally a figure appeared, standing on — or should I say *balancing* on top of — her broomstick, playing air guitar with a much smaller broomstick.

It was Frances, of course. The music was incredibly infectious, and we all started to dance along as Frances drifted closer to us with a huge grin on her face.

Her skirt was flapping in the breeze, revealing those flesh-coloured pop socks, one of which was half-mast. She seemed to know all the lyrics. It had to be her favourite band — Queen, of course. At the chorus she was singing "broomstick to fall" instead of the usual lyrics, which Mum said should have been "hammer to fall".

Out of kindness, we let her finish the song, as she loved performing. Then she gently let Wendy settle on the riverbank outside the Hall of Two Truths.

"Well, hello, bairns!" she screeched full of excitement. "Hallo, Rae," she said more warily to Mum. "It's so good to see you all. I was beginning to wonder what was going on when Wendy here suddenly tapped me on the shoulder, and we were off!"

Lois rushed over to Frances and gave her a huge hug and kiss. "I wished for you, Frances, so I could fly on your broomstick."

"But you've already done that, wee girl. Don't you remember?" Frances laughed.

"We weren't sure whether it would work, because you can't get into the Akashic Library," I said, relief filling my heart.

"You're right, of course, Rosie, but I didn't have to go to the Library to get here. The wish Lois made from the candle is very powerful magic, as it was created during a huge energy-raising event. It has the power of not just one person, but hundreds."

"Thanks to me, now we can go home," Lois stated proudly.

"We certainly can. But come here, hen. Did you get the book?" Frances asked seriously.

Adi held it aloft, its gold lettering glinting in the still-hot sun. "It's here, ready to return to the museum."

We all looked delighted. Even Mum was smiling and looking more like herself, though a little ragged around the edges due to the heat and stress of the last few hours.

Frances glanced anxiously at Mum, clearly a little unsure whether it was okay to speak to her or not.

"Frances, I'm sorry," Mum said. "I owe you a huge apology. I've been an absolute cow. I should never have tried to turn my back on my faith. Magic is part of my very bones." She tapped her chest. "It's my very essence, and I really don't think I could ever live without it." She paused, and fingered her pentacle necklace once again.

"You have your wee necklace back," Frances whispered.

Mum nodded. "Hecate brought it to me. I should never have taken it off. I'm sure that's why Mal Vine was able to get inside me and of course why I felt like I was falling apart. I don't care about the job ..."

Frances butted in. "No, no, Rae, please, you've worked hard to get this job. Don't throw it away. You don't need to make a choice between your career and magic ..."

"But what if I do?" Mum looked pensive.

"Then that job's not the right one for you. We'll figure it out. Don't be worrying." Frances squeezed Mum's hand. "Come on, enough adventures. Let's get these bairns home."

"Frances?" I asked seriously. "How are we all going to get on Wendy? Last time she could only carry you, me, and Lois."

"I've thought of everything." Frances grinned, handing the mini broomstick that she had been using to play guitar to Mum. "This is Winnie, and she'll take your mum; the rest of us can get on

Wendy. It's only one extra bum. It'll do her good, build up her muscles, so to speak." Wendy (at least I think it was her) let out a long breathy sigh, followed by a snort. Frances looked at her crossly. "And we'll hear no more about it, madam."

She gathered up her skirt and flung her leg over Wendy. "Come on, all, let's get on. Put your wee sister in the middle of you and Adi." She motioned to me. "And Rae, straddle Winnie, give her a stroke, and tell her where you want to go."

I watched Mum, delighted that her dream to ride on a broomstick was finally coming true. She glanced back at us all, slightly rosy-cheeked with nerves, and she stroked Winnie gently and whispered our address to her.

"Oh my god," shrieked Mum, as Winnie gently lifted up into the air.

We followed suit on Wendy, once Frances had berated her for pretending to play dead.

"Are you managing, hen?" Frances called to Mum.

"Yes, I think so! Woohoo!" she whooped as we all climbed up higher into the sky.

Flying a broomstick is the MOST AMAZING experience in the world. The air feels warm on your face and body, even though it's cold high up in the sky. You feel totally balanced and in control; you feel airless and weightless and without a care in the world. You feel as if anything, and I mean ANYTHING, is possible.

Frances took the lead, and as we sailed higher, I looked down and watched the river and the Hall of Two Truths become smaller and smaller, until eventually the landscape we had left behind took on the shape of a double page in an open book.

Had we really just flown out of the pages of a book?

We then flew over quite a lot of desert, and Frances shouted at us to hold on tight, as we were taking a shortcut.

Whatever the shortcut was, I wouldn't recommend it. It was like being sucked up into a vacuum cleaner in darkness.

Once we were out of that, the air became clearer, and we started to descend. I could see our street!

I gazed over at Mum, who was sitting back, her hair flying freely in the wind. She was smiling, and I'd never seen her look so excited.

We landed gently in the back garden and Frances propped Wendy and Winnie up by the back gate as we gathered in the kitchen. Unusually, both our cats fled outside once we'd arrived home; we saw them make a beeline for the broomsticks, which they sniffed and scented.

"Sit yourself down, Rae, and I'll make you a nice cup of tea like old times." Frances bossed us about, instructing us to sit down as we must be starving. (We were.)

I was about to ask Frances what had happened to Phyllis and if they'd sorted the leak out in the Tunnel of Eternal Darkness, when she gave me a peculiar look, one which said, "don't ask me about that yet."

I bit my lip and munched thoughtfully away on

the biscuits that Mum had put out on the table for us.

"I think we'll get a takeaway tonight as a treat. What do you think, everyone?" she said.

We all nodded in agreement.

"Yes, please, Mummy. Can I have spicy chicken?" Lois asked, doing her best pleading face.

"You can have whatever you like, Lois. We'll wait for Dad, though. You're welcome to stay too, Adi." Mum glanced at the kitchen clock. "Gosh, it's only 6.30 p.m.; it feels much later. How very odd."

"I'll probably have to get home soon anyway, but thanks," Adi replied, his glasses having given up and slid entirely off his nose.

I smiled to myself and wondered whether he would ever get glasses that fit him.

"Where were you, Rae, when you suddenly ended up with the bairns?" Frances asked, slurping her tea loudly.

"I had literally just parked the car in our driveway here," Mum said slowly, as if trying to engage her brain with a distant memory. "In fact, I think I must have left my bag and phone in the passenger seat. Let me go and check."

Mum grabbed her spare car keys from Dad's office and made her way outside.

Frances wasted no time. "Now listen, bairns. No word of this to your mum, okay? I'm not one for keeping secrets, but I don't think she should know about the leak in the prison. She'll only be worrying, especially as we've got to go back to the tunnels in order to get the book returned."

"What happened after we'd left you with Phyllis?" I asked, desperate to know.

"Did you take her back to the Tunnel of Eternal Darkness?" Lois said curiously.

"Is she feeling okay now?" Adi asked, his eyes widening.

"She's not too bad, hen. Jonathan has been looking after her in his area, and she's been teaching the prisoners some more songs, so that's kept her busy." Frances giggled.

We heard voices from the hall. Mum was coming back in with Dad, who must have just got home from work.

"We're going to need to pop back to the Tunnel of Eternal Darkness, I'm afraid. Hecate turned up, and when we couldn't find the leak she asked for you three to return there," Frances whispered.

I wanted to ask why we were needed to help find the leak. I was prepared to go back into the tunnels to return the *Book of the Dead*, but not to the Tunnel of Eternal Darkness — no way.

"Aaaah, Miss Fiddlesnitcher!" Dad said happily as he came into the kitchen, followed by Mum. "Nice to see you again."

Frances didn't say a word. Lois, Adi, and I caught each other's eyes and tried not to giggle at Dad continually getting her name wrong.

"I'd best be off now. I think there's plenty of stuff for me to catch up on at home," Frances said, winking at us.

"Thank you, Frances, for ALL your help today," Mum said, smiling, as Frances gathered her bag and made for the door.

"Nae problem, hen. Are you working on Monday?" she replied.

"Just one scene in the afternoon, so I'll be back around this time, I expect, Frances." I heard Mum pause in the hallway. "Oh, I've got a few missed calls from my agent. How odd."

As Mum made her way back into the kitchen, she still looked a little troubled.

"Can you call them back now, Mum?" I asked, carefully, wondering if it was about whether her contract was going to be extended on *Brightside*.

"No, darling, it's after hours. I'm sure whatever it is will wait until Monday."

That night, I lay in bed feeling a strange emptiness.

Even with the knowledge that Mal Vine had vanished, things still didn't feel quite right.

3 2

THE LEAK

T he weekend flew by and on Monday morning I was sitting with Dad in the kitchen eating breakfast, paying little attention to the TV as the news was on, when suddenly an item came up that made me almost choke on my croissant.

"In a shock announcement, one of popular soap *Brightside*'s most enduring characters, Ethel, played by veteran actress Harriet Mouret, has decided to quit the show. Ms Mouret, seen here at the Channel 9 studio entrance, refused to speak to reporters today."

What followed was a short video, clearly taken on someone's phone, of Harriet bending over in the downward-dog position, wearing a fluorescent cropped top with tassels on the front and nothing else except for a pair of flesh-coloured tights.

As the voice of the reporter asked her why she had quit, all she said was, "Sausages." We had a very close-up shot of her bottom in the air, and to be

276

honest, it didn't look as if she was wearing any knickers.

"Good lord!" my dad exclaimed, his coffee spluttering everywhere.

"We met her on Mum's FaceTime," I said, unsure what else to say given the situation.

"Really? I'm surprised you can recognise her from that angle," Dad added, drily.

"Well, she was doing that pose when we were introduced to her," I replied.

"Ha! That explains it then. She's off her rocker." Dad drained his coffee.

I felt quite glad for Harriet, even though we'd only met her once. She seemed to have felt trapped in her job, and so I guess it took a lot of courage for her to finally act on her beliefs and hand in her notice.

At that moment, Mum came rushing into the kitchen. "I've just had a text from Harriet! She's leaving!"

"Yeah, she's just been on the news," I said.

"Showing her bottom," Dad stated, smirking slightly.

"Showing her bottom?" Mum questioned.

"Whose bottom?" chimed the voice of my little sister, who was dragging Bea into the kitchen, yawning.

"Not yours for a change, young lady," Dad added, quickly grabbing his bags to head off to the station. He gave Mum a peck on the cheek. "Let me know what the agent says later, and let's have a celebratory drink at home whatever the news, eh?" he said warmly.

It was nice to see Dad being more like himself. I did sometimes feel nervous that his cloud might return at any moment, but thankfully all seemed well right now.

Lois moaned and groaned until we told her the story about Harriet on the news.

"Oh, well, that's good. Didn't she say it was like working in a sausage factory? After all, no one wants smelly sausage fingers," Lois stated.

Mum continued to read the messages on her phone. "It looks like her bravery might be paying off. She said her agent got her a huge deal to write her autobiography and appear on a new TV show about body image and yoga for the over sixties."

"That's good," I replied, following Mum and Lois out the door to go to school.

I was glad that Harriet's story appeared to have a happy ending. She'd obviously spent years doing something she wasn't happy with, and once she finally decided to be brave and be honest with herself, it paid off.

I hoped that Mum, too, was relieved that she had accepted her own truth by realising how important her beliefs were to her.

Adi had taken the *Book of the Dead* with him on Friday night, as Frances had said it was down to us, not her, to bring it back to its home, because we had completed the mission. I must admit, I was very nervous about Adi keeping it in his rucksack in his locker all day. What if Murray or Daredevil Dan got wind of it and pinched it? I could just imagine

them ripping out pages of this ancient artefact —
then we'd be in real trouble.

Thankfully, the day was uneventful and
Frances met us from school, this time wearing a ca-
nary yellow jumpsuit that had green and blue
budgerigars all over it. I had never seen her wear
such a strange outfit. She did, of course, have her
black Doc Martens on, and probably flesh coloured
pop socks, though I didn't look too hard to check.

It was quite a warm day, and we were all relieved that we didn't have to go back to the ex-
hausting heat of Egypt. In fact, the coolness of the
tunnels would be most welcome now.

The bus journey was over quite quickly, mainly
because Lois was now revved up and excited about
seeing Phyllis and Mr Foggerty, as well as Jonathan.
Frances clearly knew how to sell an idea to her. She
was also eating a ginormous piece of Madeira cake,
which she managed to get all over the seat, herself,
and Frances.

Soon we were striding into the George's Dock
Building, happy to see Uncle Vic sitting in the
ticket booth.

"Well, well, well, the adventurers return then."
He grinned at us all, squeezing himself out of the
ticket booth and reaching for the notice that said
"Tour full. Come back in one hour."

"Can I put the sign up?" begged Lois, who
loved to feel she had been given an important job.

"Be my guest, young lady," Uncle Vic said,
passing her the sign.

"No Reg today?" Frances whispered to Uncle
Vic, who shook his head and beckoned us to hurry

up and follow him down the corridor. "Off sick, as are a few other staff members."

"Oh no!" Frances replied, looking worried.

"Oh yes, and it probably is what you think it is." Uncle Vic winked at Frances but kept his face deadly serious and then mouthed, *"The darkness."*

"Are you saying the leak in the prison tunnel is affecting people in this building?" I asked nervously.

Uncle Vic glanced at Frances before answering, "Possibly, Rosie, yes, but it's all under control. We will find the source, make no mistake."

"Do you think Mal Vine has anything to do with this?" Adi asked as we reached the extractor room.

"Mal Vine is usually at the bottom of every-thing catastrophic, but unfortunately we can no longer ask him or blame him," Uncle Vic continued, raising his eyebrows at Frances.

"Of course," I said, half to myself. "No wonder Hecate was so angry that Osiris erased him. Now we can't ask him if he did cause the leak and where it's coming from."

"I think you might have hit the nail on the head," said Adi seriously, glancing at Uncle Vic, who looked like he was in agreement.

"Yes, that has rather put the cat amongst the pigeons, I'm afraid." He scratched his head thoughtfully. "We are missing something though. Hecate has turned every cell upside down looking for the source of the leak, but nothing, absolutely nothing can be found. It's most bizarre."

"Why do you think *we'll* be able to help find

it?" I asked nervously, not thrilled with the idea of having to revisit the tunnels again and experience that awful feeling of gloom and sadness.

"Hecate had a hunch you might be able to help." Uncle Vic pressed the button on the fan and we waited patiently for it to slow down to 137 before jumping through as quickly as possible.

I still hated the leap of faith I had to take when throwing myself through the spaces between the blades.

We crept past the glass-fronted office, which was packed full of people pointing out different areas on what looked like a huge map of the prison. There were red and amber lights flashing all over the place, and Frances and Uncle Vic rushed us past quickly.

"No time to gawp, please," Uncle Vic panted as we reached the clearing where all the tunnels met.

I could see Frances, like Uncle Vic, was almost out of breath. "One second, Vic, let me catch myself. I'm not as young as I used to be!" she joked.

We were just having the usual discussion of which tunnel was which, when suddenly we saw a figure coming towards us from one of them.

"Oh, is it Phyllis?" Lois said curiously.

I squinted my eyes, and suddenly it became clear who it was.

"It's Hecate!" I cried in surprise.

This time she was dressed as THE STRANGER, so we couldn't see her face properly at all. It was completely obscured by the Indiana Jones-type hat she had pulled low over her face.

"Thank you for coming, children," she said in

her deep, hypnotic voice. "I know all you need to do is hand back the book. You will have that opportunity shortly. But Lois, I need you to find Aradia for me first."

I couldn't help myself. "Aradia?" I said out loud. "Why her?"

Hecate turned to me, and I felt the familiar chill that I did whenever she was dressed as THE STRANGER. "Aradia has been working with Mal Vine, so I believe it must be her that is behind the leak in the Tunnel of Eternal Darkness."

"How is Lois going to find Aradia?" Adi asked, which, to be fair, I was thinking, too.

"You know what to do, Lois, don't you?" Hecate spoke softly to my sister, who to my utter surprise nodded innocently.

We all stared at Lois, waiting for her to enlighten us, but she stayed silent, with a smug expression on her face.

Hecate squeezed her shoulder and said, "I'll be off then, and I'll be ready." And with that she strode back down the tunnel in the direction she had come from.

"Should we be following her?" Adi asked, removing his glasses to clean them with his school shirt.

"I've no idea, bairns," Frances said. "Aye, maybe we should, at least until we reach Jonathan's area. I cannae go further than that right now. I spent too long here on Friday." Frances huffed and puffed, and we slowly continued to walk the way Hecate had gone.

I was still wondering what mysterious thing

Lois was supposed to be doing, when suddenly she stopped and looked up.

We all paused, slightly nervously, and looked up, wondering what on earth she could be looking at.

"Oh, terr-if-ic!" cried Uncle Vic, sounding furious.

We looked round and couldn't help ourselves from dissolving into hysterics, for his bald head was covered in runny bird poo. It was dripping down his rosy cheeks and threatening to slide down his neck.

"Oh dear!" cried Frances, furiously dabbing at him with a green hanky. She was the only one who was able to contain her laughter. "This place must be infested with seagulls, dirty things."

Lois shook her head. "Not seagulls, just my best friend."

And with that, we heard a familiar "caw, caw", as if laughing at us, and Paloma landed gracefully on Lois' shoulder.

33

SNAKE IN THE GRASS

"Paloma?" I cried out. "What's she doing here?"

"Shhhhh!" Lois hissed. "You'll offend her. She's my friend, and she's going to tell me where Aradia is, so we can stop the leak."

Adi, who had been fairly quiet for a while, piped up earnestly. "Lois, be careful. She might be just pretending to be your friend. What if she is going to lead us into a trap?"

Lois looked furious and, to be honest, so did Paloma, who did a little stompy dance on Lois' shoulder and cawed even more animatedly into her ear.

"Paloma is very upset you're saying this," Lois said. "I trust her, and I'm afraid you're just going to have to trust me." And with that the two of them marched on ahead.

The four of us looked at one another. Uncle Vic's face looked like he wanted to jack it all in and turn back, Frances seemed stressed, and Adi and I studied each other as if debating the situation telepathically.

Finally, I spoke. "I don't think we have much choice here. If it is a trap, how much damage can Aradia really do on her own now that Mal isn't around? Hecate is here. I can't believe that Aradia could defeat Hecate."

"Sometimes we have to just trust. There is a saying I know ..." Adi said self-importantly.

Here we go again, I thought fondly.

"Sit on the bank of the river and wait: your enemy's corpse will soon float by," Adi continued.

Frances looked confused. "But Mal has gone. There is no corpse, and which river do we choose? We've loads here."

Adi shook his head. "No, I don't mean literally. I mean, let's be patient. Aradia will reveal herself if we are patient."

"Ahhhh, I see." Frances smiled, still looking a little confused. "Clever."

She looked to Uncle Vic, I think for clarification, but he just thrust her now very mucky green hanky back at her and beckoned us on.

"Come on, let's get this over with. I need a shower," he said gruffly.

We continued walking and almost jumped out of our skin as the gate slid down behind us with a crash.

"Dear god!" panted Frances, her hand dramatically patting her chest. "Even though I know it's going to happen, it still nearly gives me a heart attack!"

Adi and I exchanged nervous smiles — there was no going back.

Soon, we saw faint orange lights in the distance,

and I hoped it was a sign that Jonathan would be greeting us.

As we got closer to the lights, the cells either side were very quiet. I recognised some of the faces from before — Colin, Fred, and Dave — but they were all silent. Most of them were lying down, completely motionless in their cells. Mickey J was the only one standing, his face blank, his eyes dead, his finger jammed up his left nostril.

Gone was the jolly atmosphere that Jonathan had tried to create. Instead, the air felt heavy and it was difficult to breathe properly.

Even as dear Jonathan walked slowly towards us with his wings outstretched, I failed to feel much joy. His pinnie today bore a picture of a cupcake with a slogan underneath that read: *Weapon of choice.*

"Darling chums, how utterly splendiferous to see you all!" We fell into his feathery arms — even Lois, who had eventually slowed her pace down so we had all arrived together. "Goodness me, it's been a trial these last few days. But hopefully we shall endeavour and come out the other side."

He was always so positive. "It's so good to see you, Jonathan," I said enthusiastically, stroking his soft feathers. "What's wrong with everyone here? They're all so quiet."

"It's the leak," he replied gravely, scratching his beak with a feathery wing. "It's coming from the main prison somewhere, where the darkness is particularly grim. We've had countless riots in the main building, and so many staff have resigned. There have been security breaches with the entrance appearing all day, as opposed to only after 6 p.m. Plus, if Phyllis was found wandering outside the prison tunnel, then this proves anyone could wander in or out and compromise the security of our prisoners."

"Security has been increased though, hasn't it?" Uncle Vic asked cautiously.

Jonathan nodded. "Yes, thankfully. The main problem right now is finding the leak. We've looked high and low, and Hecate thinks NWCs are the key."

"Non-Witchy Cargo?" Adi repeated slowly, looking at me and Lois.

"Yes, that's right, young man." Jonathan looked impressed. "Do you remember seeing things here last time that perhaps not everyone else saw?"

I shook my head. "I don't."

Lois butted in vehemently. "Yes, I remember seeing creepy crawlies all over the wall, and there was a horrid smell."

"And I felt like there were faces watching me from the walls and things. I felt awful," Adi said, looking anxious.

"You never said about the faces," I said, surprised. "I never saw any of these things."

I wondered if I should be concerned that I hadn't had the same experiences as Adi and my sister.

"Not everyone is affected, Rosie. It doesn't mean anything, except that you must have a remarkable amount of self-discipline and inner strength."

"Or it's a case of no sense, no feeling!" Adi joked.

Jonathan led us to his little office, where we sat patiently while he spoke privately to Uncle Vic and Frances. All around we could see traces of where Phyllis had been — there were several pairs of glasses strewn here and there, and a book called *Songs for a Rainy Day* by Mack Entosh. I wondered where she could be right now.

All the while I had this feeling of anxiety in my stomach, as if we were waiting for something to happen. I glanced at Adi and my sister. Adi had curled up on the sofa, looking tired and sad already. Lois was looking paler, and she reached for me.

"Rosie, I don't feel well," she said.

I touched her forehead quickly; she was burning up. "Okay, Lois, where's Paloma now? Has she told you anything else?"

"She said follow the trail, but I'm tired. She said she had to go. She would be in trouble if she said any more to me," Lois whispered.

She felt floppy in my arms, and I was worried sick. "Adi, can you help me? Lois isn't well at all. I think we will need to get out of here."

Adi didn't move. "Adi!" I called more urgently, but still he lay motionless, his eyes looking dead. I knew we didn't have time to waste. "Listen, Lois, I'm going to help you out of here. Let's see if you can find this trail that Paloma mentioned, okay?"

She nodded sleepily, and I pulled her to a standing position. She pointed weakly to the other side of the tunnel.

"What? What can you see?" I asked.

Her lips started to wobble and tears formed. "It's horrible, Rosie. I can't look."

"What is it?" I whispered, afraid, as my imagination ran riot.

"It's a silver line, like a snake's slimy trail, and there's all these horrible little spiders running up the walls. I don't like it," she stammered.

"Okay, my darling," I said reassuringly, wishing Mum were here. "Point to where the trail goes now."

We walked a little way up the tunnel, and Lois pointed to a puddle of water that gathered just by a drainage grid. "There," she whispered. "It goes in there, and there's a massive spider right by it."

Suddenly, she screamed and turned her head away, sobbing hysterically.

Frances, Uncle Vic, and Jonathan appeared in a flash.

"What is it, wee thing?" Frances soothed, reaching for Lois.

"No, leave her, Frances," commanded Jonathan, blowing on a whistle around his neck, which didn't seem to make any sound.

"What can you see, Lois?" I asked again, urgently.

"Sssssss-sn-sn-sn-snake!" She had barely uttered the words when an eagle appeared, flying towards us down the tunnel. It was terrifying to look at. Its sharp eyes scanned us all, and I wondered whether it was sizing us up to eat.

I was about to try to leg it back into Jonathan's office with Lois, when Jonathan spoke.

"Hecate, thank goodness. The child has seen it."

The eagle, which I now realised was Hecate in one of her many forms, shrieked and squawked.

Jonathan quickly translated. "Lois, tell her what you've seen and where it is NOW!" he shouted. I'd never heard Jonathan sound so bossy before.

Lois turned back to the drain area and pointed. "It's a snake coming up from the drain, and it's eating a massive spider now." She burst into more tears, and I comforted her the best I could.

What happened next was incredible. Hecate, in eagle mode, swooped down to the drain, clearly picking something up that none of us could see. As she hovered in the air, we all uttered a collective "urghhhhh" as we saw the last remaining inches of what looked like a yellow and red stripy snake slip down the back of her throat.

The bird gave a great belch, landed on the cobbled tunnel floor, and gradually morphed back into the form of Hecate dressed as THE STRANGER.

Uncle Vic, Frances, and I joined Jonathan in a cheer and clapped our hands in appreciation — even though, to be fair, I wasn't quite sure of the significance of what had happened.

"Well, that's got rid of her, thankfully," said Hecate, her voice full of relief.

"Who was that snake then?" I asked.

Before Hecate could answer, my sister turned around and spoke clearly. "It was Aradia, disguised as a snake. She was the one causing the leak, because she'd been told to by that horrible man."

Suddenly, Lois shrieked again, pointing at the opposite wall in fear.

"What is it, darlin'?" Frances cried anxiously.

"It's a giant gold cockroach!" Lois shouted.

We all looked to the wall. Frances was jumping about, brushing herself down, as if the cockroach were crawling all over her. I strained my eyes but couldn't see a thing.

Then something chilling happened. I heard his voice again in my head.

"*All right, kid. The fat lady ain't sung yet. So it ain't all over. I'll be seeing ya. You can be sure of that.*"

Mal Vine.

As his words faded, a mist appeared, floating across my vision. I blinked several times, and then I saw it.

A large gold cockroach on the wall.

I froze with fear. All I could manage was a sort of pathetic stutter. "There, Hecate, he's on the wall. A gold cockroach. It's him!" I felt like I was being strangled.

Lois had cuddled into me once again. I could feel the weight of her sinking against me, as if she were losing strength by the moment.

Hecate strode over to the wall in one swift movement, grabbed the cockroach, and dropped it into a clear plastic bag, which she zipped shut.

"Gotcha!" she said with relish. "You may have been erased by Osiris, but I knew, I just knew, you'd find a way back here, you odious little man. Be prepared for a looooong stay in a small cell."

"How can that be Mal Vine?" I asked quietly,

feeling exhausted with the emotion of it all. "Osiris got rid of him. He completely destroyed him, all except for ..."

"A gold tooth?" Hecate added.

I nodded.

"Yes, a tooth," she continued, "which funnily enough, disappeared soon after."

"Yes, I noticed that," I said. "I looked for it after you and Anubis had fought, but it had gone."

"I took it with me, because I knew if I'd left the tooth, it, too, would have eventually disintegrated. If Mal had never existed, which is what Osiris wanted, it would have affected too many other things. If the No-Laws had never formed, you wouldn't have needed to give Phyllis a safe house last year and would therefore probably have never met. The ripples of Mal never existing would have potentially been far-reaching," Hecate explained. "I wanted to safeguard the tooth here, but I must have dropped it when I returned to the prison, and of course, with all the dark energy that exists here, it was easy for him to regain a sense of himself. Darkness feeds darkness, I'm afraid. Once he had managed to evolve as a cockroach, with the help, no doubt, of his accomplice Aradia, it would only have been a matter of time before he grew in power." Hecate placed the bag into her pocket and brushed her suit down.

"I'm guessing this young lady," Uncle Vic pointed to Lois, "and the lad, will need some TT?"

"Don't know about them. I think I need it, too," sighed Frances. "But not from you, thank you very much," she added sharply as Uncle Vic's face took on a horrified look at the thought of having to tickle her.

"No need for any of that," Hecate said impatiently. "Give them some black medicine, Jonathan. It will absorb the darkness and be much quicker than TT. Plus, the book needs to get back as soon as possible." She checked her watch and gasped. "I'm late! I must go. Thank you, Rosie, and Lois, and Adi. I know I can always rely on you three."

And with that she vanished.

Uncle Vic and Jonathan carried Lois into his office and gave her and Adi some thick black medicine, which looked disgusting.

"Come along, chums, that's it. Drink it down. You'll get rid of that floppy-body feeling and be able to walk again. Then, once you're out of here, you'll feel splendiferous," Jonathan coaxed, as he poured a large spoonful of medicine down Adi's throat.

"I expect you're wondering where Phyllis is?" Frances added, gently stroking my sister's hair.

I nodded, feeling slightly worried.

"Mr Foggerty took her to Uncle Vic's office this morning. She couldn't wait to get out of here." Frances smiled reassuringly.

"Come on, Frances, let's get them back via my office. It's not far. Then they can hand the book over." Uncle Vic helped Adi up, and Frances and I held Lois' hands.

"Goodbye, Jonathan," I whispered, nuzzling my face into his warm plumage.

"Goodbye, my darling," he murmured back, pushing me away. "Go on, go, before I make a fool of myself. I think this place is starting to get to me, too," he added, wiping a tear from his round, un-blinking eyes.

We walked away, and the last image I had of Jonathan, which will always stay with me, was seeing him lift the black medicine bottle up to his lips and pour the remains of it straight down his throat.

34

MY MAGICAL FAMILY

W e arrived back at Uncle Vic's office at the George's Dock Building through the tunnel wall that Jonathan had taken us to on our previous visit to the prison. Phyllis and Mr Foggerty were already there waiting for us, and we exchanged hugs, delighted to see that she was looking more like her cheerful self.

It was such a relief to be surrounded by light and soft cushions and FOOD! My sister came alive as soon as we had sat down on the sofa. She looked as though she were in heaven as she tucked into a glass of lemonade and a huge piece of Madeira cake.

"I feel so much better," she said through mouthfuls. "This is yummy."

"I can't believe I missed all that stuff with Hecate eating the snake and capturing Mal Vine as a gold cockroach. It must have been mind-blowing!" Adi had not stopped talking since we'd arrived back in Uncle Vic's office.

"To be honest, Adi," I said seriously, "it was terrifying, and probably more so for Lois, as she could see all the spiders and the snake and its silver trail. She was in a right state."

"Mmm," nodded Lois, spitting crumbs everywhere. "I don't think I want to be the chosen one again. Paloma's gone now, too, and I miss her."

Adi and I looked at each other cautiously.

"Where's she gone to, hen?" Frances asked gently.

Lois shrugged. "I don't know. She just said she had to go before she got found out." She looked down and her lip wobbled, as if she were going to burst into tears.

"Anyway," Phyllis said hastily, diffusing the situation, "you've all been absolutely brilliant, and I believe you may have something to give Mr Foggerty and me?"

As we were all squished together on the sofa, Adi stood up and handed Phyllis the *Book of the Dead*.

"My, oh my, this is wonderful." She smiled, squeezing me and Lois. "Isn't this wonderful, Wolfie? We can make sure it's put back in its display case now."

Mr Foggerty nodded, and continued to sip his cup of tea slowly. He patted Phyllis' leg. "Got to get going in a minute, Phyl. Only a small window of time to get it back there, eh?"

She looked at him sadly, I thought, and nodded slowly. "I do hope we'll be nearer you lovely lot once this is over," she said, blinking back tears. "I do miss not seeing you all. I think we'll have to retire soon, Wolfie, and find a nice cottage where my lovely girls and lovely boy," she ruffled Adi's hair, much to his embarrassment, "can come and stay with us in the holidays. What do you think?"

"Oh, yes please, Aunty Phyllis. But you'd need to get my biscuits. Oh, and as long as I can bring Bea, I'll come," Lois said excitedly.

"Enough chatting now, we really have to go." Mr Foggerty stood and waited for Phyllis to finish hugging us before the two of them left, clutching the precious *Book of the Dead* — the book that we had faced so many challenges to eventually get.

I was relieved our adventure was over. It had been pretty scary at times, but I felt sad if this marked the beginning of another period of not seeing our witch friends.

"What's wrong, hen? You're very quiet," Frances asked, putting her arm around me.

"Will we still see you all again, now that the *Book of the Dead* is found and going back to the museum? Or will you be posted somewhere else?" I asked sadly.

"We've no plans to go anywhere right now, Rosie." Frances squeezed my hand in hers. "Head-quarters are staying here. Wherever we are posted, we will always be found here at some point. I've never had a chance to show you our living quarters, have I?"

I shook my head, wondering where the space was for that.

"Maybe next time. But I still have a job as long

297

as your mum is working, and even if she isn't, I will make sure I'm around. Don't you be worrying about that." She dropped a kiss on my head and sniffed. "Come on, gang, let's get you home. Your mum and dad will be back soon."

As a last special treat, Frances said we could fly home on Wendy, and Uncle Vic would drop Adi off at his house, so we said our goodbyes to them both.

Uncle Vic, who liked to pretend he didn't want a fuss but secretly loved it, went red and sweaty. "It's not goodbye, it's *au revoir*. Come along now, you can pop in anytime and see me. I'll still be here doing maintenance and keeping Reg on his toes." He guffawed as if he'd cracked the funniest joke ever.

Adi high-fived me and Lois, and I smiled to myself as I watched him throw his leg with gusto over Uncle Vic's broomstick. He looked like he'd grown in confidence so much. I guess swimming in a river full of sharks and surviving does that to you.

We got settled on Wendy, who gave a groan under the three of us.

"That's enough, young lady. Perhaps you'll no' be so quick to moan now when it's just me," Frances nagged good-naturedly.

As we hovered above the floor, Frances' music blasted out. Queen, of course, and the song was "You're my Best Friend". We all listened in silence, as we held our breath during the unpleasant blasting through the ceiling bit.

Once we were up in the sky, I felt overcome with joy. I listened to the words of the song and thought how lucky I was to have such a great family and wonderful friends.

I don't think Frances wanted the journey to end any more than we did, for she did a few extra swirls and sweeps about Liverpool. We flew over Anfield Stadium, hovering in particular over the Kop, the River Mersey, the big wheel, and of course the Liver Building.

As the song ended, Wendy gently touched down in our back garden, and we silently got off the broomstick and stood in a little circle all holding hands.

We were all a little bit teary.

"You're *my* best friends," Frances spluttered, trying to hide her emotion with some coughing and throat clearing. "Come on, bairns, let's get inside and wait for Mum and Dad."

Mum had left Frances a note telling her not to do any tea for us, as she had taken a shepherd's pie out of the freezer for us all. So, while Lois played on the computer, Frances and I sat in the lounge watching TV.

Newsround came on, which I would not normally watch, but I saw a quick flash of the British Museum and decided to turn the volume up.

"Historians across the country are celebrating this evening as the stolen *Book of the Dead* has miraculously reappeared, completely undamaged, back in its locked display at the British Museum. Curator Beowolf Foggerty had this to say."

The TV screen cut to footage of our own Mr Foggerty talking to the journalist, with Phyllis hovering behind, smiling.

"Yes, of course we are delighted that the book has been returned."

He held the book towards the camera, flicking through its colourful pages.

"It's a complete mystery how it was stolen in the first place."

"Oh wow!" I exclaimed as Mr Foggerty gazed into the camera and seemed to be looking straight at me, a knowing look on his face. "It's a fake," I gasped.

"A fake?" Frances cried, leaning in towards the TV to get a closer look.

"Yes," I added, excitedly. "In the real *Book of The Dead* you couldn't turn the pages over until you had completed that part of the challenge. I think Mr Foggerty was purposely flicking through the book to show us it's not the original."

Frances gave a tut and leaned back in the armchair. "Well, I never did. This doesn't surprise me one little bit." She smiled and shook her head.

"Why?" I asked curiously.

"Do you remember Anubis saying he was the one who took the book, because he wanted it to be back where it belonged, in Egypt?"

I nodded slowly.

"Well, the cheeky doggy face has kept the real

book. He gave youse a copy to bring back, so that the British Museum would still think they had the original." She laughed. "I like your style, Anubis! Good for you."

I thought about it, and I decided I agreed with Frances. The book did belong in Egypt, not here, and I felt a smile of satisfaction, knowing that I was part of a very select few that knew the truth. Did it really matter that it was a fake on display? After all, no one could touch it or read it anyway.

We both started to laugh at how we'd been "had" by Anubis, who I'm sure was feeling the wrath from Hecate for doing things his own way.

As we chuckled, we heard the front door open, and Mum, followed by Dad, traipsed in.

"Hello!" Mum called, poking her head round the door. "My goodness, what's so funny, you two?"

I looked at Frances, and we both started laughing again.

"Nothing, Mum, honestly, just something silly," I said.

"Hello again, Miss Feathertickler," said my dad, beaming for some reason.

We fell about, so much so that Lois appeared at the door looking most put out that she wasn't in on the joke.

"What's so funny?" she whined, scratching her bum with Bea's nose.

"Nothing, Lois, honestly," I said, suddenly feeling that I might cry now Frances was about to go.

"I'll leave you all to it then," Frances said, wiping the tears of laughter from her eyes and heaving herself off the sofa. She glanced at my mum, who looked like she was about to burst with excitement. "What's going on with you?"

Mum glanced at Dad, who squeezed her arm encouragingly. "My agent said that *Brightside* would like to extend my contract by a further six months!" she shrieked, hugging us all.

"That's amazing news, Mum!" I shouted, practically jumping up and down with Lois, who was doing a happy dance with Bea.

"And even better," Mum continued, "is that Donna is leaving in a few weeks."

"Where's she off to then, Miss Watlington?" Dad spat her name out as if it was an unpleasant piece of gristle he'd just found in his mouth.

"She's going to America," Mum said, raising her eyebrows.

Dad laughed. "Lucky America!" he replied sarcastically.

Mum hugged me and Lois to her tightly. Dad's arm was loosely around her shoulders. "This is thanks to you all," she said softly, kissing both of our heads. "I was in real danger of losing myself in this job. I was silly enough to try to pretend to be someone else, afraid that if people knew who the real me was, that they wouldn't like me or let me stay on."

"But who were you being if you weren't being *you*, Mummy? Were you being Donna's sister?"

Mum laughed and she and I exchanged a look of understanding that had obviously escaped Lois.

"I suppose in a way I was," she continued. "I thought that if I was more like Donna, then maybe people would like me. But it made me ill and I started to lose myself. All of you, including you," she motioned to Frances, "helped me realise that the most important thing is being true to oneself."

"And now you have your reward. Your job is extended, Rae, and I'm so happy for you," Frances crooned. "Not least because it means I'll be able to stay around and mind your two bairns a bit longer, if you'll still have me?" She looked to Dad for his approval.

"You're already part of the family, Miss Fungusfighter," Dad replied, to my horror, as he headed out to the kitchen.

"Come and have a celebratory drink with us, Frances," urged Mum, as we heard the pop of a champagne cork.

"Well, I'm sure you can twist my arm," Frances giggled.

We joined Dad in the kitchen, and Lois and I had lemonade in posh champagne glasses.

"I want to do a toast," Dad said exuberantly. "To Mum and her work and to us all!"

"Cheers!" we all shouted, clinking glasses.

"To us all," Mum said, smiling warmly at each and every one of us. "To my magical family."

"My magical family," Lois and I whispered to each other.

Suddenly we all stopped mid-toast and stared in wonder at one another. The fridge magnet, the Scottish fridge magnet, the one that had been mute for the past six months, since our last adventure, had suddenly regained power!

We all looked at each other in shock.

"I haven't touched it!" Dad protested, wide-eyed.

"Come on, John, you have to join in. It's the rules!" shouted my mum, as she hoicked up her skirts, and we all started Scottish dancing wildly.

Even Dad.

EPILOGUE

It had taken many days and nights of gnawing and nibbling away, but at last the gold cockroach was free. He pulled himself out of the plastic bag and scuttled into a corner of the cell, where he soon found a crack in the wall into which he could crawl.

He waited and waited. Time was of no consequence.

He didn't need food. He didn't need water. He just needed darkness to fill his dry body with sustenance and help him grow in strength.

When the time was right, he would make the journey through the tunnels, through time to 1215, to the Trevillet River, just east of Tintagel, Cornwall.

Here he would regain his power and find strength through the ancient lore of Arthurian magic.

ACKNOWLEDGEMENTS

Thanks again to my family for their patience whilst I scoured Egyptian Mythology as part of my research and to Karen at Temple of Light who introduced me to Sekhmet and her wonderful healing powers. I hope I have done her justice in this book. The guys at the Tunnel Tours in Liverpool were brilliant and their expertise gave me lots of inspiration when writing the tunnel segments.

Peyton, thanks for your insightful editorial notes, which you gave with sensitivity and understanding.

Lastly, a massive thanks to my agents; Silvia at PFD, and Melanie and Amanda at Urban for all the tireless work you do on my behalf in so many different ways.

LOVE AGORA BOOKS?
JOIN OUR BOOK CLUB

If you sign up today, you'll get:

1. A free novel from Agora Books
2. Exclusive insights into our books and authors, and the chance to get copies in advance of publication, and
3. The chance to win exclusive prizes in regular competitions

Interested? It takes less than a minute to sign up. You can get your novel and your first newsletter by signing up at www.agorabooks.co

facebook.com/AgoraBooksLDN

twitter.com/agorabooksldn

instagram.com/agorabooksldn